About

Amy Lord is a writer, blogger and digital marketer from north-east England. She won a Northern Writers' Award in 2015 for *The Disappeared* and was also longlisted in the inaugural Bath Novel Award. An earlier manuscript saw her shortlisted for Route Publishing's Next Great Novelist Award. Amy is currently working on a new novel, which was developed as part of a year-long mentoring scheme with Writers' Block NE.

Praise for *The Disappeared*

'Provocative and prescient, *The Disappeared* is an unflinching tale of resistance in dark political times. Set in a near-future Britain where books are banned, this is a thought-provoking dystopian debut.'
– Caroline Ambrose, Founder of The Bath Novel Award

'*The Disappeared* grabs you by the scruff of the neck with its gripping narrative. But as well as that, it breathes down your neck with the eerie probability that this bleak dystopian universe will soon reflect the world that we inhabit. With populism and the misuse of technology on the rise, this novel is as harrowing as it is enthralling.'
– Matt Abbott, poet and activist

The Disappeared

The Disappeared

Amy Lord

unbound

This edition first published in 2019

Unbound
6th Floor Mutual House, 70 Conduit Street, London W1S 2GF
www.unbound.com

ISBN (eBook): 978-1-78965-028-0
ISBN (Paperback): 978-1-78965-027-3

Cover design by Mecob

Printed and bound in Great Britain by Clays Ltd, Elcograf S.p.A.

For Ste, for the best half of my life

*With grateful thanks to Susan Robson
for helping to make this book happen.*

Super Patrons

Carolyn Maughan
Marie McGinley
John Mitchinson
Anth O'Malley
John-Michael O'Sullivan
Kwaku Osei-Afrifa
Justin Pollard
Shaun Robinson
Michael Robson
Alison Simpson
Laurie-Ann Spencer
Lucy Sullivan
David G Tubby
Philip Whiteley
Louise Wilkin

Part One

One

I was eleven when my father disappeared. It's almost twenty years since the night I last saw him. I still remember that knock at the door; it echoes down through the years, as it echoed that night through the walls of our home.

I use the word 'disappeared', but it always feels like a lie. My father didn't vanish. He didn't walk to the shops for a packet of cigarettes and fail to come back. He didn't run away to start another life somewhere, another family. He didn't even leave behind a body, washed up on some riverbank, or slowly spinning from a straining tree branch.

That last night with my father was like every other. He returned late from his job at the university, where he lectured in English Literature. Public transport was unreliable in those days, when the regime was still taking hold. He would walk the five miles home each day, carrying his bag, heavy with papers. I would watch from our sixth-floor window as he made his way across the car park, past the burned-out shells of old hatchbacks, where the braver children would sometimes play army, machine-gunning each other with sticks or old bits of piping. His ragged hair would take on a life of its own in the breeze, his thin shoulders tensed beneath the weight of his students' words, twitching uneasily at every fake bullet that came his way.

By then we had been moved into the flat. Shared accommodation, they called it. We weren't allowed to live in our house in the suburbs any more. My mother mourned the loss of her rose garden and the expensive paper that lined our living room walls, its delicate floral pattern climbing from oak floor to corniced ceiling. She wept about the silverware she was forced to leave behind, a wedding gift from the grandmother who passed away weeks after her marriage.

Our new home became a one-bedroom flat, former housing association detritus that stank of cat piss and had holes in the plaster the size of fists. I slept in the bedroom while my parents shared an old sofa bed in the main room, which was littered with piles of my father's books, the vibrancy of their spines bringing life to the beige world we found ourselves adrift in. He had salvaged as much as he could from our house, but my mother wouldn't let him risk rescuing anything more. He would fret sometimes, struck by a jolt of longing for a particular book that had been abandoned.

We hadn't long fallen asleep when the knock came. I sat up in bed, disorientated. The knock came again. It was dark, but I could hear my parents whispering in the front room, my mother's voice low and pleading.

'You can't let them in. Think of Clara.'

My father snapped, 'I have to, Lucia.' I listened to them half-dressing in haste. I could picture my mother smoothing her hair as he opened the door, a nervous smile on his face. I crept out from beneath the covers to peep through the slit in my bedroom door. The sudden light made my eyes water.

They barged in without invitation: four men in the black and grey uniforms of the Authorisation Bureau. The door was flung back hard; there was a crack as it hit the wall. My father was jostled as they marched into the living room, where there was barely enough space to stand.

They were all much taller than he was, with broad shoulders and thick arms. They were young too. I didn't realise how young until years later, looking back.

There was another man with them. They saluted him stiffly. 'Major.'

He barely acknowledged them. 'Please, excuse the interruption. I'm sorry we had to call so late, but we need to ask your husband some questions.'

He addressed my mother, who hung back, clutching her thin dressing gown closed over her nightdress. The width of the sofa bed was between them, yet she took a step back as his eyes raked over her.

My father moved forward, his body shielding her from the major's gaze. 'What's all this about?'

Without speaking, the major turned his back and began circling the small flat, taking in every detail. He ran a finger over the piles of old paperbacks that lined the walls. 'So many books...' With a flick of his wrist he sent them tumbling, sliding across the floor in a wave of yellowed paper and dust.

There was a pause; the air still after an avalanche. He stooped to retrieve one of the novels from the floor and examined the cover. He held it up for my father to see. I was too far away to read the title of the book, but I recognised the colours on the jacket. It was the memoir of a South American poet who had spent much of his life as a political prisoner. I knew it was banned.

The major flung the book at my father's chest. It landed with a dull slap and ricocheted back onto the floor. He signalled his men, almost casually. They didn't speak, just moved forward as one to take my father by the arms, fingers digging into his flesh.

In a blur of satin and bare legs my mother dashed across the room to clutch at his clothes. 'No, please. You can't take him. You *can't.*'

They shoved her away and she stumbled on the carpet of books, catching her feet and falling back onto the sofa bed, her dressing gown falling open to reveal the nightgown, almost sheer from age under the harsh lights. All the soldiers stared at her. She might as well have been naked. She moaned softly and I could feel the air in the room begin to boil.

My father went to help her up. It was a mistake. One of the soldiers drew his weapon and brought it down quickly on the back of my father's head. He fell, his knees crumpling, a rush of air escaping from his mouth. His face landed against my mother's stomach and she clutched at him, trying to draw him closer.

All four soldiers came to life. They gripped his arms and heaved him up, but he was dazed and couldn't stand. The back of his head was bloody. They were forced to support him, a dead weight, bare feet trailing behind. My mother was crying and saying his name over and over, trying to hold on. One of the youths released his hold on my father and pushed her back onto the bed, looming over her as she tried to shuffle away. With him between us, I couldn't see her face.

The others dragged my father outside. Our neighbours huddled behind the cracks in their own doors. They stayed hidden in their darkened flats, too afraid to emerge, although we all knew they were watching.

And he was gone. My final image of my father was not his face, but the soles of his feet as they disappeared through the door. I remember vividly how dirty they were. I felt tears on my cheeks and my body shook as I tried so desperately to stay quiet.

My mother was crying too, trying to pull herself up off the

bed, to pull her clothes together. Her eyes flickered wildly from the doorway to the man leaning over her. A strangled noise escaped from the back of her throat.

I had almost forgotten the major, when he put his hand on the soldier's arm. 'Go and make sure they have the prisoner under control.'

When my father was gone, the major sat on the bed beside my mother, who huddled with her knees crushing her chest and a fist in her mouth to muffle the sobs. She turned her face away. Slowly, he reached out a hand and touched her hair.

'I wish you didn't have to see this, Mrs Winter. But I hope you understand. Your husband broke the rules and we can't allow that.'

His fingers twined through her hair softly, pulling strands loose from their clip. She had beautiful hair, long and dark; it shone in the light.

'I know it's difficult, but really, this is the best thing that could have happened. You've got the chance to redeem yourself, away from your husband. You can have a new life.'

A sob choked its way free from my mother's lips. She clamped her hand over her mouth as his fingers stilled in her hair. He sighed heavily.

'Perhaps this isn't the best time to talk. It might be better if I came back another day.' He released her hair and stood, brushing his hands over his uniform to make sure it was all in order.

He looked at her for a long moment, as though he wanted to say something more. But he settled for 'Good evening.' With a nod, he turned to leave. The door stood open behind him.

I burst from my hiding place to close it, caught the echo of his boots as they strode away and down the stairs; caught the whisper of the neighbours as they faded back inside their homes.

I tried to force the door shut, but it wouldn't go. The soldiers must have broken something when they forced their way in.

'Mama,' I wailed, looking to her for help. But she was lost to me too, curled up on her side, the soft fabric of her dressing gown rippling as her shoulders trembled. I cried harder. Clutching a chair, I dragged it across the room and braced it under the door handle so that no one else would be able to come in.

I crossed the room in a rush, my eyes blurring as my feet slid on the discarded books. I could fall at any second; fall and never get up. I flung myself on the bed next to my mother, tried to curl my body around her but she tensed at my touch and pulled away.

Cold, I lay alone on the edge of her bed, listening as she sobbed herself to sleep. I stayed awake all night, staring at the broken door handle. Just before dawn there were footsteps in the hallway. They stopped outside our door. I held my breath as someone rattled the handle. But the chair held and the rattling stopped. I listened to the footsteps trail away into the night.

Part Two

Two

It was mid-morning and the streets were quiet. I kept my head down as I walked to the university, carefully avoiding the cracks in the pavement where weeds had broken through, threatening to catch my feet and make me trip.

Outside the Employment Bureau office on the corner there were still a few men huddling in the hope of work. An armed guard watched them lazily. Usually the vans came early to collect them and transport them out of London to work in the fields, or take them to a building site to haul breeze blocks, or to clear rubble from a demolition site. Sometimes the jobs involved disposing of bodies from a recent purge, but no one was supposed to talk about that. Those who were particularly desperate for work would linger throughout the day, waiting for something, anything that would help them feed their kids that night.

I glanced at my watch and began to walk a little faster. I was due in the office soon, ready to receive a line of students who all wanted to discuss their latest grades. Usually the ones who came to complain were those with rich parents. But it was only those with government jobs whose grades I would end up changing. It was a dance; a game we played. I'd give them a bad grade to highlight their lack of study or the laziness of their ideas and they'd come to see me, arrogant and secure enough to know I'd have no choice but to give them a higher mark if I wanted to keep my job.

There was a commotion ahead and I glanced up, my pace slowing abruptly. Two black vans had screeched to a stop, surrounding a small car. Soldiers were hauling a woman with grey hair out of the car while she yelled and hollered. They shoved her face down on the bonnet and her shouts stopped. I crossed the street quickly, looking away. Traffic shifted like water around a stone as everyone on the street diverted their attention from what was happening.

I hurried down a side street instead, somewhere I didn't usually venture, even during the day. Tightening my grip on the bag slung across my body, I felt my shoulders tense. My eyes began to dart from side to side.

The acrid smell of burning filled the air and my nostrils flared. I walked by an underpass where a group of men huddled around an oil drum, warming their hands over the flames. They looked up at me as I passed, their eyes blank and sunken. I tried not to look at them, but it was a compulsion. Whenever I came across a group of men broken like this, I always looked for my father. Sometimes I'd imagine I saw the curve of his cheek or the colour of his eyes, but it was never real. So many years had passed, but I still missed him every day.

There was a patch of scrubland further along the street. There had been a children's park there at some point, but it had been vandalised so many times and there was no money to repair it. Gradually anything of value was stripped away. Now it was a place where homeless people sometimes lived, albeit briefly. This wasn't a city where it was safe to stay in one place for too long.

I heard the voices first, before I saw them. A sense of dread awakened in my stomach.

A family was hunched together on the wasteland, a flimsy tent that had seen better days behind them, quivering in the breeze. An old shopping trolley sat beside it, with what I assumed to be everything they owned in this world.

There were four of them: an older couple and a teenage boy and girl. They had lilting accents that I struggled to place. A group of boys were dancing around them. I could hear the taunts they were flinging, the insults, the racism. Most of the boys appeared to be in their mid-teens, but some were younger.

The family sat there silently as the boys' cries grew louder. I stopped, caught in the web of tension that filled the air. The father looked like an old man. His face and hands were scarred and he had a vacant stare that made me wonder if he was even aware of what was happening. His wife cowered behind him; the children stared at the floor.

The boys continued their dance. At this time of the day, they should have been in school; there were penalties for truancy. Usually the only children who skipped classes were already abandoned or alone, or living in poverty. Society had little for them. This group had found someone with even less and they revelled in the power that gave them, however fleeting. I could picture them all in the sleek black and grey uniforms of the Authorisation Bureau, taller and throwing blows at their victims, not just words.

'Whatchoo fuckin' lookin' at, eh?'

The pack turned towards me and I froze. The siblings looked at me, their eyes demanding my help.

'I...'

I didn't have any words. I didn't have any breath. My mouth opened and closed and I wondered how it had come to this.

I'd never forgotten what it felt like to stand in the darkness behind my bedroom door and fear what was about to happen. I'd never forgotten what it felt like to witness violence.

It still shocked me when it came. Most of the boys were looking furiously at me when it happened. The youngest of the gang, who couldn't have been more than eight or nine, picked up a rock that was lying on the ground at his feet. I watched him as he weighed it in his hand, studying the smooth texture of the surface. And then he threw it.

The rock arced through the air and struck the girl on the temple with a sickening crack. She didn't cry out, just crumpled to the ground, a burst of blood on her skin. Her father didn't flinch. The mother cried out and ran to her daughter, fussing over her prone body.

The boys all began to laugh and catcall, cheering the young one who had thrown the rock. A few of them moved closer to the family. I couldn't help myself: I took a step forward.

The brother stared at me, his anger palpable. I could see he wanted to do something; there was violence brewing beneath his skin, but he knew it was futile, against these boys. His mother wept.

'Leave them alone!'

Their attention was on me then and, instantly, I knew I'd made a mistake. They turned towards me.

'Fuckin' bitch,' shouted one of the older ones. 'You want a piece too?'

He gestured obscenely, grabbing at his groin, as the others circled closer.

I looked at the girl, struggling to sit up as her mother pulled at her arm. Blood ran down her face and she didn't wipe it away. The boy's eyes burned into mine.

'I'm sorry,' I whispered. And I turned my back. Clutching the bag across my chest, I let my feet carry me away, head down once again. I listened for footsteps behind me, poised for the attack, but it never came.

As I reached the end of the street and turned back onto a busy road, I heard a faint scream and howls of laughter. I paused on the corner to look back, but the street was empty. Heart pounding, I hurried away, shame and sickness twisting in my gut.

My hands were still shaking an hour later as I sat in my office, trying to control my breathing. I couldn't forget the faces of the family: the emptiness of the father and the anger of the son. I couldn't bear to think about what might have happened to them. I couldn't bear to think about what I might have done to help.

There was a knock and the office door opened. I turned, expecting one of my students, but the new head of department stood in the doorway. His brow furrowed.

'Clara, are you alright? You look awfully pale.'

I took a breath. 'I just…' It all flashed through my mind again and the words were about to tumble out. But I tightened my lips instead. I wasn't sure what Brian would understand less: my shame at walking away from someone who needed help, or my desire to stop and help in the first place.

I pulled my shoulders back and met his eye. 'I'm fine, just a bit of a headache.'

He nodded. 'It is a bit stuffy in here.'

I didn't reply and the silence stretched on a moment too long.

'I wanted to have a word with you, about Luke Campbell.' There was a sheaf of paper in his hand, which he held up between us. 'You've given him extremely poor grades recently. His father has been in touch to complain.'

Brian waved the papers at me. I assumed they were examples of Luke's work. He continued, 'I really can't see why you would deem it necessary to mark his essays so poorly.'

I lifted my chin.

'I gave Luke low grades for a number of reasons. His work is always handed in late and without apology. His spelling is atrocious. His ideas are simplistic and even, frankly, offensive. I get the impression that he only refers to the first books he finds in the library and doesn't bother to consider an idea in any more depth. I could go on.'

Brian's mouth pursed. Again, the papers in his hand fluttered.

'I'm disappointed in your attitude, Clara. Luke's father believes you have some kind of grudge against his son and, from that display, I'd have to agree. I don't recognise any of the problems you've just listed in this work.'

He shuffled through the papers and pulled one out to show me.

'And what you say about work being handed in late simply isn't true. Just look at the sign-in sheet.'

He held the paper out to me. Feeling suddenly queasy, I took it from him. It was a list of essay submissions from Luke's student record. According to the dates listed and signed off by the records officer, every piece of work had been handed in early.

I stared at it in disbelief.

'This can't be right.'

I looked up at Brian. 'Can I see those?'

I held out my hand for the rest of the papers and he gave them to me wordlessly. I rifled through them, recognising the titles of essays I'd set. But none of these were Luke's essays. I'd never seen them before.

'This can't be right...'

Luke's father was a high-ranking official; he actually worked in the office of the First General, although I wasn't sure what he did there. I'd met him once, at an open day for new students and their families. He was a short man, with a barrel chest and a sharp voice. He wasn't affectionate with his son, but he clearly had high expectations for him.

It looked like his influence extended to bribing university officials on his son's behalf. It wouldn't do to have a child who wasn't even capable of stringing a sentence together, not if he wanted to maintain a certain level of respect.

A wave of fury swept through me. I thought of the family in the abandoned park, of the brightest students in my classes, who were without exception also the poorest. I thought of my father and how he had given everything for his principles, while I wrote glowing reports on idiots and cheats.

Brian was watching me. I really didn't know him well at all. Perhaps he was the one who altered the records.

I forced myself to smile apologetically. It didn't stretch to my eyes.

'There must have been some... misunderstanding,' I heard myself say. 'I'll be sure to mark Luke's work more carefully in future.'

Brian nodded. 'I'm pleased to hear that, Clara. I'll be keeping an eye on Luke's grades myself; just to make sure this doesn't happen again.'

My smile grew rigid, but I didn't let it slip. There was a twitch in the corner of my eye. 'Of course.'

It looked as though Brian wanted to say something more, but instead he smiled. 'Alright then.'

When he left, he closed the door behind him. But he'd opened something in me, something that had been building for a long time without me even knowing. My father had risked so much to teach his students the truth. He'd made a difference to their lives, however small, when he broke the rules to share his books with them. There was no reason I couldn't do the same.

Once I'd had the idea, I couldn't stop thinking about it. People didn't read now, the way they used to. I missed the lure of a new book, the afternoons spent in the library after school finished, wandering among the shelves searching for another world, another life to inhabit. I needed that more than ever.

I roamed the library again, tracing my finger over the smooth, uncracked spines of the books. They were all sanitised, carefully chosen for the warped version of the truth they presented to the world. We didn't have stories about controversial or difficult subjects; there was no diversity in the voices that inhabited the library. Each one was a friend to the regime, at least on paper.

If they weren't their book was banned. Perhaps not officially; there was no rule, no law that prevented you from reading certain things. But you risked yourself all the same. Certain books disappeared from the shelves, as their authors disappeared from sight. Political books, historical books, biographies, many vanished overnight. But fiction was the worst. The government didn't like any story that explored revolution or protest, or even gave its characters too much personal freedom. They didn't want us to remember, to get ideas outside of their control.

I'd spent years hunting for a copy of *Doctor Zhivago*. My father had encouraged me to read his copy when I was young and we had spent hours discussing it, but it was left behind when we were forced to move to our flat. I still didn't know how the story ended. Every time I entered a bookshop or a library I would search for it, but the book was never there.

The librarian watched me from her desk as I scrutinised the shelves. I pulled out a copy of the First General's *Manifesto* and pretended to flick earnestly through the pages. Turning my body, I angled the cover so she could see what I was reading. After a moment, her attention shifted to one of the students, who was whispering a little too loudly to a friend.

With a shove, I put the book back and moved deeper into the library, into the dusty corners where the students rarely went. There was a shelf on the back wall where the academic publications were kept. A copy of Brian's dissertation on the social influence of a state-sponsored poet was there, the cover gritty and untouched. Lips pursed, I plucked it from the shelf and scanned a few pages. It made me hate him even more.

As I replaced it, another book caught my eye. I glanced over my shoulder. Marcus Nielsen was a Danish poet who once taught English Literature at the university. He was a good friend of my father's. But he disappeared too, a few months before my father did. His crime was publishing a book of poetry critical of the First General. The imagery he used was so opaque that the book went unnoticed for over a year before a disgruntled colleague published a critical analysis. Both men ended up in the Authorisation Bureau's hands. It broke my father's heart and ignited his activism, his rebellion. His disappearance.

I sank to the floor, opening the cover and flicking quickly through the pages, devouring the densely structured stanzas, the poet's fire bursting off the page. When footsteps rang out along a neighbouring aisle, I shoved the book into my bag, heart pounding. Guilt stained my face.

Clutching my bag, I hurried back along the shelves, snatching a couple of safe titles to check out. A different librarian served me, a young man in a bright t-shirt and glasses. He smiled as he stamped the books and handed them to me. I emerged from the library into the afternoon sun, the light dazzling my eyes after the dull interior of the old building. Hugging the books to my chest, I made my way to the main lecture hall to meet Simon, anxiety fizzing in my veins.

Three

When I first met Simon, he was one of the university's stars: a charismatic man who delivered passionate and intelligent lectures, pushing at the boundaries of the curriculum that the government had assigned but never straying into territory that might attract the wrong sort of attention.

I'd recently completed my master's programme and was anxiously anticipating the first day of my new job as a junior lecturer in the English department. It had been a difficult job to secure, with round after round of interviews and assessments and background checks. Somehow I scraped through and was assigned an official position, along with a room in an accommodation block on campus that was reserved for staff.

The night before I was due to start, I was invited to a welcome event thrown by the university, where new staff could mingle with existing employees. I arrived late, after finding myself hopelessly lost among the narrow corridors of the economics building. After a slightly unnerving detour into the echoing depths of the basement, I managed to find a caretaker who gave me directions to the main hall, all the while looking sideways down my top.

It only took me another two wrong turns before I found the

right place. I stumbled into the room, hot and bothered from my prolonged journey through the building. The room was surprisingly full, as knots of people gathered together, deep in conversation. I lingered in the doorway, scanning the hall for anyone familiar.

On the far side of the room, the head of the English department – who had interviewed me for the post – had spotted my entrance. I'd always enjoyed working with George: he was the first man I met, other than my father, who was driven by his love of books. But they were his downfall too, in the end. Writing a memoir about his life under the regime wasn't the best idea; leaving the manuscript in his office was worse. None of the staff ever admitted responsibility for reporting him, but one of them was guilty. The Authorisation Bureau didn't manage to arrest George though. In his hurry to escape them, he tripped and fell down a flight of stairs, opening his skull on the stone steps. Instead of taking him, they took his things, obliterating his presence. Over twenty years at the university, gone.

George raised a hand above his head, clutching a narrow-stemmed glass of wine in the other. 'Clara!' he called, making his way towards me.

I waited for him, my smile turning rigid as he came closer.

'How nice to see you again! We'd almost given you up for lost.'

I blushed. 'It did take me a while to find the right place, sorry.'

He patted me on the arm. 'Oh not to worry, it can seem like a bit of a maze until you find your way around.' He leaned towards me confidentially. 'When I first started here, over twenty years ago now, I once managed to get locked in the building after classes. I lost track of time in my office and then couldn't find my way out. By the time I found the exit, everyone had gone home. Fortunately I managed to find a number for the caretaker and he came back and let me out.'

I smiled. 'Oh no, how awful. It must be eerie being alone in the building like that.'

He gave a bark of laughter. 'Yes, yes, I suppose it was.'

His eyes glazed over for a moment and I could almost see him remembering. Then he snapped back to the present. 'Well, we must get you a drink. Would you like something to eat?'

He steered me towards the buffet table in the corner. A pile of paper plates sat beside a thin-looking spread of sandwiches and snacks. While he busied himself pouring me a drink, I took a plate and selected a couple of dry sandwiches, along with a few cocktail sausages and a mini Scotch egg.

'Here you go.' He handed me a glass of wine and I smiled gratefully.

'Thank you.'

I took a sip and almost winced: the wine was overwhelmingly sour. But I swallowed, glancing about me for somewhere to put the glass while I ate one of the sandwiches.

I made my way through the food slowly as the head of department chatted away, telling me stories about some of the students and pointing people out to me across the room. Once I had finished eating and stowed my empty plate in an appropriate place, he took my arm and began to guide me across the room.

'Let me introduce you to a few of the staff here, Clara.'

The other English lecturers were gathered together in a huddle in the corner of the room. As we approached, they began to laugh uproariously. I hung back as the head of department marched straight into the tight circle.

'Everyone, I'd like you to meet Clara Winter. She's our new team member, starting tomorrow.'

He gestured about the group, introducing me to each of my colleagues. I nodded and mumbled my hellos as they greeted me in turn, clutching the wine glass against my stomach. I was so nervous that I took another gulp, forgetting how foul it tasted.

To my relief, the head of department didn't leave me alone with the English staff. Instead he whisked me off around the room, introducing me to as many people as he could. After five minutes I'd already forgotten the names of everyone I'd met.

My head was reeling when a petite woman with mousy hair approached us. 'Excuse me, George, but there's a call for you in the office. Would you mind?'

He apologised profusely for leaving me and hurried off with her, leaving me alone in the hall with my glass of rank wine. I took another sip for something to do. My taste buds were already scarred so I barely noticed the flavour.

I was wondering if it was too early to make my escape when someone appeared at my side.

'I must be the only person in the room George didn't introduce you to. I'm Simon.'

He held out his hand and I shook it. 'Clara Winter.'

He tutted gently. 'I can't believe you're drinking that rubbish. Here, give me your glass.'

He didn't wait for me to respond, but took the glass from my hand and turned surreptitiously away. We were standing by a window where a lone plant was wilting on the ledge. He dumped the wine into its pot and reached into his jacket pocket, pulling out a small silver flask.

'Ssh!' He put my glass on the window ledge and held a finger to his lips, before pouring something gold coloured from his flask. He tucked it back into his jacket and handed me the glass. I looked at him.

'Go on, take a sip.'

The whisky burned a little as it went down, rich and smooth. It felt hot in my stomach. It was only the second time I'd ever drunk spirits.

Simon smiled at me. There were creases at the corners of his eyes that I found endearing, salt and pepper threaded through his beard. 'Good isn't it? Hard to get hold of though. I keep it for special occasions.'

I looked around the room at the academics picking at their buffet, sipping the disgusting wine as they chatted quietly about the year ahead.

'This counts as a special occasion?'

'I got to meet you, didn't I?'

It took a second for his words to sink in. My cheeks reddened and I had to look away. I felt like a girl, embarrassed by her first crush on a teacher. He brushed his fingers against my shoulder and my skin tingled.

'Come on, let's get out of here.'

I didn't know where we were going. Simon led me outside and across campus, towards the university library. It was an imposing granite building, built in Victorian times. A set of wide steps led up to a pair of heavy wooden doors. They were shut tight, the building in darkness.

'Isn't it closed?' I asked, as Simon started up the steps.

He grinned at me over his shoulder. 'I've got a key.' He patted his pocket.

A flood of envy rushed through me. 'How did you manage that?'

As I followed him up the steps, apprehension shivered across my skin. 'Should we be doing this? What will happen if we get caught?'

Simon laughed, wrestling the key into the lock. 'Are you

always this much of a worrier?' He swung the door open with a long creak. Inside was pitch darkness. He gestured for me to go ahead. I stepped into the blackness.

My footsteps rang out on the stone floor. After three or four steps into the room, I had the sense that I was inside a vast cavern. I could make out the outline of some furniture to my right; I squinted into the dark. The door closed behind me and the remaining light disappeared. I stood completely still, feeling as though my body was wobbling as I tried to gather my senses.

Somewhere behind me I could hear Simon moving around. My heart was racing. Then light flooded the room. I blinked rapidly.

We were standing in the library's entrance hall, a small space with a stone floor and a cubbyhole on one side that led through to an office space where the librarians must work. The hall was lined with thick mahogany beams that had been polished to a shine.

'Have you been inside the library yet?' Simon asked, coming up behind me.

I shook my head, too busy marvelling at the space to answer him. He grinned.

'You'll enjoy this then.' In front of us was another double door. The wood was carved elaborately and trimmed with strips of black metal. Simon opened the doors wide; the library was cavernous.

'It's beautiful!' I followed him into the main room, staring up at the high-domed ceiling, which was painted with a historical frieze. Bearded scholars pored over thick, leather-bound books while regal-looking men stood by.

And the shelves! The shelves stretched out around me like the spokes of a wheel, each one lined with books. I was amazed.

'I've never seen so many books all in one place! Even my university, it was nothing like this.' I ran forward into the stacks, tracing my fingers along the spines as I went deeper into the room, stopping occasionally to read the name of a text or an author.

Simon followed leisurely behind me. His voice was strong in the silence. 'This is the biggest collection of books anywhere in the country. There are books here that you can't find anywhere else. That's one of the reasons the university is so strict about access. They don't want just anyone coming in here. And you have to have signed approval to check anything out, which is rare. Usually students come in and work directly from the books.'

I came to the centre of the room where there were half a dozen sets of stairs leading up to a raised platform. I waited for Simon and we climbed to the top, where I spun around in awe, gazing out over the shelves.

'How many books do they have here?' My voice was breathy.

He shrugged. 'No one knows, officially. They don't keep proper records any more. But some people say there must be millions, not including the ones in storage in the basement.'

I stared at him. 'Millions!'

He came and stood beside me and we looked out over the rows and rows of books, his hand so close to mine that it brushed against me whenever he moved.

'How did you get a key for this place?' I asked quietly. 'Surely that isn't allowed.'

'Of course, not officially…' He leaned his elbows against the railing that ran around the platform, cupping his hands against his chin. He looked up at me coyly. 'I had a short-lived relationship with one of the librarians, years ago now. She gave me a key so that we could meet here, after hours.'

He raised an eyebrow and I flushed.

'Anyway, things burned themselves out fairly quickly, but

she never asked for the key back. I think she forgot I even had it. I meant to give it back of course, but it's so peaceful here at night, I like to come and think. Not to mention the reading.' He sighed. 'And eventually she went away. I think her mother fell ill, so she went back home to take care of her. There was no reason to return the key after that.'

He smiled up at me. We stood too close; his pupils expanded slowly.

'I bet you bring all the girls here.'

'No, not since the librarian. And she brought me.' He moved closer. 'You're the first one.'

Four

I sat in the back of the lecture hall, watching Simon as he paced in front of the whiteboard, animated gestures accompanying his words. Each time he paused, pens scratched across paper as his students hurried to capture every syllable.

'At first, it was a slow thing, the way the country changed. After the banking crisis in 2008, the economy never really recovered. The new government began austerity measures, cutting public services to reduce national debt. A few years in and the cuts really began to bite. Ordinary people felt out of touch with the political class. They were angry that no one would listen to them, while they lost jobs and their standard of living fell. Housing became expensive and the cost of a university education grew, pricing many young people out completely.

'People needed someone to blame for the lack of opportunity. And that blame fell on the immigrants who were moving to the UK and, according to certain politicians at the time, stretching the NHS and the education system. The country voted to leave the EU, which only made the economic situation worse. At the same time, there were a string of terrorist attacks across Europe, and war broke out in Syria. A wave of people fleeing the violence tried to cross the Mediterranean, but rumours of terrorists hiding among the refugees spread and there was real reluctance to help those who wanted to find sanctuary here.

'Suicide bombings and attacks began to happen regularly across the UK and the fear of terrorism threatened to tear the country apart. There was a series of bombings on election day, at polling stations in Sheffield, Enfield, Harrow and Brighton. Almost 100 people were killed. That threw the election into chaos, as polling stations across the country shut down early, keeping the previous government in power. But with barely any authority left, they struggled to control the situation. The real defining moment came after the Whitehall bombing, when the prime minister was almost killed by a suicide bomber, who stepped in front of her car. Right-wing groups instigated riots, demanding tighter controls on anyone from a migrant family. People were too terrified to do everyday things. Sporting events and concerts were cancelled; shopping centres began to close as custom dwindled. More and more people stopped going to work, refusing to use public transport.

'Finally there was nothing for the government to do but impose martial law. The army took to the streets, and a fragile order was restored.'

Here Simon stopped, removed his glasses and rubbed his eyes. I knew him well enough to recognise his exhaustion as he remembered what came next. His students were too young to recall the junta's rise to power, but we could never forget that time. We couldn't forget the people who disappeared as the First General gave his rallying speeches, calling for a new way of life, a freedom from terror. He promised to take back control, to restore the country's economic standing and make it great again, but he only made things worse.

Simon had to choose his next words carefully. There would

be spies in the room; some might even be genuine students. There are so few opportunities for them now.

They had stopped writing; their pens caught up to Simon's words, captured them indelibly in ballpoint ink. They leaned forward almost imperceptibly, waiting for him to speak. Some of them sensed that he was conflicted. I could feel the ache of expectation in the room.

The bell rang and the room was jolted from its reverie. Many students looked relieved, others disappointed. They began stuffing their notepads into rucksacks and shuffling out of the room in twos and threes, wrapped in the soft murmur of conversation.

Simon stood at the whiteboard, his back to the room. I waited until the lecture hall was empty before I approached him. The plans that had begun to form earlier in the day had solidified as I listened to him speak.

'That was a good talk today.' I placed my hand on his back.

He didn't turn to me. 'It was the same as every other day.' Tension radiated from his body; I could feel it through the palm of my hand. 'How can I call myself a history teacher when I only lecture in lies?'

I moved closer, wrapping my arms around him and pressing my cheek against his back. My body was still jittery with energy. 'You tell them what you have to. But we all know…'

'Do we? Some people seem to find it easier to forget.' Simon spun around angrily, and I was reminded of the emotion in my father's voice when he was passionate about a cause.

I'd noticed recently that Simon was showing signs of exhaustion: he had bruises under his eyes, the grey flecks in his hair were starting to spread, his shoulders slumped beneath the weight of so much history.

I took a deep breath. 'I've been thinking…'

Out of habit I glanced around the room, checking for stragglers. Rows of empty seats stared back at me.

'There is something we could do.'

Our eyes met. I opened my mouth, but something stopped me. Simon touched my cheek.

'It's been a long day; I'm tired. Let's go home.'

He nodded, his eyes searching mine. 'Are you alright?'

I shifted my bag on to my shoulder and took his hand. 'Let's just go.'

He flicked off the lights one by one as we left the lecture hall, plunging the room into an eerie blackness that echoed with suspicion and strangled dreams.

Five

Simon slept beside me, his face crumpled against the pillow. It was four in the morning and I still hadn't managed to get any rest. My mind was churning with anxious thoughts. I watched the clock beside the bed as each hour ticked by.

That evening, the journey home from the university had passed in silence. We took the bus, watching the city streets roll by, consumed with shuttered windows and the shuttered lives of the people we passed.

We drove along streets lined with grotty-looking takeaways and pawnbrokers. Signs advertised easy-to-access loans; I didn't need to see the small print to know the interest rates would be huge. Despite what was advertised, most of these loans were consolidated through a government scheme: fail to pay your debts and you'd be hauled off to the north somewhere to do manual labour on one of the new infrastructure projects, roads or railway bridges needing to be built.

I couldn't bear to look at Simon. My nerves were blazing, anticipating the conversation we would have. Instead I stared at the other passengers, wondering if there was an informer among them. I felt eyes on me wherever I looked.

When our stop appeared it was a relief. I staggered down

the steps, blinking against the late-afternoon sunlight as Simon shouldered his bag, heavy with student philosophy and marking. The bus shelter was lined with old posters encouraging residents to report suspicious behaviour among their neighbours, the paper faded and torn. The slogan *We're taking back control* screamed at me from the page.

We walked in silence past the park at the end of our street, the military checkpoint on the corner overseeing all our lives. Simon strode ahead as I tried to build up the courage to set things in motion. He paused at the door to our building, waiting for me to catch up, and pressed a soft kiss to my forehead as I stopped to look up at him, my heart heavy and my arms tired.

'Here, let me carry your bag,' he said, the familiar smile flickering suddenly across his lips. I didn't resist as he held the door open for me. I shuffled inside and began to climb the stairs, rummaging in my jacket pocket for the door key.

Our flat is small, smaller even than the one I lived in as a child. Years ago it would have been called a studio apartment – one room contains our double bed, a shabby sofa that has been reupholstered half a dozen times, bookshelves and a work desk that we fight over most days.

While Simon dumped our bags on the floor and flung himself onto the bed, I crossed the room and opened the windows onto our rickety Juliet balcony. The last of the day's warm air wafted into the apartment. I could hear the family who lived below us laughing as they cooked dinner, the rich smell of spices billowing through their open window.

We kept a small second-hand television set, although there wasn't much to watch; all the channels were state controlled. I had once managed to tune into a French news programme. It was fuzzy and faint, but I stared at the screen in amazement, letting the unfamiliar language wash over me, until the screen abruptly filled with static. I searched for hours, but never did find it again.

Desperate for a diversion, I flicked on the television. The evening news was just beginning: two presenters sat in the studio, poised to read from an autocue. A title banner flashed across the screen: *Night-time News with David G. Tubby and Susannah Smart.* As it faded, the man began to read, his face serious.

Reports of a planned attack by a terrorist group emerged today, after they were thwarted by the Authorisation Bureau. Members of the public are advised to report any suspicious behaviour in their neighbourhood to the confidential hotline.

Lips pursed, I turned the volume right down. The newsreader finished his piece and smoothed a hand over his carefully styled hair, smiling confidently at his co-presenter as she began to speak. His suit looked expensive, probably more expensive than everything on the single rail that served as my wardrobe.

'Are you going to tell me what's been bothering you?' Simon asked.

I turned away from the television to find him watching me, his expression contemplative. I shook my head slightly. 'I don't... it's just...'

My heart fluttered in my throat; I was acutely aware of my own pulse. For an instant I was back in the bedroom doorway all those years ago, deafened by the blood thundering in my ears as I saw my father arrested, our home drowning in discarded paperbacks. Sometimes I felt as though I'd never escaped the confines of those walls.

'I saw a family get hurt today.'

The shame came rushing back. I pressed the heels of my hands hard against my eyes, forcing myself to breathe.

'I think... they might have been killed.'

Simon looked horrified. 'God, Clara, that's awful. Are you okay?'

'See, that's exactly the point. *Am I okay?* I just told you that I saw someone get attacked, maybe even killed, and you're worried about how that affects *me*. I walked away, Simon. I fucking walked away.'

I sat beside him on the bed. 'I could have done something, said something, told somebody – but I just walked away, because I was scared. For years I've been cursing our old neighbours for not helping my father, but I did exactly the same thing. I saved myself. And they were kids. I saw this little boy chuck a rock at a girl's head, while his friends were threatening her family. When did that become okay? When did we stop and turn our backs? We closed ourselves off from the world and it doesn't help anyone.'

Simon pulled me close. The familiar scent of his skin wrapped itself around me. I buried my face in his neck, in his comfort, his protection. My mother had always been scornful of our relationship. Simon was fifteen years older than me and she dismissed him as a replacement for my father. Sometimes I hated her.

We sat there, our bodies pressed together, Simon's hands stroking my hair. The sounds of life on the street outside filtered up to us: the voices, the cars rolling by, a dog barking. The sense of shame receded and was replaced by something else, something stronger. I was certain.

'I want to teach a new class – outside the curriculum. I still have some of my father's books that I can use.'

Simon stared at me. I could see him processing my words, taking them apart and putting them back together in his head, unable to make them fit.

'You can't.'

I shook my head. 'But *we* can. History, literature – it all ties together. Think how powerful that message would be.'

He sat up and swung his legs over the side of the bed. 'Clara, I love you, you know that. But you've gone insane. Where has this come from?'

My eyes burned. 'It's always been there. My whole life, there's been this sense of inevitability. Like a black hole drawing me slowly in. How could I choose anything else?'

His lips were a thin line. 'This is about your father, isn't it? It's always been him. Nothing else in your life has even come close, certainly not me.' He choked on the last words and I couldn't breathe.

'That's not true.' My voice was a whisper.

'For an intelligent woman, you can be frighteningly obtuse when it suits you. Reading you is like reading a bloody psychology textbook.'

I jumped up from the bed. 'Are you saying that I'm not capable of making my own choices? That I have to copy everything my father did?'

My words grew shrill.

'But what other choice is there? I can sit here for the rest of my days, with you, in this apartment. We can go to work and pretend that our lives have meaning. Who are we kidding? Every day we lie; we skim over the most important parts of the subjects we teach. We're always walking that tightrope. Well I can't do it any more. There has to be something… and what weapons do we have? All I have are books. Books and the things my father taught me. And when you think about it, what else do we need? The cracks are there.' I waved my hand vaguely at the window, at the world outside. 'If we can force them, just a little, they might grow deep enough to do some damage.'

Simon's face was raw with emotion. It hurt to look at him,

but I forced myself to hold his gaze. 'And what if I don't want to do it? What if I refuse to let you?'

'You don't own me, Simon. *I'm not your wife.*' He looked as though I had slapped him. 'If you don't want to, that's fine. I understand. But you won't stop me. I have to do this.'

I took a step closer, imploring him with my eyes. 'You don't know how it feels. To have someone you love taken away like that. You come from a safe, suburban family who always played by the rules. You've never felt that agony, the not knowing...'

He erupted to his feet so suddenly that I felt a thrill of fear. He grabbed my arms tightly, drawing his face down close to mine.

'You don't have the monopoly on pain, Clara. Maybe I didn't lose a parent, but don't treat me like an outsider, like I'm too sheltered to understand you.'

He paced away from me, yanking at his hair as he moved. He spun round, jabbing a finger towards me.

'God, I've spent how many years listening to you cry about losing your daddy. You've told me again and again how special he was, how much you love him, how you would do anything to have him back. But what about me? I'm right here, in front of you, right now. I've been here for years and you don't bloody *see* me. You're fixated on the past.'

I stood open mouthed. The family in the flat below had fallen silent. I burst into angry tears and slammed the window shut.

When I turned back, Simon had gone. The front door hung open.

I crumpled to the floor as the tears came. It was nearly twenty years since I'd lost my father, but the pain still felt fresh. It was clearer than my memories of him; so much had faded or become lost altogether. But Simon was so like him: his sleeves pushed up his forearms, his hair flopping forward over his glasses, brow furrowed.

A falling sensation hollowed my chest. Maybe that was why I was so keen to push Simon, to make him do what my father had done. I was putting him in shadow. But what if he was right?

I pictured my father being hauled off into the night; my father but with Simon's face.

When he came home after our argument, Simon refused to speak to me. I waited up for him, staring at the wall as the clock ticked relentlessly onwards into the night. It was obvious that he stayed away to avoid me, expecting me to be asleep.

I was still waiting days later. The mornings had become an agonising dance around the tiny space of our apartment. He would try to rise early, before I woke. But the muffled sound of his alarm or the floorboards creaking always broke my fitful sleep.

We ended up getting ready at opposite ends of the room, our eyelines purposely out of sync. I stared at a photograph of us that was taken at his dad's birthday party the year before. The three of us and Simon's mum stood in their garden, arms round each other's shoulders, grinning for the camera. Simon's dad was wearing an old-fashioned party hat that his wife had crafted from coloured paper. It had been a family party, full of Simon's cousins and their children. We'd cooked sausages in the garden and got raucously drunk on his mum's homemade sloe gin. It was a wonderful day. I felt a pang as Simon's back blocked my view of the picture. I missed him desperately, but my attempts at conversation were always met with silence.

On the fifth day, he came home from work late smelling of alcohol. I was propped up in bed marking a pile of essays, my hair scraped up into an untidy topknot. The television played in the background.

He banged the door closed behind him, unsteady on his feet. 'You win,' he slurred. 'I'll do it.'

I put the papers down. 'Do what?'

'I'll teach your bloody class.' He slumped into one of the kitchen chairs. 'I know it's the right thing to do.'

Pushing back the covers, I got out of bed and knelt on the floor in front of him. 'I don't want us to argue over this. I never did.' I reached up to touch his face.

He gripped my hand. 'I'm sorry. For all of it; I never should have said those things about your father.' He pressed my palm to his lips. 'I don't want to lose you.'

His eyes stared into mine, wet with unshed tears. My mind drifted away, planning for the first of the new classes.

Six

Simon had still never returned his library key. We explored the shelves after hours, searching the furthest corners for material to share with our students. Tucked between two ancient encyclopaedias, I found a copy of Brecht's play *Fear and Misery of the Third Reich*, which clearly hadn't been touched for years. I wondered if it was listed in the catalogue.

'Look at this.' I showed it to Simon. He had to peer at the cover – it was dark outside and we hadn't dared to switch the main lights on. Dim lights lined the end of each aisle and they were just about enough to illuminate our search.

'I read that at university,' he told me. 'I haven't seen a copy for years.'

The book went into my bag with a collection of Yeats' poetry and two intriguing historical books Simon had found about the rise of nationalism in Europe and America early in the twenty-first century.

We'd been combing the bookshelves for two hours already and my back was aching. I stretched, feeling the tense muscles relax. Smiling, Simon touched my face.

'Do you want to look in the basement?'

I felt a thrill of excitement.

'Don't they keep things there they don't want us to see?'

'That's the rumour. I've never been down before. But if we're going to do this, now seems as good a time as any.'

I took a deep breath. 'Let's do it.'

The stairs to the basement were dark. Simon took my hand and we felt our way down. As we made it to the bottom, there was a soft buzzing sound and the overhead strip lights slowly came to life.

'There used to be cameras down here,' Simon told me. 'But one of the admin staff told me the system failed a few months ago and the university never bothered to replace it.'

I scanned the walls for a blinking red light. 'Let's hope so.'

The corridor was lined with storage spaces, filled with shelves and boxes of books behind criss-crossed metal gates. We began to walk.

'Do you know who you're going to invite to class?' I asked.

Simon was frowning at a shelf of philosophy books.

'I have a couple of people in mind. The way they write, their ideas. They're bold.'

Anxiety shuddered through me. This was happening.

'I spoke to one of the girls in my Introduction to Poetry class today. It was terrifying.'

Simon took my hand. I could see that he was nervous too.

'There's still time to back out, if you want.'

His eyes studied my face. I tilted my chin. 'No. It doesn't matter that I'm scared, we need to do this.'

He didn't reply at first. But then he nodded.

'I'm with you, Clara.'

It was raining when the inspectors came. I was sitting alone in my office, watching the water as it ran down the outside of the window. A volume of banned poetry lay open on my desk.

There was a knock at the door and I jumped, shoving the book under a pile of papers. I spun round, guilt plastered across my face as the door opened to reveal one of the other English lecturers, breathless, his hair wet.

'They're here, the inspectors are here.'

I stared at him, not taking it in.

'They're here to audit the department.'

My stomach dropped. I had begun working on my class, putting together all the materials I would need, but it had taken time to find the right books. Most of them were banned, so it was impossible to find them in the library, or the campus bookshop. But there were other places you could go and my father had left me several from his collection. A pile of those books sat in my desk drawer, wrapped in other, more innocuous dust jackets: novels by Ray Bradbury, Kurt Vonnegut, George Orwell, Margaret Atwood and Alan Moore. A volume of poetry called *The Life of X*, whose author still fell victim to the void, despite publishing her work anonymously. Even now, her name is not known.

'What are they doing?' I asked. 'Do they want to speak to everyone?'

He nodded. 'They're holding a meeting in the lecture hall now. It's compulsory.'

I got to my feet, feeling light headed. Grabbing my bag, I followed him out of the door, only pausing to lock up my office.

The rest of the English department were already gathered when we got downstairs. They sat in a cluster in the middle of the room, muttering amongst themselves. Four stern-looking men in suits stood at the front, unpacking their documents, along with a clunky laptop computer.

Gradually the room fell silent. The four inspectors stood in a line, looking at us. Their faces gave nothing away. I shrank

42

down in my seat as one of them caught my eye. He didn't flinch. My heart fluttered, too high, caught in the back of my throat.

Then one of them stepped forward and the spell was broken.

'We are from the Educational Standards Bureau,' he said. His voice wrapped around us like a shroud. 'We're here to ensure that this university is maintaining the standard of teaching that the government expects from all its academic institutions. On this occasion, our focus is on the English department.'

All around me, I felt my colleagues tense. It was possible this was a spot check. But it was equally possible that there had been a report of some kind, or there were suspicions of inappropriate activity. I tried to keep my breathing even.

'We will be here for as long as it takes to confirm the legitimacy of your activity. During that time, we will speak to each of you at length about your classes, your own research and your students. If you have concerns you wish to raise, that is your opportunity.'

He paused, his gaze raking across each member of the team. I clutched my hands tightly in my lap so he wouldn't see them shaking.

'You must make your office space, your research materials and your computers available to us on request. We will attend your lectures and classes at random. You will not be notified about this in advance.'

He stopped speaking, and instead began to arrange a stack of papers on the desk, obviously ignoring us. One of the other inspectors clapped his hands.

'You may return to your duties.'

Silence hung in the air for a moment; no one moved. Then, as if triggered by some invisible signal, the English staff jumped up from their seats as one and filed towards the door. No one dared speak, but I could feel the tumble of words building.

Once the door was safely closed and we were in the stairwell, the frightened whispers began, steadily growing louder as the anxiety rang in my ears.

It felt like the audit would never end. Even after two weeks, the inspectors were still a stifling presence in our department, present in every lecture, every seminar, every class.

I arrived at work one morning to find my office already unlocked. With a feeling of dread, I pushed open the door and went in. A uniformed inspector was sitting at my desk – drawers open haphazardly – flicking through the pages of a book.

She turned sharply as I came into the room.

'Ah, Ms Winter, good morning.' Her smile unnerved me.

I wished her good morning, unsure of what else to say. The office felt small with us both in it. With her at my desk, I hovered uncertainly.

'I haven't read this, is it any good?'

She held up the book for me to see. It was one of the set texts from the first-year course. *The Lost Ones* told the story of a family killed in the Whitehall bombing. I'd always found it horribly overwrought, but that was the point. You were supposed to be moved by the narrative, to be angry that a young family died so senselessly; it justified the First General's takeover of the government.

'I've always enjoyed it,' I answered, in a flat tone. 'It's a very powerful story.'

She nodded. 'So I've heard.'

As I watched, she turned her back on me and continued pulling things from my drawers. My stomach churned, despite the knowledge that each of the banned books had already been purged from the office. They sat in two piles beneath the floorboards of our apartment.

With the drawers empty, their contents scattered across the desk and the floor around it, she turned her attention to the folders where I kept my lesson plans. My papers were soon scattered around her. She wasn't careful.

The room was warm and sweat began to prickle the small of my back. I was still wearing my coat and scarf, unable to remove them, or relax at all in her presence. My heart rate was too high; I worried she could hear it racing.

She made a noise, a little gasp of triumph that whistled between her teeth. It jolted me back to the moment, every nerve jangling.

'Well, what's this?'

She turned in the chair, brandishing the paper in her hand. I couldn't see what it was, but terror flooded my system. I had begun making a list of potential students for the class one night, when I was at the office too late and too tired. It was foolish, but I was sure I'd disposed of it. As I searched my memory, doubt began to set in.

When she opened her mouth again, I noticed her teeth. They were stained yellow with nicotine and lack of care.

'These notes appear to refer to a book that you shouldn't have access to. Are you familiar with Plato's *Republic*?'

My body stiffened. I remembered the basement storage space and the piles of philosophy books there. I hadn't taken it away with me, but I had spent an hour tracing my finger across the pages as Simon hunted for something, absorbing these words that spoke to me across more than two thousand years.

I'd been compelled to take notes.

And now an inspector sat in my office with them tight in her hand, this evidence of my wrongdoing. I didn't know what to say, or how to justify this. I thought of the half-dozen students I'd invited to a seminar in a small, isolated room later that week. My mouth opened, but no words came out.

She fixed me with a disapproving stare.

'While possession of this book would be enough to justify a warrant for your arrest, having notes is not, technically, a crime.' She got slowly to her feet. For the first time I noticed that she was tall. She pulled her shoulders back and seemed to fill the space around her.

'Fortunately for you, Ms Winter, I can't see this book among your possessions. But I will be confiscating your notes. Your file will be updated.'

She brushed deliberately past me as she left the room, leaving behind the faint tang of body odour. At the door, she paused.

'And we will be monitoring you.'

She let the words hang in the air. I couldn't breathe. And then she was gone, her heavy footsteps fading along the corridor. Every instinct told me to run and find Simon, to warn him. But I held back. It was all too easy to picture the inspector, waiting in the lobby for me to burst from the stairwell and reveal more of my secrets.

I forced myself to breathe. Instead of running, I went through the papers she had left discarded across my office, organising them carefully and returning them to the correct folders. As I worked, my fear began to turn to anger. How could anyone imagine reading a book was enough to ruin someone's life and remove their future? Especially when that book contained a wisdom that was centuries old, far older and more impressive than this regime would ever be.

As I returned the last folder to the shelf, my resolve hardened. I'd spent my whole life afraid of this government, of what they might do to me, what they'd already done to my family. They had taken my father away once, but planning these classes, I felt more connected to him than I had in so long. I wouldn't let them take that away too.

When enough time had passed that it wouldn't be suspicious, I went to look for Simon. I found him in the Humanities staff room, with a pile of essays and a red pen, immersed in his work. He looked up, startled, when I came through the door.

'God, you scared me!' He studied my face. 'Is something wrong?'

I was still furious about the invasion of my privacy, but looking at Simon, I faltered, ashamed of myself for making such a basic mistake. I could choose to ignore it, but this put us in danger.

Simon was up out of his seat, papers forgotten on the floor. He took my face in both hands. 'Clara, what's wrong?'

I dragged a stuttering breath into my lungs.

'They know.'

His pupils went black. 'What do you mean, they know?'

He kept his voice low, glancing quickly around the room. No one was there but us. I put my hands over his, our eyes locked.

'I'm sorry. I couldn't help it, I took some notes on one of the books from the basement and I forgot... The inspectors just found them in my office.'

Simon pulled away abruptly, spinning round like he couldn't bear to look at me. He paced, like he couldn't believe what I'd just told him. For a second, I stood there like a scolded child, shoulders slumped and tears ready to flow. But crying wouldn't do any good, I had to be strong.

I straightened. 'I'm sorry,' I said again, my voice firmer. 'I didn't mean for this to happen. But it doesn't have to change anything; we'll just have to be more cautious now.'

The look he gave me was worse than anything he might have said.

'This was your idea, all this risk...' His hands trembled.

'There's no way you can be involved in teaching this class. They'll be keeping an eye on you now. You're a bloody fool to think you can carry on.'

Angry colour flushed my cheeks. It masked the sting of his words. 'This is too important for us to stop now. I *need* this, we all do.'

He lifted a hand to silence me.

'This is bigger than you, Clara. The work we've done...' He turned to stare out of the window. 'Teaching this class is important, you were right about that. But I'm not sure you can be there. And not just because of this. You're too emotionally involved, you aren't thinking clearly. What's to stop you making another mistake and setting the bag squad after us all? It's not just you and me now; there are students involved. The risk is too great.'

I was boxed into a corner. If I argued, I only proved his point.

Without another word he gathered his things and left me alone in the staff room. I was furious with him, and with myself. But underneath, a different emotion stirred that I didn't want to acknowledge. I flung myself into a chair, heartsick and terrified of this thing I'd set in motion.

Seven

Two meetings passed unnoticed, before the inspectors completed their audit and left the university. Things had been tense between Simon and me, but I'd done what he wanted and stayed away from the classes, leaving him to teach alone. But the longer I stayed on the outside, unsure of what was happening, the more afraid I became.

By the third session, the anxiety was beginning to affect me. I had to know, to be involved. This was my idea and I should be the one taking responsibility for it. The connection I'd felt to my father had ebbed, my grasp on his memory faltered. I needed to get it back.

I was the last one to arrive at the meeting. It had already begun when I crept in and tried to hide at the back. Simon noticed my arrival and raised his eyebrow, asking me a silent question. I looked away, focusing on pulling up a chair beside a girl who was gazing at him with open admiration. He was talking about the riots that broke out shortly after the military took over the country. Riots that had been brutally put down.

'Many have tried to make an accurate count of the death toll, but it's always been impossible. Death records were falsified or abandoned. Families were too afraid to report their loved ones missing. It was the beginning of the disappearances.'

The students began to murmur. I wondered how many of them had lost someone. It made me sad that they were probably too young to remember what life was like before. They wouldn't know the freedom education could provide, or how to cultivate their own opinions without the government watching over their shoulders.

Simon's whole demeanour had changed. He was no longer the frustrated professor, peddling lies to his students, worn and close to giving up. Instead he was alive; everything about him seemed vital. The girl beside me never once took her eyes from him and I understood her feelings. My heart fluttered at the passion in his voice.

Apart from my neighbour, all the students were taking notes. I looked at them uneasily as they scribbled down these words that had the power to destroy lives. I couldn't help but wonder who else might have access; if they guarded their books or were careless with them.

A young man sitting across from me raised his hand. 'What do you think things would be like now, if the military hadn't taken over?'

Simon gave a wry smile and looked out of the window for a moment, as he gathered his thoughts. 'That's a difficult question, Jerome. There are so many things that were affected when the new regime took over; for example, they completely strangled innovation throughout the country. Overnight, whole industries were gone. Now any new technology is developed solely by the government and sold abroad. And the internet is a shadow of what it was twenty years ago. The government quickly killed off social media and access to any unapproved websites. It's become merely another tool for propaganda. We might as well be living in *Nineteen Eighty-Four*.'

The students looked sideways at each other, not understanding the reference. Simon caught their confused expressions and began to elaborate. '*Nineteen Eighty-Four* was a novel written by a man called George Orwell, published in the late 1940s. Orwell imagined what the world would be like in the future, as surveillance technology became commonplace and the government grew more controlling. It's ironic really. He was thirty years or so out with the date, but his vision was surprisingly accurate.'

Simon gave a sharp laugh. 'And that's another difference for you. When I was at university, *Nineteen Eighty-Four* was considered a classic. Almost everyone had heard of it, even if they hadn't read it. Now it's banned and none of you are aware that it ever existed.' He rubbed his eyes. 'Do you know what reality television is?'

The girl beside me spoke up tentatively. 'The programmes that follow everyday people going about their jobs, to give young people an idea of what to do after they finish their education.'

Simon smiled and she flushed. 'That's what reality television is now, but when it first began it was very different. George Orwell's vision actually played a huge part, as one of the earliest reality shows was called *Big Brother*, a term that had been coined by Orwell in his book.'

The students sat forward, fascinated by this snippet of cultural information. I shook my head, remembering a few episodes of *Celebrity Big Brother* I'd seen as a child, back when we still had a television and six hundred Sky channels.

'The programme followed a group of people who were brought to live in a house built inside a television studio. There were cameras in every room and the contestants were filmed around the clock. They had to perform various tasks and each week someone would be voted off, until the public decided on the winner, who received prize money of... what was, I think, about £100,000.'

The students gasped. I looked around the room at their shocked expressions. That was more money than they could hope to earn in twenty years, with wages so low. I remembered when, not long after the First General's takeover, it had cost almost £100 to buy a punnet of strawberries. The ports and airports were closed to foreign trade and there were few people to pick the fruit. It withered in the fields.

Simon nodded. 'That's right. Where the programme started supposedly as a social experiment, many people entered the house in the hope of getting famous. Quite a number succeeded – to some extent at least. And *Big Brother* was only one reality show. There must have been hundreds.'

'Were these people very important or talented? If they became famous by going on television like that,' one boy asked.

Simon smirked. 'I'm afraid not. In fact, as reality TV became a phenomenon, it was seen as a way for anyone to become rich and famous, mostly through doing very little. That's one thing I'm not sad to have consigned to history.'

The students seemed inspired by these random pieces of information and asked endless questions, wanting to know all the gory details. Simon answered them with good humour, often making the group laugh loudly. I could see why he enjoyed teaching them.

It had been growing dark for a while before anyone appeared to notice. Simon glanced at his watch, his eyebrows raised. 'Well, I didn't realise it was so late. I think this would be a good place to finish for today. Shall we meet again this Thursday, at the same time?'

Murmurs of assent ran around the room as the students

began closing their notebooks and stuffing them into bags. They left quietly, in pairs or alone, calling out their goodbyes. The girl beside me was the last to leave. She lingered, tidying her things agonisingly slowly and throwing surreptitious glances my way, as though waiting for me to leave. I folded my arms and gave her a level gaze. With a sigh, she got up and put on her jacket.

'Bye Simon; thanks, that was so interesting.' She beamed at him.

He smiled back at her. 'Goodnight Elizabeth. I'll see you on Thursday.'

I stood up and crossed the room to stand beside Simon. As she left the room, the girl glared at me over her shoulder.

I put my arms around his neck. 'I think someone has a little crush on you.'

His back was stiff. 'She's just eager to learn.'

'I don't think she'd be as keen in one of my classes,' I teased.

His voice was cool. 'As long as she learns something, I'm happy.' He broke free of my embrace and began to clean the whiteboard. 'And you aren't the one teaching this class.'

A pang of guilt washed over me. 'You know I'm sorry about that, I didn't mean for it to happen.'

He made a disgusted sound. 'You could have got us both caught with your carelessness. You know, I'm not sure you ever really wanted to do this.' He paused. 'Did you get caught on purpose so you'd have an excuse to stop?'

His words were like a punch in the gut.

'Of course not!' I exclaimed. But even as I said it, I wondered if it was really true. I knew better than to take notes – I'd had to be careful my whole life. And just when the stakes were raised for both of us, I messed things up.

But it must be worse for Simon. I'd pushed him into this. I'd made him start this class that he had no desire to teach, and then

I'd been forced to pull out. I had no choice, it was true. But that didn't make me feel any better, when I lay in bed beside him, gazing at the hard curve of his spine, at his body, pulled as far away from me as it could get on the narrow mattress. I was too afraid to touch him after the first rejection, the tensing of his shoulders and the way he shifted from beneath my fingertips.

I embraced him more tightly, relieved that he was allowing me to get this close. Resting my cheek against his chest, I spoke softly. 'I don't know any more whether I meant it to happen and that's the truth. Coming to your classes, it makes me realise things I never thought of. I see all the things that could go wrong. Did you see them all taking notes? What happens if someone else sees what they've written? It could be dangerous for you… and for them.'

He sighed heavily and his breath ruffled my hair. 'What did you think would happen? You must have realised we'd be taking a risk: us and them. They're all responsible young adults, I wouldn't have invited them here if I thought they would be careless with the knowledge I'm sharing. They're all well aware of the consequences.'

I broke away from him. 'How aware can they be? None of them have ever been to the prisons. I bet they're all from nice, respectable families who have never put a foot wrong.'

He scowled. 'Like me, you mean?'

I looked away. 'That's not what I'm saying.'

'Actually, there are several of these students who have lost relatives. You only have to look around you to see that we're all victims of this regime, not only the ones who have been kidnapped.'

I shook my head. 'It's not the same and you know it. How old are these kids? Eighteen? Nineteen? They were babies when things changed. This world is all they've ever known. It doesn't mean the same thing to them as it does to us.'

He was angry now. 'That's where you're wrong. Maybe they don't remember what it was like to have a smartphone and a Facebook page. To be able to go out drinking on Saturday nights, go backpacking round South East Asia or get a mortgage. But they know that things in this country *aren't right*. They can see that people are suffering, that things are broken and we have to make a change. In a few years, no one will remember what it was like before. That's why we need them to care. You were right about this, Clara. *You were right*. We need to educate them, to tell them the truth, because it's going to fall to them to change things.'

He stared at me heatedly, waiting for my reaction. I began to cry. 'I'm worried about you, Simon. Can't you see that? I couldn't take it if anything were to happen. I made you do this.'

As suddenly as it had begun, his anger was gone. He grasped me tightly, clutching me against him as though this embrace would be enough to prevent anyone from tearing us apart.

'Nothing is going to happen to me, darling. I'm not going anywhere. I promise.'

I wished I could believe him.

Eight

Sometimes we would sit together, on the roof of our building, watching the world as it went slowly by.

We had discovered one day – completely by accident – that one of the other residents kept a garden upstairs. It wasn't much to speak of: a few evergreen plants in plastic pots; a small, blossom-covered tree that was dangerously close to overgrowing; an old wooden bench that was cracked and weather worn. But it was peaceful.

The garden was carefully tucked away around a corner, where there was no reason for anyone to go. There was a steam pipe there and the heat helped the plants to thrive, bringing a splash of tropical colour to the dreary setting. Someone had begun to paint flashes of graffiti on the wall; there was an elaborate heart, anatomical yet stylised, with a rising sun emerging behind it. A scrollwork banner unfurled across the front, with the word 'Lumière' written on it. It reminded me of the retro tattoos that were popular when I was young.

And the view: ours was a tall building, taller than those around it. From the roof, you could see for miles across the city. We would bring a bottle of wine and a couple of candles upstairs with us and drink as the sun went down, watching the lights twinkling as the city drifted towards the night. Sometimes there would be a power cut and we'd sit for hours with only the stars for company.

That evening we were drinking wine, straight from the bottle. I put it to my lips and took a long swallow, wiping my mouth with the back of my hand. I passed the bottle to Simon.

Most of our conversations these days revolved around the class. We'd both grown to accept that it was his now. Although I had pushed him into it, I'd never seen him this enthusiastic about something. I'd never seen him this alive. He bloomed, while my insides shrivelled with worry.

'But how did you find them all? How could you know that they would be willing to join the class?'

I waited while he drank. Instead of handing me the wine, he put the bottle on the floor and stared out at the city.

'It's hard to say. It was like osmosis; a feeling that they might understand. I had no intention of going through with it, at first. I only agreed to keep you happy. But you wore down my reservations. And once you'd suggested it, the idea was always there, just below the surface. That gave me time to develop a sense of my students. I would notice the details: the things they would say during class, or in their essays, the subjects they chose to write about.'

He got up and wandered over to the roof edge, his elbows on the wall as he took in the view. I picked up the wine and went to stand beside him.

'Some of them play it so safe, only writing about things that won't draw any attention to them. They keep to the core parts of the curriculum – the empowerment of the working classes, or the return to family values, regurgitating the party's ideas. They would never be interested in my classes. But the ones who skirt the boundaries of what they are permitted to study, they're much cleverer. They never actually *say* anything they shouldn't, but a practised eye can trace the thread of their idea, beyond the bounds of propaganda. Some of them still value human rights. Those are the students who know how to think for themselves. Their discontent is almost transparent.'

He turned to me earnestly. 'In a sense, I'm helping them. If I can see what they're thinking, it won't be long before someone else manages it; someone more dangerous. I don't just talk about the past, I teach them how to hide; how to hold onto themselves and their private thoughts, without revealing them.'

I leaned forward to take in the view, so I could hide my face from him. It made sense. You didn't need to verbalise a thought for it to make you a target; attitude was enough.

We were silent for a long time, growing cold as the night deepened its hold. The sounds of the city seemed far away. We finished the wine, passing the bottle back and forth until the last dregs were gone. My cheeks grew warm; I threaded my arm through Simon's and pressed my cheek against his shoulder. He brought his other hand up and gripped mine tightly.

Somewhere in the distance there was a flash of light. A volley of gunfire rang out, the sound carrying across the city. We stood frozen, wondering who was out there, in the night.

When the sirens came, we blew out the candles and retreated downstairs in the darkness, still holding on to each other.

'When the military first took to the streets, I don't think anyone realised how serious the situation was.'

Simon was sitting on the desk at the front of the classroom, his students gathered around him in a semicircle. Behind him, the blackboard was covered in obscure mathematical calculations, some of them erased where a hand had wiped them away. A faded poster for a maths challenge was stuck on the wall, curled up at one corner. I sat beside the desk, so I could only see one side of Simon's face as he spoke.

'The military hadn't been active in our own country for so long, it was outside people's scope of experience. At first, some people took it as a joke. Others were offended and railed about it in the newspapers. Many more ignored the situation, trusting things would soon be back to normal. It was only after the change in government was announced that we began to worry, that creeping sense of doubt giving way to unease. That's when the people began to take to the streets in protest.'

It was late in the afternoon and darkness was beginning to descend. Simon had pressed me to come along to his next class, to find out more about the things they discussed in their classroom, after everyone else had gone home.

Elizabeth raised her hand. 'What happened to those people? The ones who protested – were they all killed?'

'Actually, no, they weren't.' Simon gave a tight smile. 'At first the new regime was civilised. Don't forget, the soldiers on the ground were a part of the previous army. They were regular young men and women with families, who had enjoyed the same freedoms as the rest of us. They could vote, they could buy a house, go abroad for holidays, whatever they wanted. At first, they were following orders from their commanders, and those orders seemed reasonable. There was a real threat of terrorism that had been growing for years. It reached the point where people were afraid to go on public transport, or visit certain places. The media whipped everyone up into a frenzy of hysteria. So those soldiers, they thought they were protecting us from an outside threat. They didn't realise then that it was their own leaders who were about to do the damage.'

Elizabeth frowned. 'So how did they get all the soldiers to behave the way they did? Killing ordinary people and stuff?'

Before Simon could respond, Jerome stepped in to answer

the question. 'There was a lot of retraining, cajoling, threats to their families, that kind of thing. But they also made examples out of people.'

Simon was nodding. 'Yes, Jerome's right. The soldiers were like everyone else in that, if they didn't support the junta, if they didn't follow orders, they were punished. Often their whole family would be wiped out, or sent to prison too, as an example to the others of what could happen. That particular tactic had always worked well in the Communist states.'

'That wasn't all though,' Jerome interrupted. He looked angry. 'It was before I was born, but my mum told me the story. Not long after the coup, when the protests were starting to take place, my uncle was out on the streets with some of his friends. He wasn't much older than I am now. They were all students; my mum said it was almost like a lark for them, a day out to London to join in the protests.'

He paused to gather his thoughts. 'Mum said Uncle Josh was always a bit of a lad. He'd been a joker since he was young, class clown, you know? Well anyway, they'd all had a couple of drinks on the bus on the way down, like it was a normal day out. His friends told my gran that afterwards.

'They'd been marching for about an hour when they came to a barricade of soldiers. They all had guns, but they weren't doing anything, just stopping the people from getting any-where near Parliament. The crowd was fairly good natured: they shouted a few insults, chucked a couple of empty cans, but there was no real violence or anything.

'But Uncle Josh thought it would be funny to try to take a picture on his mobile phone – they all had them then, right?'

He glanced at Simon, who nodded.

'Well, the thing was, he tried to grab the gun off one of the soldiers. He was larking about, being stupid. He didn't mean anything by it. I think the soldier must have been surprised, 'cos Josh even got the gun off him too. His friends were all laughing and taking pictures. Other people in the crowd had started to notice.

'The soldier whose gun it was didn't even react too badly. They said he seemed to realise it was a joke. He took the gun off Josh and went back to his post. But Josh didn't leave it. He was flushed from the prank, trying to play the clown. He grabbed the gun again, laughing the whole time. But the soldier didn't let go. They wrestled a bit and Josh slipped and went down – he'd been drinking, after all. As he fell, somehow the gun went off. When he got back up, the toe of his shoe was missing where the bullet had gone right through – without hitting him.'

The students were all smiling, amused by the story.

'They all went mental, thinking it was so funny. The soldier was in shock; he didn't know what to do. The crowd around them was laughing and cheering. Well, one of the commanding officers had seen what had happened. He was one of their core people, the junta. Before anyone realised what was happening he had walked over, took his gun out and shot Uncle Josh in the head. Then he turned round and blasted the soldier in the face.'

There were gasps from his classmates. Jerome fell silent, his lips pressed together in a tight line. The air in the room felt heavy.

Simon got up from his perch on the desk. 'Thank you for sharing that, Jerome.' He put his hand on the boy's shoulder. 'I'm sorry about your uncle.' There were murmurs around the room as the others agreed.

'But Jerome's story is actually the perfect example of what we were discussing. When the army resorted to violence, we weren't prepared. These soldiers were ordinary men; they were a part of our families. They hadn't been indoctrinated or grown up with war and horror. But this still happened. The army still became a monster, from the head down. It was all the more powerful, all the more sudden, because we never expected it. Things changed while we were sleeping and we no longer had the power to change them back.'

Nine

Once a month, we would meet my mother for Sunday brunch at a local restaurant. It was a place that she disapproved of, but we continued to go because it was convenient. Every time we visited she would sneer delicately at the traditional decor and the black and white cityscapes that lined the walls. She preferred her eateries chic and minimalist, all glass and exposed steel, with expensive wine lists.

She always ordered the same thing: braised kale frittata with a Bloody Mary. The drink would disappear quickly and be replaced with another, over and over, as we pretended not to notice. She would pick at her food while we scoffed mounds of American-style pancakes with maple syrup or French toast covered in cinnamon, food we wouldn't have been able to afford without the fifty-pound notes she would slip into my pocket, leaning in to kiss my cheek.

'Tell me, Simon,' she asked, taking a sip of her crimson drink, 'how is the manuscript coming along? Surely you must be almost finished by now?'

Simon swallowed a mouthful of sticky pancake and wiped his mouth. 'Actually, I haven't had much time to work on it lately. I've been teaching some extra classes and that has rather monopolised my time.' He smiled. 'The students are very keen.'

A heavy pearl bracelet slid up and down her wrist as she cut the frittata into tiny pieces, without taking a bite. 'Really? How nice.' She smiled thinly, the blood seeping from her lips as she pressed them together in a tight line. 'But you must make the time to work on your book. It's so important as an academic to be *published*. Isn't that right, darling?'

I sighed inwardly. 'Well, of course it's lovely to have written a book, mother, but it isn't everything. And you know that Simon has had over a dozen articles published in journals over the years. He's even won awards.'

I squeezed Simon's hand under the table. He squeezed back and gave me a quick wink as my mother put down her knife and fork and stabbed instead at her phone, which had shrilled self-importantly.

She scrolled through to read the incoming message and frowned. Shoving the phone into her designer handbag, she picked up her glass and drained it, a thick drop of tomato juice sliding down her chin. She banged the glass unsteadily onto the table and waved her other hand for the waiter to bring a refill.

'Honestly,' she muttered. 'Your father knows that I *always* come here to meet you for brunch. I don't know why he insists on pestering me, asking where I am.'

A lump of toast caught in my throat and I gave a sharp cough. My voice hoarse, I said, 'Why do you insist on referring to him as my father? You know how I feel about it.'

She wafted her hand at me dismissively, accepting a fresh glass from the waiter who had scurried over from the bar. 'Oh don't be ridiculous, Clara. Darius is your father, even if you refuse to use his name.'

When my mother remarried, I had been forced to take her new husband's surname, effectively wiping my own father out of existence. It was only when I left home and began teaching that I reverted back to Winter. No doubt my name would be on a watchlist somewhere, as the child of a disenfranchised academic. The name change would only have drawn attention to my existence, but it was the one act of rebellion I could safely commit. In fact, if my stepfather hadn't been an important member of the Authorisation Bureau, I would never have been permitted to abandon my father's name. They didn't like it when people tried to hide the true nature of their identity.

She was beginning to sway a little now, a sign of impending drunkenness. I changed the subject. 'And how is Will? Is he enjoying the academy?'

My half-brother was sixteen and had recently finished school. He had followed in his father's boot prints by deciding to join the military and was currently enrolled at an academy for elite officer training, which was widely known as a recruiting ground for the Authorisation Bureau. We had never been close. He was too like his father.

She stiffened slightly before she replied, avoiding my eye. 'He's fine; he seems to be getting on well there. Your father has a friend on the staff; he said some extremely favourable things about Will.'

There was a lull in the conversation. Unsure of what to say next, I busied myself with my food. Beside me, Simon did the same, while my mother busied herself with her fourth Bloody Mary.

I remembered Will as a child, tormenting the frogs in the garden pond with a stick. Once he caught one and trapped it in a glass jar until it suffocated. He left the tiny corpse in my bed, under the pillow. I still recall the sensation of its cold flesh against my skin as I slipped my hand beneath the pillow, trying to get comfortable. Even at seven years old, Will had found my screams hilarious.

I put down my fork, no longer hungry. My mother was staring into space, glass in hand, tomato residue clinging to the sides. 'What time did you tell him you'd be back?' I asked.

She didn't seem to hear me. 'Mum,' I said, reaching out to touch her hand. She jumped, brought back to the present moment. 'What time do you have to leave?'

She flicked her wrist, glancing at the face of her gold watch. 'About twenty minutes, I think. The driver will be collecting me.' My mother rarely went anywhere alone.

I nodded. 'Do you want a coffee before you go?'

She squinted at me, as though deciding whether or not to be insulted.

'I'm having one,' Simon said, gesturing for the waiter. 'Lucia?'

She nodded. 'Yes, alright then. A latte.'

Simon ordered the drinks and the waiter hurried away. I watched as the girl behind the counter began pulling levers on an elaborate but aged coffee machine, slowly filling three cups.

We sipped our coffee in silence. My mother had that washed-out look that comes after drinking too much alcohol, when it starts to seep into your bloodstream and make you nauseous.

Simon was at the counter paying our bill with the fifty-pound note when my mother's phone rang. She glanced at the screen, 'It's the driver.'

I waited while she spoke to him, a brief conversation that consisted of barely half a dozen words on her part. 'He's outside,' she told me, hanging up.

I nodded and picked up her coat, which was hanging from the back of her chair. I held it out for her as she struggled to get her arms in the right place. She fastened the buttons as I shrugged into my old leather jacket and wrapped a scarf around my neck.

66

She stepped around the table and gave me a hug. I was surprised, but returned the embrace. I caught Simon looking at us over her shoulder; he raised his eyebrows and I smiled in return.

My mother pulled back and looked at me properly for the first time that day. Lifting a hand to touch my cheek, she said, 'We should get you a proper coat, Clara. You must be cold, always wearing that old thing.' She tugged both sides of the jacket together and fastened the zip. 'There, that's better.'

She gave me a soft smile. 'You look after yourself, darling. I'll see you again soon.'

Then she tottered off, the heels of her suede boots clicking on the wooden floor of the restaurant. She didn't say goodbye to Simon, but then she never did. He would always retreat to the counter to pay the bill so that she could make her escape without acknowledging him.

He came back, tucking his wallet into the pocket of his trousers. 'You ready to go?'

'Yep.' I smiled and he bent to give me a kiss, his lips lingering against mine. He took my hand and we made our way outside, shielding our eyes as we emerged from the dimly lit restaurant into the bright autumn sunshine.

On Sunday evenings, we had a ritual. Simon would cook a meal, usually something vaguely exotic from a cookbook he found in the library. Sometimes he had to improvise, if he couldn't get hold of all the ingredients. So we ate bizarre versions of dishes we remembered from our childhoods, like chicken curry with most of the spices missing.

It was an unspoken rule that we would take a day off from our work, the university and our students.

That evening, Simon had prepared a casserole. The television played in the background, a familiar theme song signalling the start of that day's news. I don't know why we insisted on watching it, when it only made us both angry.

I'm David G. Tubby, and I'm Susannah Smart. In tonight's news, we reveal the secret plan to bring down our government, which was averted thanks to the swift intervention of the Authorisation Bureau, who arrested a dozen suspects today.

Simon slammed a cup down on the counter. I hurried across the room to silence the television. We were moving around the kitchen in a well-rehearsed dance when there was a knock at the door.

'You expecting someone?' I asked, gripping a serving spoon in my hand.

He shook his head. 'It could be your mum.'

I actually laughed. 'Don't be stupid. When has my mother ever been here?'

The knock came again. Wiping his hands on a dish towel, Simon answered it. I hovered in the kitchen, keeping a firm grip on my spoon, craning my neck to see round him.

I raised my eyebrows. It was the girl from class. She was dressed for a party, in a short dress that clung to her body but her hair was wild and she was breathing hard. She jittered in the corridor, shifting from one foot to another. My eyes were drawn to the delicate tattoo that curled around her ankle.

'Elizabeth! What are you doing here?' Simon asked.

She rushed in, eyes darting around the room. I folded my arms.

'Can we help you with something?'

Simon threw me an exasperated look. 'What's wrong?'

There was a pause. 'Jerome's disappeared.'

We both stared at her. Simon's brow puckered. 'Disappeared?'

She nodded, running a hand through her hair. 'I was supposed to meet him for a few drinks, but he didn't turn up. I waited, like, nearly an hour.' She started to pace. 'So I went over to his place. When I got there his room was empty and the door had been kicked in.'

She was shaking. 'Here,' I guided her to the sofa. 'Sit down. I'll make you a cup of tea.' She nodded, eyes glistening.

As I filled the kettle, Simon began questioning her. 'Did you see anyone else when you were there?'

'No. If anyone was home they were inside. The guy in the next room is friends with Jerome. I knocked, but he didn't answer.'

Simon was walking in circles around the kitchen. 'When did you last see him?'

'I think it was, mmm… Tuesday. We had a lecture together. We went to the library afterwards and arranged to meet up tonight.' She fiddled with her hair again. 'It's not like Jerome not to turn up. Something must have happened.'

'Let's not panic.' Simon held his hands up in front of him reassuringly. 'Maybe he went out somewhere and lost track of time, forgot he'd agreed to meet you. Or there could have been an emergency.' It was obvious he didn't believe it.

I gave Elizabeth her tea and perched on the other end of the sofa.

'Is there someone we can get in touch with? What about his parents?' Simon said.

She shook her head. 'They live up north somewhere. I don't think they have a phone. It's easier to avoid the surveillance.'

'He must have friends you can contact?'

'There might be one…' She fidgeted, twisting her hands together. 'Ronnie might know. He works with Jerome, at a bar near the university. We go there sometimes after lectures.'

'Where can we find him?'

'He'll be at the bar; he works Sunday night.'

Simon was already putting on his coat.

'Do you think it's a good idea to turn up and start asking questions?' I said softly. 'You don't know who else might be there.'

'If something's happened to Jerome, we need to know about it. And this lad might have information. So we go.' Simon was wrestling with the buttons on his coat. 'You don't have to come if you don't want to, Clara.'

I jumped up. 'Of course I'm bloody going. I'm not going to sit here wondering where you are and if you're okay.'

'Fine.' He didn't look happy. He pulled my jacket off the hook behind the door and held it out. We left the apartment; the Sunday evening casserole cold and congealing on the hob.

The bar was a mile or so from our apartment. It was Sunday night so there were few buses. We made the journey on foot, Simon striding ahead.

It took almost half an hour to find the place. We stood across the street, watching as people went in and out. The bar patrons seemed young. They looked like an edgy crowd; I caught a glimpse of metal piercings glinting under the flickering neon signage, of tattoos and elaborately shaved hair. Elizabeth shivered in her thin jacket.

It was me who took the initiative. 'Let's get this over with.'

I strode across the street and past the sullen bouncer in his leather coat. He eyed me as I walked by but I ignored him, pushing the door open and descending into the depths of the bar, the heat beating at me like a wave. Simon and Elizabeth scurried at my heels.

The stairs took us into what must have once been an old cellar, with a low brick ceiling. The club was small and dark, the air thick with smoke. The beat of the music pulsed in my chest. The bar was tucked away in a corner, crowded with people. I pushed my way forward, reaching back to grip Elizabeth's hand.

'Which one is Ronnie?' I yelled into her ear.

'What?' she shouted back.

'Point him out to me.'

She stopped, straining to see over the mass of drinkers gathered around the bar. 'There.' She pointed at a tall guy who was emerging from a back room, carrying a crate of lager, a beanie hat pulled low over his eyes.

Elizabeth stiffened. 'That's him!'

'Wait here.' I wound my way through the throng of bodies, until I was close enough to lean on the bar. I waited for my turn, waving away a young girl with a pierced septum when she tried to serve me. She shrugged and shifted her attention to the couple next to me.

Eventually Ronnie met my eye and nodded. I beckoned him closer. He leaned over the counter towards me and I got close enough that my lips brushed his ear. I had to shout to be heard over the dull pounding of the music.

'You know Jerome, right?'

When he understood what I was asking, he pulled back and stared at me with open suspicion. The pierced girl glanced over with interest, then went back to her drinks order.

I twisted around to point at Elizabeth. 'I'm with her.'

He frowned, his eyes roaming across the crowd until they fixed on the right girl. He took a step closer and rested his elbows on the bar, his face close to mine.

'Not here. I'll meet you outside in ten minutes.'

He pushed a glass towards me and turned away to serve someone else as though I had never existed. I picked up the glass and took a sip. It was water. I threaded my way towards the exit, slipping the glass onto a table as I went.

I emerged onto the street, dead sound rushing in my ears. The cold hit me full force and I shivered violently, tightening my coat as I walked slowly back across the street, waiting for Simon and Elizabeth.

They weren't far behind me. A burst of noise escaped from the bar as the door opened; when it swung shut the sound stopped abruptly.

'Where are you going? What did he say?' Simon hissed as he came alongside me.

'We have to wait for him,' I said, moving along the street away from the bar. We stopped in a doorway, huddling together out of the light.

Eventually Ronnie came outside. He paused to say something to the bouncer, lighting a cigarette. They shared a brief joke and then the doorman ducked into the bar. Ronnie finished his smoke.

As he flicked the stub to the pavement, Simon put his fingers to his lips and gave a low whistle. Ronnie glanced up quickly, catching sight of us loitering on the other side of the road. He looked over his shoulder and then jogged towards us.

'Follow me,' he said, without stopping.

He hurried away round another corner and ducked into an alleyway. Simon followed without hesitation, Elizabeth and I now trailing behind. I glanced around nervously. The street was fairly quiet, but there were several cars parked further along. I stopped, trying to see if there was anyone inside, but the street lights were dark. Rolling blackouts affected a different part of the city each night.

'Clara,' Simon hissed, beckoning for me to follow.

They were standing in the alley, hidden from the street.

The only light seeped from a window three floors above them, where a row of candles burned behind the glass.

Ronnie was leaning against the wall, with one foot flat against the brickwork. His leg jiggled nervously. When he saw me enter the alley he stood up straight and began to speak, his voice a whisper.

'We have to make this quick. I don't want anyone finding us here.'

The four of us moved closer. 'We need to know if some-thing's happened to Jerome,' Simon said. 'He was supposed to meet Elizabeth here for drinks, but he didn't show up. We haven't been able to get in touch with him.'

At the mention of her name, Elizabeth said something so softly I could barely hear. Colour rose in her cheeks as we all turned to look at her.

'Sorry,' she mumbled, voice wobbling. 'I'm just worried about him.'

Ronnie took another long look around. I began to think that this was more about avoiding whatever he was going to tell us, rather than checking for spies.

He leaned forward. 'He's gone. The Authorisation Bureau kicked his door in during the night and dragged him off.'

'But how do you know? Were you there?' Simon's voice was disbelieving.

'Heard it from one of the lads who lives on the same corridor. There was a big ruckus about two in the morning; he looked out of the peephole to see Jerome being carted off with a bag over his head.' He shook his head. 'Apparently one of the other neighbours stuck his head out to see what was going on and got a kicking for his trouble. Guy's from China; got a rich daddy who wangled him a place at the university. Don't think he realised the situation so he tried to intervene.'

Elizabeth started to cry. Simon put his arm round her shoulders and shushed her gently. His face was grave.

Ronnie looked at each of us closely. 'I don't know what it is you're all involved in, but if I was you, I'd be careful. They've got Jerome now, and once they've got someone, they always make them talk.'

It was late when we arrived back at the apartment; Simon insisted on taking Elizabeth home first. She didn't live on campus, but in a dilapidated block of flats several miles and two train rides away.

'It might be better if you take a break from lectures for a while – go home and see your parents,' he told her.

She sniffled. 'Won't it look worse if I run away?' She pulled out a tissue and wiped her nose. 'Besides, if I go home, what's to stop them coming there to find me? No, I couldn't do that to my parents.'

'You need to stay safe, that's the most important thing.'

We parted ways outside her block of flats, trudging back to the station in silence. Simon had his hands deep in the pockets of his coat, shoulders hunched against the cold. I threaded my arm through his, snuggling against him. My stomach churned; I wasn't sure if it was with hunger or worry.

The streets were dark, many of the lighting columns broken. It would be an ideal place for someone to stop and drag us into the back of a van with darkened windows, never to be heard of again.

But my nightmares weren't realised. We made it to the station, the sickly yellow lights casting eerie shadows on the faces of the waiting travellers. A lone man in overalls stood at the far end of the platform with a long-handled roller, diligently painting out graffiti. He had covered most of it up, but I could still make out the design, a tag used by one of the anti-government groups. A heart motif with intricate lettering that scrolled across the design. Underneath it read: *You don't control me.* The artwork appeared mysteriously around the city, under the noses of officials, as fast as the government could have it removed.

When we arrived home, the apartment was dark; the smell of casserole lingered, sickly and unappetising. I scraped the hardened food into the bin and left the pot to soak in the sink.

We went to bed without eating, lying awake in the darkness.

'Do you think Jerome will be okay?' Simon said. He sounded like a little boy.

I found his hand under the covers and squeezed it tight. I didn't have the heart to tell him what I really thought. Instead, I murmured, 'I'm not sure any of us will be okay.'

Ten

That week I went to Simon's class as normal, but the room was empty, the lights turned off. I flicked them on one by one, the cold classroom staring back at me. Fear shuddered through me. He should be here. My life felt like a series of empty rooms, haunted by missing people.

I glanced at my watch. The time was right, I wasn't late. Simon hadn't said anything to me about moving to a different room, or cancelling. He'd debated it after our excursion with Elizabeth, but had said nothing more. I hadn't seen much of him since, as he'd taken to working late, leaving me to get the bus home alone.

A noise in the corridor outside made me jump. The cleaner was pushing a supply cart through the double doors. She looked tired and unhappy, her feet dragging as she laboured along.

'Excuse me,' I called. My voice cracked with anxiety, too quiet, and she didn't look up. 'Excuse me,' I tried again.

She stopped abruptly, looking up in surprise.

'Sorry pet, you gave me a start. I wasn't expecting anyone down here.'

I switched off the lights and let the classroom door close.

'Wasn't there supposed to be a seminar here tonight?'

She shook her head. 'I'm not really the one to ask.' She patted the pockets of her tabard. 'Oh hang on, I've got a schedule here somewhere, let me check.'

With a huff, she pulled the piece of paper out and unfolded it.

'Let me see… looks like the room was booked, but it's been crossed out. Must have cancelled. Doesn't say what the class was though.'

I thanked her, worries about Simon filling my thoughts. More than anything I felt guilty for starting this. As I pushed through the doors, the squeak of her cleaning cart began again.

It was almost midnight when Simon got home. He came into the apartment stealthily, expecting me to be in bed. Instead I sat rigid on the edge of the sofa, with only a reading lamp illuminating the room. He jumped when he saw me. There were scratches on his face and hands.

'Clara! I thought you'd be asleep. I was trying not to disturb you.'

He shifted his gaze away, fascinated by something on the kitchen wall.

'Where have you been? I was so worried about you,' I said quietly.

'Oh I told you, I had a lot of work to do…'

My sense of guilt abruptly turned to anger. I knew that Simon had never really wanted to teach this class, that I'd pushed him into it, but he'd spent a lot of time blaming me. I'd accepted that; I felt like I deserved it. But allowing me to be afraid for him was something else.

'You expect me to believe that you've been in your office until almost midnight. Just like every other night recently.' I snorted. 'You must be really busy, Simon. Been giving your students extra research assignments?'

'Clara, please…'

I held up my hand. 'Don't bother lying to me. You're bleeding! What's going on? I went to class tonight and no one was there. Did you forget to tell me it was cancelled?'

He dropped his briefcase onto the floor. 'I was trying to protect you.'

I stared at him, my face blank. 'Do you think it will be better for me when one day you don't come home? I can pretend that you never existed either, just like your bloody group.'

He groaned. 'Oh come on; let's not have this discussion again. I don't want to argue with you.'

'Fine.' I got up from the sofa and climbed into bed, turning my back on him. His footsteps hurried across the room and the mattress dipped as he sat beside me.

'Listen, I found something out, Clara,' he said urgently, close to my ear. 'I've been looking for Jerome. Mine wasn't the only group he was a part of. Apparently he was involved with some kind of protest group. You remember that minister who was carjacked outside Birmingham? That was them.'

I sat up. 'Are you telling me that one of your students is a bloody freedom fighter?'

He nodded eagerly, leaning towards me. 'Yes, apparently he was involved in all sorts.'

'And how do you know all this?'

'Ah, well,' he ducked his head and started rubbing the bridge of his nose. I frowned. 'One of his… colleagues… approached me.'

For a moment I was at a loss for words. 'Is that what you've been doing these last few days – meeting with terrorists?'

'They aren't terrorists.' His voice was stern. 'They're a group of people who believe in doing what's right, in making things better, for all of us.'

'I can't believe what I'm hearing. You didn't want to be a part of this. I had to force you to even consider taking this class, and suddenly you're out there in the middle of the night joining terrorist groups.'

'I haven't joined them. Not yet.'

I stared at him. 'Simon, this whole thing scares me to death. I know it was my idea, but seeing you teaching that group, you reminded me so much of my father. You had the same conviction he had. It terrifies me that you could end up the same way. And it would be my fault.'

He shrugged. 'It's worth the risk.'

Frustrated, I flung myself back on the bed. 'I'm sorry, but I don't agree.'

We avoided the subject of missing students and militant groups for days, but it hung between us like a heavy weight.

It was early on Saturday when Simon suggested that we do something together. 'Let's go and find somewhere to have lunch and we can spend the afternoon exploring, like we used to.'

I remembered the early days of our relationship, how we would walk for hours around the city, discovering hidden gardens and quiet streets away from the bustle of daily life. We would search out street art and abandoned buildings, striking architecture and memorable views. Places that were still untouched by the creeping hand of urban decay. I had an old camera that I would tote around, capturing everything I saw, seeing the city anew through its lens. Simon joked that I couldn't fully appreciate any sight, any moment, unless it had been immortalised on film.

We had a photograph of the two of us, framed beside the bed. I had managed to take a self-portrait, as we laughed uproariously during a picnic in the park. We'd been discussing the future and what we wanted out of life. The conversation had turned to marriage and how people took it far too seriously. Simon remarked that it would take him years to save up for an engagement ring on his salary and I joked that I'd rather have a jelly ring, because at least I could eat it if I changed my mind.

We were still in bed, warm beneath the covers despite the bite of autumn in the air. I rolled onto my side so I could look at him. 'I'd like that, I miss exploring.'

I leaned forward and brushed my lips across his. He slipped his arms around me and pulled me close. We lay like that for a long time, my head resting against his chest, his breath ruffling my hair.

It was late afternoon when we tired of wandering aimlessly. The sky was growing dark and I was getting cold, despite wearing a long winter coat and a scarf over my dress. I had resurrected my old camera and couldn't handle it properly in gloves, so I'd opted to leave them at home.

We were walking through a small park close to our neighbourhood. Simon watched me as I photographed a dog playing ecstatically in a pile of fallen leaves, tongue lolling out of its mouth.

Across the park, there was a whistle. The dog pricked up its ears and shot off in a cloud of dried leaves, which rustled and crackled as it went.

'You're shivering.' Simon put his arms round me and I snuggled against him, enjoying the warmth. 'Do you want to head back?'

I smiled tiredly. 'Yeah, I think so. I'm ready to curl up on the sofa with a cup of tea and a book.'

'Okay, let's go.' We started walking across the field, feet sinking slightly into the soft earth. Simon caught my hand as it swung at my side, my camera slung over my shoulder.

As we approached the street, I caught sight of a park bench covered in intricate graffiti. My pace slowed as I gazed at it, imagining how I would frame it in my viewfinder.

'Do you want to take a few more pictures?' Simon asked.

I glanced at him guiltily. 'It's okay; we said we'd get back. It's getting dark now anyway.'

'Don't worry, Clara, take your photos.' He looked across the street. 'I might call into the corner shop and grab a couple of things while you do that. You never know, I might even get you a little surprise for later on.'

His eyes twinkled and I laughed, happy that we had put our argument behind us. 'That sounds interesting. How could I say no?'

He gave me a kiss and jogged across the street, avoiding a car manoeuvring into a parking space across from the shop. The bell chimed faintly as he pushed open the door and went inside.

I turned back to the bench, intent on my photography. After snapping away for a few minutes, Simon still hadn't returned. I looked up as he emerged from the store, carrier bag in hand. He was grinning as he scanned the street, looking for me. I waved, slinging my camera strap across my shoulder and starting towards him.

As he stepped into the street, eyes still fixed on me, the car that had been idling at the edge of the road suddenly screeched forward. It was a sleek black off-roader, with tinted windows and no number plates.

The driver accelerated hard into the street and then slammed on the brakes, forcing the car into a skid. The doors flew open and four men in uniforms piled out, shouting, guns in hand. They ran towards Simon, who was staring at them in shock. I watched as comprehension dawned on his face and he turned to run, but they were already on him.

They grabbed him roughly by the arms, forcing his head down as they dragged him towards the car. I was frozen to the spot. It was almost dark now and I didn't know if they'd seen me, standing at the edge of the park.

As they bundled Simon into the back of the car a voice in my head screamed at me to move. I sprinted across the street, but they were already speeding away. Simon was framed in the back window, as one of the men delivered a blow to the side of his head.

Shaking, I grabbed my camera and started taking picture after picture, before the car turned a corner in a screech of smoking tyres and disappeared from view. I stood there, in the middle of the road, staring after them for a long time, still clutching the camera, finger on the button.

Part Three

Eleven

I should have known from the beginning that she would be my downfall.

That night wasn't the first time I had seen her. We had her husband under surveillance for quite some time before his arrest. I'd seen her coming and going, laden with shopping or hauling dirty clothes to the launderette.

But I never realised she was beautiful; not until she was cowering in her negligee beneath the strip lights in the bedroom they shared, watching as we dragged him away. I couldn't look away; I knew then I had to have her.

As I followed the others down the stairs, my head was full of her. I wasn't thinking about her husband's arrest, or the long night of interrogation ahead. Not then. I thought about the curve of her thigh and the way the light cast a halo around her hair. It was so soft. I could feel my fingers burning where I had touched her.

I was sitting in the front of the transport before I came back to myself. The men were in the back of the van with the prisoner. The noise was unbearable in the enclosed space.

I pulled an old contraband iPod from my pocket and meticulously unravelled the wires, slotting the earphones into my ears.

The swell of Mozart's *Requiem* filled my head. I closed my eyes and allowed myself to drift on the current, closing out everything else.

When I was younger I hadn't realised that music could make a man feel this way. I'd wasted hours raging with the shrieking rock songs of my youth, turning up the volume until the distortion was an angry snarl in my chest and I couldn't tell the thunder of the bass from my own heartbeat.

I was angry with everyone then: my parents, the teachers who had failed me and the government that deprived me of opportunity. That feeling still simmered beneath the surface, but along the way I learned how to use it. It gave me a focus that other people lacked.

The driver pulled away, tyres screeching on the slick asphalt. I lay my head against the back of the seat, feeling the vibrations as the soldiers' boots beat out a rhythm on the prisoner's body.

They didn't stop us at any of the checkpoints, the unmarked van gliding through, occupants hidden behind tinted glass. The eyes of the people waiting slid away, unseeing. It's a kind of self-preservation.

When we arrived at headquarters, the driver swung us expertly down a narrow tunnel, into an underground parking area. It was deserted, except for two armed men, standing either side of the entrance. The metal gate rolled down behind us. The guards stared ahead, unflinching, as the driver and I exited the vehicle.

Tucking my iPod away inside my jacket, I heaved the van doors open. The four soldiers jumped out, their feet slapping on the floor. Bloodstains smeared the concrete where they landed.

Without waiting for instruction, they hauled the prisoner out of the vehicle and tried to force him upright. His head lolled sickeningly forward, face already swollen. His wife wouldn't recognise him now.

I jerked my head towards the entrance. 'Take him inside and make sure his details are recorded. Then put him in one of the interrogation rooms.'

They dragged him towards the cells.

The driver appeared at my side, a bucket full of cleaning gear in his hand. He scowled at the interior of the van.

'Do they 'ave to make this fuckin' mess every single time?'

He was a gorilla of a man, his thick neck straining the collar of his shirt. His tie was always fastened obscenely, too tight around his bulging Adam's apple; it looked like it was strangling him. He dragged his knuckles across the dark stubble on his scalp and swung himself up into the back of his van, cursing loudly.

'Can you 'ave a word with them, Sarge?' he asked. 'I'm sick of cleaning up this shit every time. At least make 'em clean the fucking van themselves. It's not me in 'ere kicking the shit out of some poor bastard, is it? So why should I be the one scrubbing 'is blood off the floor?'

He and I had joined the army at the same time. It was years since I'd been a sergeant, and he was the only one who could get away with using that name. It was his way of reminding me that we both came from the same place.

I bent down and retrieved a rag from his bucket, tossing it into the van. He caught it one handed.

'Tell them yourself, Duke. If you want to get them out here on cleaning duty, that's fine with me. But watch who you sympathise with in future.'

I strode towards the building, leaving him to scrub at the mess. I could hear him complaining loudly, until the guards swung the door closed behind me and I found myself in the void.

The entrance to the Authorisation Bureau headquarters was stark and cold. I walked alone along the corridor, following the intermittent trail of blood left by the prisoner. In places it was smeared where one of the soldiers had trodden in it.

When I eventually reached the end of the corridor, I stared up into the camera positioned in front of the door. Slowly, I held up my badge to the lens and identified myself.

There was a pause and the door clicked open.

I pushed my way through onto a metal staircase. My steps echoed as I jogged deeper into the bowels of the building, into the cells.

The silence was eerie. I wasn't expecting it to be this quiet.

One of the young soldiers was waiting for me. He stood to attention and saluted sharply.

'In here, sir.'

He was tied to a chair, wrists knotted tightly behind his back. He was slumped forward as far as his arms would allow. I couldn't see his face.

Pulling on my leather gloves, I grasped his chin and lifted his head. His face was caked in blood. I pulled my hand away, feeling the wetness sucking at my fingertips. He groaned.

'Professor Winter,' I said softly. He moaned again, but didn't open his eyes. 'Professor.' I nudged him with my toe. When he didn't respond, I kicked him sharply in the shin.

He gasped and sat up, eyes wide.

'Where am I?'

His voice was little more than a croak, caught in the back of his throat. He strained to swallow and winced. When he tried to reach a hand to his mouth, he realised that he was restrained. He began to panic.

'Where am I? Where's my family? What happened?' His eyes darted frantically around the room. 'Where the hell am I?'

His breathing was laboured, chest jolting with the effort.

My voice was smooth. 'You needn't worry about your family, they're fine. They're right where you left them. Do you remember what happened?'

He screwed his eyes closed. As though *that* would help. When he spoke, I could barely hear him.

'You arrested me.' There was accusation in his voice.

'Now, Professor.' I tut-tutted. 'Let's not pretend you've done nothing wrong. We both know you've been very naughty… teaching things you're not supposed to.'

He tried to keep his face impassive, but I could see it. I could *see* it there in his expression; guilt poured off him in waves.

'No. Who told you that? No. It isn't true.'

I smiled. 'Now Matthew, that's a lie. I'd prefer it if you didn't insult my intelligence.'

I flexed my knuckles, adjusting the gloves so they fitted snugly against my hands. He watched in wide-eyed fascination as I clenched my fist.

'We've been watching you for a while now. We've listened to your lectures, read your notes. There are photographs. Not just of you, but all those things that you shouldn't have. Rows and rows of books, all of them fit for nothing but the fire.'

His face darkened. 'You won't burn my books.'

I laughed. 'You think you can stop me?'

He didn't answer.

I took a step towards him. Behind me, the young soldier tensed.

'Perhaps there's something I can do. If you're prepared to help me.'

He didn't meet my eye; the pulse in his neck worked double time.

'Tell me who you're working with.'

He jerked his head. 'I don't know what you're talking about.'

I punched him in the face. I felt his nose break as my fist connected. Blood and gristle exploded, spraying across my uniform. I stared down at the mess as he tried to breathe, the air wet as it struggled through his twisted nostrils. I flicked a piece of flesh onto the floor.

'Well?'

He spat. 'Get… fucked.' It didn't sound right, coming from him.

Mouth pursed, I turned away. The soldier was watching me. I nodded. He drew his baton. His whole body was poised.

'I'll come back tomorrow. You might be ready to talk by then.'

I hadn't even left the room when the soldier's footsteps rushed forward. I pictured the first blow bearing down across the prisoner's temple. Then the second that would follow to his jaw.

As I made my way towards the exit, I counted each blow.

Twelve

Occasionally I indulged in the surveillance of my subjects before their arrest, if their files intrigued me. The first time I watched the professor, he was enjoying a rare night out with his wife, at the theatre where she worked.

I followed them discreetly as they left home, dressed in their sad finery. They didn't notice me sitting half a dozen rows behind them on the bus, staring at the wife's reflection in the glass window as she rested her head against her husband's shoulder. They sat like that for the whole journey, not talking but sitting with their heads bent towards each other, hands entwined.

I slipped off the bus amidst a group of chatty middle-aged women. By the time I got onto the street, the professor and his wife were already disappearing around the corner. Loitering by the bus stop, I pretended to be reading the timetable, allowing them to pull ahead. By the time I turned onto the next street, their slow-moving figures were small in the distance. I followed them carefully, hands tucked deep in the pockets of my coat, collar turned up against the cold night air.

They arrived early at the theatre and had a drink at the bar. That evening there was a performance of *Swan Lake* by a celebrated Russian ballet company. They were still permitted to perform each year in the capital, thanks to a recommendation from their government. They may once have extended the tour across the country, but most of the provincial theatres were forced to close years ago. Theatre was regarded as too divisive; it wouldn't do to give the people ideas. But the First General kept a few venues open in the city to indulge his wife's thirst for the stage, and as a place for the select crowd now filling the bar to congregate.

As the professor and his wife sipped house wine in the corner, coats folded over their arms, I ordered a glass of tap water. Beside me, a large woman in a diamond necklace and voluminous purple dress loudly ordered a bottle of champagne. I assessed her covertly, and wondered who she was married to.

It was only by flashing my identification at an usher that I gained entry to the theatre. He found me a seat at the back of the dress circle, a few rows over from my subjects, who were squashed into a pair of seats partially obstructed by a pillar. Theatre staff might get to see the shows, but they weren't entitled to a seat that actually had a decent view.

The lights dimmed and the hubbub in the auditorium fell silent. The curtain rose and I was aware of the dancers' movements across the stage, but it was the professor's wife who caught my attention. I was transfixed by the rapt expression on her face as she leaned forward to get a better view. Even in the darkness, her eyes sparkled.

It was a long time before I remembered the presence of the professor. Reluctantly, I switched my attention to him. He wasn't watching the production either. Instead, his gaze rested on his wife, his hand on her back protectively. As I watched, she glanced at him and smiled. A thrill of jealousy tightened in my gut, but I knew that their time together was growing short.

I found the commander in his office. He sat in front of a cluster of monitors, watching interrogations with the sound turned off. I lingered in the doorway. He leaned forward in his seat, chin buried in his steepled fingers. The blue light from the screens flickered across his face.

I cleared my throat. He turned sharply, breaking into a grin when he saw me waiting for permission to enter.

'Darius! Come in, come in.' He jumped up from his chair and beckoned me into the room. As I closed the door, he grabbed a spare chair and pulled it across to the desk beside his.

'Sit down.' He resumed his seat and went back to the bank of monitors.

'Look at Farnsworth's technique.' He pointed to one of the screens, where a colleague was questioning a prisoner. It was a woman, with close-cropped hair and wide eyes. She had bare feet; they were curled up beneath the chair, toes clenched inwards. She was trembling, but even with the volume turned down it was clear she was talking. Her lips were moving quickly.

I leaned in for a better look. There were a number of dark swirls on the picture that I thought were marks on the monitor.

'Is that...?'

'Her hair? Yes.' The commander inclined his head. 'It didn't take him long to get her gabbing once he started with the clippers. What is it with women and their damn hair?'

I made a noise of agreement in the back of my throat, but all I could think about was how soft her hair was: Professor Matthew Winter's wife.

'Darius? Are you with me?'

I snapped back to attention. 'Sorry, sir. What were you saying?'

He frowned slightly. 'I was asking how your interrogation went. Did the prisoner give you anything useful?'

I shook my head. 'Not yet. He's awfully stubborn for a book-worm; refused point blank to say anything. I left one of the bag squad down there with him.' I couldn't help but smirk. 'He might be feeling a bit more cooperative after an hour or two of special attention.'

The commander laughed. 'Quite right, Darius. Let the young ones flex their muscles a bit; gives them a taste for it.'

When they joined the Authorisation Bureau, new recruits were sent out in small groups to arrest a target, usually under the direction of a commanding officer. Often that involved snatching people off the streets or kicking down their door and dragging them screaming out of bed. They would be zip tied and shoved into the back of an anonymous van, a hood over their faces. That's where the bag squad name came from. We encouraged it quietly because it gave the recruits a sense of mythology; they felt feared. They walked into those houses with a swagger and a sense of invincibility, a righteousness that made them drunk with power. It was intoxicating. Once they had a taste of that life, that superiority, they only wanted more.

I glanced at my watch. 'I might give him another hour or so, then leave the prisoner until the morning.' My eyes settled on one of the screens. The professor was taking quite the beating. His chair was on one side on the floor; I couldn't tell if he was still conscious. The soldier had been joined by another two recruits. There was blood up the walls.

The commander nodded in approval. 'You won't get much out of him after this. Let him sleep for a few hours. He'll be feeling a little more... pliable... in the morning.'

He slid the drawer of his desk open. 'Fancy one? Single malt.' He pulled out a bottle of whisky and started pouring before I had a chance to respond. His measures were always generous.

It was good whisky too, gave that nice burn on the way down. We drank slowly, watching the monitors. It was funny how quickly the violence became hypnotic.

The fugue was broken when the desk phone rang. The commander sighed, tipping back the remainder of his drink.

'That'll be my driver, come to whisk me back to the wife.' He began flicking off the monitors one by one, ignoring the phone. My hand itched with the urge to answer it.

'Can I drop you at home?' the commander asked, tugging on his jacket. I downed the last mouthful of whisky.

'If you don't mind, that would be great.'

'Anything for you, Darius.' He winked. The phone abruptly stopped ringing.

We made our way into the corridor. I always walked slightly behind him; it wasn't out of deference, it was safer to keep your distance.

'You should have a woman waiting for you at home,' he said. 'It's good to have someone there when your blood's up – healthier that way.'

I blustered a little, muttered about having a couple of women that I saw occasionally. But she was there again, in her negligee. Every time I closed my eyes I could see her so clearly. I wondered what she was doing behind her broken door, all alone without her husband. My skin felt hot.

'Actually, I might not go home,' I heard myself say. 'Do you think your driver would drop me off in town?'

The commander slapped me on the shoulder. 'He'll drop you off wherever I damn well tell him. Maybe I'll even come with you, wherever it is you're sneaking off to.'

For a split second I was horrified. It must have been apparent on my face, because he laughed uproariously. 'Oh, it's a joke, don't look so worried! I'm not going to steal her from you. The wife would never stand for that kind of behaviour.'

I smiled and nodded. His wife was twenty-three and hated him. She probably wished that he would find another woman to play with and give her some peace. No doubt he would get tired of her soon enough; he usually did. But she wouldn't much like the outcome of that.

The commander's car was sleek and expensive. I enjoyed the luxurious feel of the leather seats, the way they moulded to your body as you reclined against them. I stared out of the window as the streets flashed by; there were few people out at this time of night.

'Where do you want to go?' the commander asked.

I gave him the name of a bar that was notorious enough to attract my interest and not arouse his suspicion. It was only a few streets from the professor's home.

I made the final part of the journey on foot, my breath heavy in the darkness. I had forgotten that the lift in her building wasn't working. By the time I'd reached the sixth floor my blood was singing, adrenalin flooding every nerve.

I approached the door cautiously. Everything was dark, but I could still see the way the frame had buckled when the bag squad forced their way in. I reached for the door handle. It was stuck. I rattled it and the noise echoed along the corridor. My breathing was too loud.

I gave one last twist but the door held. She must have shoved something against it. Somewhere a door slammed. Suddenly I felt exposed; somewhere I shouldn't be.

The adrenalin carried me down the stairs and onto the street. I stopped to stare up at her window. My body was on fire.

It took me two hours to get home. I forced myself to run, to burn away the excess energy flooding my body. It was the darkest part of the night, the streets empty and silent as I charged through them, the soles of my boots slapping on the ground.

I remembered the way we ran in basic training, matching our strides to the men beside us, feet pounding a rhythm, shoulders heavy beneath the weight of our packs. I forced myself to keep going, long after my lungs began to burn and my legs started to cramp. I ran past checkpoints so fast that the men waiting there didn't have a chance to stop me. They recognised the uniform and let me go.

I raced through dead streets, avoiding potholes and broken glass. Silent windows stared down at me. I saw no one.

When the buildings began to thin out and the streets grew wider and leafier, I knew I was nearing home. The last few miles were difficult in almost complete darkness. I knew the curve of the roads, followed them like second nature. As I crested the hill at the edge of the village my heart felt like it might burst.

The house was silent but for the sound of my breathing. I switched on a light in the hall and had to shield my eyes from the glare. My uniform was soaked with sweat and plastered to my skin. When the light became bearable I took my hand away and caught sight of myself in the mirror. My face was red, veins bulging. I turned away.

Moving through the house, I began to strip off my damp clothes, leaving them in piles on the floor. The air was cool; I felt goosebumps stir on my arms and chest. There was an old hooded top hanging on a hook on the wall. I pulled it on and wandered into the kitchen without bothering to switch on the light.

I pulled a bottle of vodka out of the cupboard and unscrewed the cap. In the darkness I could see through the deep-cut windows, out across the gardens. They stretched away into the shadows. Stepping closer, I took a swig from the bottle.

I stared out of the window for a long time, drinking straight vodka and thinking about her. It was slowly growing light by the time exhaustion hit me.

Leaving the vodka in the kitchen, I went upstairs to take a shower. The discarded clothes stayed on the floor downstairs; the maid would collect them when she came in later that morning.

When I eventually slid into bed, I was too tired even to dream.

Thirteen

The building looked different in the daylight. At night, it was intimidating: a prison that swallowed people whole. But there was something pathetic about it in the light. The sun picked out the sad state of the paintwork, grey flakes crumbling away to dust. The windows were streaked with dirt, a handprint smeared against one of the panes of glass.

From the outside, the building looked abandoned. As far as the rest of the world knew, it was. When we took people inside late at night, they rarely re-emerged.

My office wasn't as large as the commander's. I didn't have a bank of computer monitors arranged for my viewing pleasure. What I did have was a single report waiting on my desk. It told me in great detail what my prisoner had said and done since the moment I left the room the previous night.

After I had gone, he had been beaten for over an hour, resulting in several broken bones and a loss of consciousness. The duty physician was called to deal with a deep gash on his temple that bled profusely. He now had twelve stitches stretching across his forehead, in thick black nylon thread. These stitches, it was noted, would leave an ugly scar. I knew from experience that they would be painful to remove. At no point during any of this had the prisoner said anything coherent. He had, however, managed to mumble his wife's name several times.

I was distracted by the possibility of her presence. I couldn't help but wonder how she felt this morning, what the world looked like without her husband.

Shaking my head, I returned to the report. It informed me that the prisoner was permitted three hours' sleep, before being woken. He had then been subjected to an hour with one of our interrogation specialists, who had several unpleasant tricks involving water.

I tossed the report onto the desk. Somehow the desire for the interrogation room had drained away. Normally I approached the cells with a sense of determination, the knowledge that I would do whatever it took to force the truth out of whichever miserable specimen was waiting there. This was different. I couldn't think of Professor Matthew Winter without thinking of his wife. I dragged my hand through my hair, tugging at the roots, trying to shock myself back to reality.

It was no use delaying; I had my duties to carry out.

A different soldier stood to attention at the cell door when I approached. 'Sir.' He saluted sharply and opened the door for me. I thanked him and went inside. The door swung shut, leaving me alone with the prisoner. But I knew that somewhere, someone would be watching.

Matthew Winter was slumped forward, head lolling on his chest. The stitches were as ugly as I had imagined. They were uneven and pulled the skin too tightly. The doctors here weren't used to fixing their patients.

I took off my jacket and draped it across the chair in the corner. I placed my hat on top of it and slowly removed my tie. I rolled up my sleeves. All the while, he failed to make a sound.

When I turned to face him, he was staring at me sideways, from the corner of his eye.

'Good morning, Professor. And how are you this morning? Making the most of our hospitality, I hope.'

His bloodshot eyes followed me across the room, narrow in that swollen face. Still he didn't say anything.

'Did you sleep well?' I smiled. There was no bed in the room, only that chair. His clothes were crumpled and covered in bodily fluids. He smelled awful. I had to remind myself that he had only been here one night.

'I thought you might be ready to have a little chat. Nothing too serious, we'd just like to know the names of your co-conspirators, the people who supplied the contraband materials you were distributing.'

On a normal day, if his face hadn't been so mangled, he might have frowned. He opened his mouth, but whatever he was trying to say, the words emerged as nothing more than a croak. He swallowed painfully.

I put my hands on either side of the chair and leaned in close to make out what he was saying.

'Don't know... you mean... what contraband?'

His eyes bored into mine.

I smiled. 'Now Matthew.' I turned away, casually readjusting my sleeves so they sat more comfortably on my forearms. 'You don't mind if I call you Matthew, do you?'

I didn't give him time to respond. I don't think he could have summoned the energy to refuse me anyway.

'You know full well that certain... texts... are not permitted. We've done our best to ensure that our university students have access to the best curriculum we can provide. Books that will develop their understanding of our great country and its history, its place in today's world. We want them to have texts that challenge and provoke them, that teach them how to pursue a line of thought and make a sound argument. We want them to learn. But there are some books that would undermine that. They were written in a different time, when certain… attitudes… were acceptable. They aren't relevant to our young people today. And we can't have them corrupting our future, can we, Matthew?'

He swallowed again.

'Everyone has… freedom… to read. Books are…'

He couldn't finish the sentence. His words trailed off into a rattle in the back of his throat. He started to cough violently. I waited until he had finished.

'That's where you're wrong, Professor. Books aren't about "freedom". Books are a tool for enhancing the First General's message and they should only be used as such.'

His breath was a sharp gasp. 'Poetry. It was poetry. Beautiful…'

I snorted. 'So you risked your life and everything in it for some poetry? I don't believe that.' I closed in on him again. 'You had an agenda. And you had help. Tell me who was helping you.'

But he was gone. His breathing grew laboured and his eyes began to roll. I couldn't tell if he was faking. I slapped him hard across the face but his head only swung loosely sideways. I slapped him again. He didn't react.

With a sigh, I straightened up and began to roll down my sleeves neatly. I called for the guard. He hustled into the room and stood to attention, awaiting my orders.

'Have someone keep an eye on the Professor here. It's time we took a little field trip.'

His office at the university was piled high with books. I had never seen so many all in one place, even in the days before. It was like he was building his own library. I spent a long time going through the titles, as my men waited impatiently in the corridor, more used to gathering prisoners than reading material.

So much of it was banned. I don't know how he could have got hold of it all. There was even a copy of *The Call of the Wild*. I remembered my grandfather reading it to me as a child. We would escape into the story whenever I stayed with him, when my dad was too drunk to know, or care, where I was.

Some of the books were decades out of print. Others had been purged on the orders of the First General. It was possible that a few copies remained, but the cost would have been exorbitant. There was no way someone on a lowly professor's salary could have got hold of such a thing. Not without help.

I was about to call for the bag squad when I saw it. There was a photograph of her on the desk. It was a family portrait; she stood beside her husband, an arm wrapped around a young girl who I assumed was their daughter. I vaguely recalled seeing something about a child in his file.

Picking up the frame carefully so I wouldn't disturb the contents of his desk, I removed the picture, folding it so that only her face was visible. I tucked it into my pocket and shoved the frame into a drawer.

Straightening my jacket, I went to the door and called the waiting soldiers into the room.

'Pack up the books.'

They looked at me blankly for a moment.

One of them piped up, 'All of them, sir?'

'Yes, *all of them*. Find some boxes and get them in the van, we're taking them back with us.' I smiled. 'They might be a useful way of getting some information from the professor.'

I didn't bother to wait as they scurried off in search of boxes and packing materials. I knew it would take them at least a couple of hours to complete the task. Impatient, I radioed for a driver to collect me from the university. As I waited for him to arrive, my fingers strayed to the picture in my pocket, its rigid folds tucked against my chest.

It was evening when the bag squad arrived back at headquarters with the books. Boxes and boxes of them, piled precariously high in the back of the van. It took almost an hour to unload them. For once, Duke was happy. There was no blood for him to clean up.

'Take them out into the yard and pile the boxes up,' I ordered.

Matthew Winter was where I'd left him, drowsing upright in his chair, arms still cuffed. A lone soldier was stationed in the corner of the room, watching him emotionlessly.

'The key.' I held out my hand.

He came forward, digging into his pocket. The metal was hot in my palm as I unfastened the cuffs. The prisoner wilted forwards, slipping onto the floor without the restraints to hold him up.

'Get him on his feet.'

The young soldier struggled with the dead weight. Winter's arms flopped uselessly around, his eyes barely open. I shifted my feet, growing increasingly impatient.

'For fuck's sake.' I stormed across the room. 'Put him back in the fucking chair if you can't get him on his feet.'

I had to help. The soldier huffed loudly as we wrestled the professor's unconscious body back into a sitting position. As soon as we let go, he began to slide down the seat of the chair, head slumped unnaturally far back.

'Go and get the doctor.' I turned to glare at the boy when he didn't move quickly enough. 'Don't make me ask you again.'

He returned minutes later with the doctor by his side: a wiry man with thick glasses and dead eyes.

I nodded at the prisoner. 'Wake him up.'

'Of course.' He was carrying a small leather bag. He placed it carefully on the floor and opened it. It was full of neatly organised jars and tubes, a stock of hypodermic needles. He selected a small glass vial with a rubber stopper. Approaching the unconscious man, he removed the plug and wafted the container under his nose.

Matthew Winter woke with a start, a horrible gurgling noise bursting out of his mouth, hands clawing at his throat. It took a couple of minutes, but eventually his breathing began to slow and his eyes focused.

'Professor, it's about time. I've got something I think you'd like to see.'

They had the fires going by the time we came outside. His books were piled up high in the centre, lit torches lining the yard.

I had the professor in chains, his wrists cuffed together, the skin chafing into blood. I held the shackles in my hand like a leash, yanking him along behind me.

When he saw the books out there, he paled. Even in the growing darkness, I could see his skin change colour. I let him stagger closer to the mountain of books. The bag squad had evidently grown bored with arranging the boxes in tidy stacks; many of them were simply thrown in the direction of the original piles, boxes split, books spilling out across the pavement.

One of the men struck a pose before the bonfire, reading Neruda aloud to a raucous crowd, his voice pitched high and falsely effeminate.

The professor staggered closer, hands outstretched. The bag squad roared, their faces wild in the half-light. The poet closed the book and with a grin flung it to another man, the pages fluttering over the unfortunate prisoner's head. He leapt for it clumsily but they whisked it out of his reach. His hands shook. He had to turn away.

I allowed him to bend down and pick up one of the books. He stared down at the cover for a long time, one hand pressed against it. When he opened it, I could make out the scrawl of an inscription on the first page.

He turned to me, the whites of his eyes enormous. 'You wouldn't...'

He clutched the book against his heart.

I surveyed the scene, watched the men as they watched us, waited for a reaction. The torches burned brighter.

'We paid a visit to your office, Professor. I can't believe you managed to fit all these books into that small room.' I scratched my nose slowly. 'A man of your position, you'd think they could find something a bit bigger than that cupboard. Maybe even something with a view.'

He was staring at me. I could feel the heat coming off him. Surrounded by all these damn books, it was the first time he had even seemed alive.

'Take a look around. They're all yours. It took the lads all afternoon to get these packed up and back here. They wanted to make a nice display for you. They know how much you care about your books.'

Their feet began to shuffle against the concrete. They weren't even aware of it; this desire to come closer. They wanted blood. Blood and scorched ink.

He grasped the book tighter, hunching himself protectively around it.

'Please. You mustn't.'

I kept my face impassive. 'You know what you have to do. Just the answers to a few questions.'

I could swear I saw a tear roll slowly down his cheek.

I gestured to one of the men. He plucked a torch from its holder, the fire dancing as he held it ready.

'You choose.'

The panic was written across his face.

'There was no one else. Only me.' He came towards me, his voice pleading. 'Look at them, look at those books. There are worlds inside them like you've never known. Insights, emotions, stories. Knowledge. How could I not share them? How can you deprive the world of something so beautiful?'

I smiled. Reaching out, I tugged the book from his arms.

'You think that's enough?' I turned to the bag squad, coiled around us. 'Light 'em up, boys.'

They were like hyenas, flames leaping as they snatched up the torches, the light dancing across their ghoulish faces. They wanted to destroy something. They could smell blood.

I threw his book onto the pyre.

The first books caught, the burn flaring quickly. He cried out, charging forwards, trying to rescue his treasures from the flames. He clutched at anything that was within reach, piling them up against his chest until his arms were overflowing.

I still held the chain in my hand. I yanked him backwards without warning and the books tumbled into the fire. He kept trying to reach for them. I could smell his flesh burning as he forced his hands into the flames.

Most prisoners broke when you threatened their families, when you caused them physical pain. This one wept when we burned his books. I couldn't keep the disdain from my face.

It was a long time before he gave up, the bonfire raging. He seemed to crumble in on himself, sinking down onto the ground, staring deep into the heart of the fire. Nothing we did could rouse him. In his mind, he was the one who was burning.

Fourteen

After we burned his books, the professor wouldn't speak to me for days. He turned completely inward, shutting himself away.

More and more, I wanted to hurt him. My frustration grew deeper, more difficult to control, but I could never reach him. It didn't seem to matter what I did; the books were the breaking point.

I couldn't hurt him the traditional way, so I decided to find another way. I went to see her.

But I'd be lying if I said that was the only reason. After the bonfire, I went home and removed the photograph from my pocket, smoothing it out as best I could. I sat and stared at it for an hour, nursing a whisky as I studied the shape of her face, the curve of her body.

When I went to bed, I propped her picture up on my bedside table. I could feel her there, in the dark.

All the way to their flat, I stared out of the car window, trying to concentrate on the details of the neighbourhood. Anything to distract me from the churning in my stomach.

It was a long walk across the car park outside the building. I had the driver drop me off around the corner; I needed time to collect myself. In the lift, I took off my hat and tucked it under my arm, but it felt unnatural and stilted. I put it back on.

By the time I reached her front door the hat had found its way back under my arm. As I waited for her to answer, I pulled it free and began to twist it in my hands, fingers running across the brim.

When she opened the door my breath caught and I couldn't speak. She stared at me in horror. There was fear in her eyes; I caught my own reflection there. I swallowed.

'Mrs Winter.' She stepped back and I followed her inside. 'I thought I would stop by and see how you were.' In daylight, the flat looked different. Without the stark glare of the overhead light, it didn't look as shabby. The afternoon sunlight filtering through the curtains gave the room a warm glow.

'You're the one who…' She didn't finish. We both knew what she'd been about to say. I tried not to stare as she fussed with her hair and rubbed her cheeks, which flushed with colour. 'How thoughtful of you…'

'Major Jackson, madam. Darius.'

She smiled. It looked real enough to me. 'Darius.' She was wearing an oversized dressing gown, the belt tight around her slender waist. When she moved the fabric shifted; I saw a flash of skin on her inner thigh and felt the heat rising in my own cheeks.

'Could I get you a drink, Darius?' There was an intoxicating lilt to her voice. I remembered from the files that she was born in Italy and had moved to Britain with her family as a child. The first time I saw her, I remember thinking she was too alive for this grey place.

'Clara, sweetheart. Make the Major a cup of tea, please.'

The girl was in the corner of the room. I didn't see her until she stepped forward into the kitchen, eyes black in her narrow face. Where her mother had olive skin and soft curves, she had her father's pale, angular complexion. She glared at me as she passed.

I knew they had a child, but I'd never seen her during my long evenings of surveillance. I couldn't recall seeing her the night we arrested her father. I wondered if she was here somewhere, if she saw. A flicker of guilt sharpened in my chest.

But she was calling me and my attention returned to more pleasant things. 'You must call me Lucia. Madam makes me think of my grandmother.' She smiled at me, eyes sparkling, and pulled out a chair for me to sit on. 'I hope I haven't grown her whiskers.'

The girl banged a cup down in front of me, milky tea sloshing out onto the table, dark little eyes needling me. She made me uneasy. I had the feeling that she didn't miss much. But she was quick to hide her arms, which were covered in bruises.

'I understand you work in a theatre, Lucia.'

She nodded. 'Yes, yes I do. I work in the offices now, but when I was young, I was on the stage. I loved the lights, the rustle of the crowd in their seats, taking everything in.' Her eyes took on a faraway quality. I could almost feel her sadness as she glanced at the child. 'But these things, they can't last forever.'

I wanted to reassure her, even as I longed to see her standing bright in front of her audience. No doubt marriage and pregnancy had forced the career change. 'That's probably for the best. It can be difficult to live life so... publicly.'

She gazed at me with sad eyes. 'Life on the stage does bring with it so much attention.' I could hear in her voice how much she missed it. 'Things are different once you have children.'

I struggled for words but the right sentiment evaded me. 'Much better to live a quiet life, to dedicate your time to the needs of your family. That's the best thing a woman like you can offer society.'

As soon as the words left my mouth I knew they were wrong and I tensed, angry at myself. I didn't want her to think me uncultured. She wasn't made to be a mother, this one, she was made to shine.

The girl continued fidgeting in her seat, throwing me sullen glances every once in a while. She looked like she needed a good wash. She had nothing of her mother's grace. All of it, wasted.

I left as the light began to fade. The driver would be waiting for me around the corner, where I had left him, studiously completing the crossword puzzle in that week's newspaper.

She touched my arm as I crossed the threshold and I felt faint. 'Goodbye Darius.'

Her tongue curled around my name and I shivered. I wished her goodnight and began the slow walk to the lift. When I turned back, she was standing in the doorway watching me go.

The following evening I collected her in the car. She had agreed to join me for dinner at a fancy restaurant the commander had introduced me to. It was a favourite of his wife, who adored the sleek, industrial-style decor and the high ceilings adorned with expensive-looking chandeliers. It was popular with the city wives, those that could afford it.

But I began to regret my choice of restaurant as I got dressed. There was no way to know if it had swayed Lucia to spend an evening in my company, or whether she actually cared for me. As I knotted my tie, I told myself firmly that it was me she was interested in.

As we followed the hostess to our table, I could see Lucia gazing around with wide eyes. She tugged at the hem of her plain black dress as we walked past a woman whose cerise outfit hugged every one of her enhanced curves. Light glinted off the diamonds at her throat. I grew tense as Lucia dropped her head. Her outfit was clearly the best she had, but it was nothing next to what the other women in the room wore.

We sat down and the hostess tottered away on her stiletto heels. She was quickly replaced by a waiter, who handed us each a menu.

'Madam,' he nodded to Lucia. 'Can I get you something to drink?'

Before she could reply, I said loudly, 'We'll have a bottle of white wine. What can you recommend?'

He turned to me and rattled off a list of French wines. I caught sight of the wine list and winced inwardly at the prices, but gave him a fierce smile and ordered the most expensive one.

He gave a little bow and hurried away. Lucia gave me a shy smile and bent over the menu, studying it carefully. I watched her read, but she didn't look up. Perhaps she was aware of my gaze; I thought I noticed a faint blush rising up her throat.

The waiter returned with the wine. He opened the bottle carefully, offering it to me. I waved for him to pour her drink first. He filled our glasses and slotted the bottle into an ice bucket. Then he noted down our orders and disappeared back to the kitchen.

We made small talk over the wine, but we never got to enjoy our food. Before the waiter could bring it, my phone rang. That was never a good sign.

Lucia fell silent as I answered, watching me with her kohl-rimmed eyes.

When the conversation ended, I smiled weakly. 'I'm so sorry, I'm afraid there's been an... incident. We'll have to leave; I need to get to the office.'

I swear she held her breath. I knew she was thinking about

her husband; she was worried that something had happened to him. A rush of anger hit me full force.

Hands trembling, I forced the mobile phone back into my pocket. Hearing it ring, the other patrons in the restaurant had turned their heads toward me. They couldn't help themselves, the sound so unfamiliar, dredging up memories of a different world. Now few people outside the Authorisation Bureau carried them.

As we made our way outside, people avoided my gaze, dropping their eyes to their food. Conversations fell silent as we passed by. I steered Lucia to the car, my hand in the small of her back, a knot of emotion burning in my chest.

She climbed in first, sliding across the seat to make room. I stared ahead as the driver whisked us back to the city, not taking anything in except her body beside me. As she stared out of the window, she worried the ring on her third finger.

The driver pulled up outside the block where she lived and opened the door.

'Goodnight,' she whispered, twisting her legs to climb out of the car.

I reached over and gripped her upper arm impulsively, drawing her back inside.

'It's not him. It's *not him*.'

Her eyes met mine in alarm. I let go, feeling the touch of her skin sear into my fingertips. She stared at me, caught like a wounded bird. Then she nodded. Her hand brushed my knee – so softly I might have imagined it – and she was gone.

As we drove away, I turned to watch her through the rear window. She stood at the entrance to the building, watching as we drove away into the night.

At headquarters, it was chaos. The place was on high alert. We were stopped at three checkpoints before we were even permitted to enter the compound. I had to exit the car while the guards searched it. They searched the driver too, forced him across the bonnet as they checked he wasn't carrying anything suspicious. We stood together as they ran mirrors underneath the car.

After fifteen minutes, we were cleared to enter the building.

'I'm not sure when I'll be back,' I told the driver. 'It might not be until morning.'

His face was impassive as always. 'I'll be here, sir.'

I left him sitting in the front of the car, staring at the wall with a cigarette in his hand.

The noise inside the building was unbelievable. It sounded like a riot was breaking out on the cell floors. I grabbed the arm of a young soldier as he rushed past me. He jolted to a halt, baton clutched in his hand, breath thundering.

'What the fuck is going on?'

'Sir?' He looked at me.

'Why does it sound like the prisoners are about to break out of their fucking cells and massacre us?'

He looked afraid. 'You'd better speak to the commander, sir. I've got to go.'

He bolted down the stairs, as screams echoed up from the bowels of the building. I pushed on towards the commander's office, hand poised on the grip of my gun.

I found him pacing his office, red with fury as he screamed into the faces of three sergeants. They stared into the middle distance, trying to let the abuse roll over them. I looked at the man closest to me; his eye was twitching.

The commander finished his tirade. 'Now get the hell out of my office you useless fucking bunch of bastards.'

I waited until the three men had left and the commander

had taken a few breaths. I let him pour a generous measure of whisky. 'What's the situation, sir?'

'It's a right fucking balls-up, Darius. That's the *situation*.' He swallowed the liquor in three long gulps and poured another. 'Three bombs went off in the city, all of them at checkpoints. Dozens of men wounded. And to bloody top it off, turns out one of the prisoners brought in earlier this evening was a fucking plant. He played dead in the van with the bag squad, gets into a cell and goes mental. Before they can restrain him, he grabs a gun off the guard and shoots three men in the face. Fucking mess. Not to mention they almost kicked him to death before someone with a brain stepped in and pointed out that he might have some useful information.' The second drink disappeared as quickly as the first. 'The prisoner's in the infirmary in a coma with bleeding on the brain. Meanwhile, I've got three dead soldiers in a cell, bloody bits of brain up all the walls, and every checkpoint in the city in chaos. And the rest of the scum down there are trying to rip the cell doors off and get their hands on whoever happens to be passing by.'

He shook his head. 'I've got good men dead. Bloody waste.' This time he didn't bother with the glass, just stuck the bottle straight between his lips. I stared at the monitors over his shoulder. It was like watching apes in cages rattling the bars, teeth bared in frenzy.

The commander fixed his narrow eyes on me. 'And you, where the fucking hell have you been all night?'

I coughed. 'I was off duty, sir.'

He was in my face then, whisky fumes burning my nostrils. '*Off duty?* I know you were fucking off duty, Darius. But that doesn't mean you get to be unreachable.'

He was so close to me I could see the broken veins in his nose, the yellow tinge to his eyes. I lowered my gaze.

'I was... on a date.'

He was incredulous. 'A *date?* There's a major fucking incident occurring, and you're out on a date. In all the years I've known you, Darius, you've never once taken a woman on a date. I know you fuck them occasionally, and I'm sure they enjoy it, but you don't make nice.'

I was on fire. I wanted to punch him in the face, to see that fat nose burst open.

'This is different, sir.'

He came even closer, forcing me to meet his eye. He lowered his voice. 'Well, I hope it was worth it, son. But right now, you belong to me. Got it?'

He spun away, guzzling again from the whisky bottle as he brooded over the screens. 'I want to know who was involved in this.' He turned to thrust a finger at me. 'Now, you get down there and break some fucking heads.'

Fifteen

It was mid-afternoon the following day before I left headquarters. I was exhausted, but so wired I knew I wouldn't be able to sleep. And there was only one thing I wanted to do.

The driver was still waiting for me in the underground car park. I had no idea if he'd been there all night or if he'd slept, but he looked as sharp as usual. He took me home, where I showered and changed my clothes. Instead of the uniform, I pulled on a pair of jeans and a jumper. I spent fifteen minutes fiddling with my hair in front of the mirror, slicking it one way, then the other. In the end, I gave up and went out.

Walking to the theatre where Lucia worked cleared my head. The streets were busy with additional patrols and I nodded to the soldiers.

I waited outside, staring up at the windows hoping to catch a glimpse of her there. The sun was beginning its descent, the light fierce when she emerged. I had to shield my eyes as she made her way down the stone steps. She didn't see me waiting across the street. I watched as she reached into her bag and began rummaging around, pulling out her purse.

When I called her name, she looked up with a start. I jogged towards her. Her hair billowed in the breeze; she pushed it back away from her face, clutching her bag to her chest.

'What are you doing here?' She sounded uncertain.

'I wanted to apologise for leaving so abruptly last night,' I said. 'And I hoped I could make it up to you. Would you mind if I walked you home?'

There was a pause. 'I think... that would be fine.' She gave me a small smile.

We turned in the direction of her home, walking side by side. A few minutes passed by in silence. There were so many things I wanted to say, but even in my own head they sounded ridiculous. She looked at her feet as she walked, both hands holding tight to the strap of her handbag. I watched her out of the corner of my eye.

When we reached the end of the street, she automatically went to turn right and follow her usual route home. I touched her arm; it was like being electrified. I felt her muscles tense beneath the press of my fingertips.

'Let's go this way instead.' I pointed in the opposite direction. 'There's a footpath along the river.'

She thought for a long time before she answered. I could almost see her turning each word over carefully in her mind, wondering if I might take offence.

'I'm not sure that's such a good idea.' She tucked her hair behind her ear. 'It's not safe down there. Something bad might... happen.'

She implored me with her eyes.

'It'll be fine, you're with me.' I felt a surge of confidence; enough to reach out and take her hand, pulling her along behind me.

The path that led to the river was overgrown. I pushed aside branches that threatened to scratch our faces.

'Watch your feet.' There were the cracks in the concrete

where tree roots had broken through. She stepped carefully, still holding my hand.

When the narrow path ended in a flight of stairs, I encouraged her downwards. The steps opened out onto an old towpath that ran alongside the river. The water was still. Office buildings lined the river bank opposite, empty windows staring down at us.

We carried on walking, enjoying the silence. Somewhere in the distance, there was a screech of tyres. Raised voices carried through the air, before falling away.

'It's peaceful here,' Lucia said softly. 'I never realised. I thought it would be full of... people.'

I laughed. 'You mean you thought there would be tramps or kids from gangs everywhere, waiting to pounce on unsuspecting passers-by.'

She blushed. 'Perhaps something like that...'

'Not many people come here. There's no reason to. This path doesn't go anywhere. And the view was much nicer... before.'

She looked around, eyes exploring the dilapidated buildings and empty passageways. 'Don't people live here?' We were walking past a row of apartment blocks that had been built in the days before the old government fell apart.

I shook my head. 'The builders finished work, but no one ever moved in. The apartments became too expensive; not many people had that kind of money to burn.'

She looked at me brazenly. 'So why didn't you choose to live there? You decided where people should live, took their homes away. You could have had your pick, surely.'

I met her eye. 'Most of us don't live in the city. We didn't think it would be safe. And the committee wanted something nicer for their families. They reward those of us that do well with a house in the country.' I laughed. 'The old status symbols still apply.'

She went quiet. 'They made us move away. I never understood that.' She gazed up at the abandoned block. On the surface it remained a desirable place to live, but look close enough and you could see the scars: the shattered windows, the crumbling brickwork, the loose tiles.

'I loved that house.'

I stood behind her. 'I'm sorry you had to leave it behind.'

She didn't respond. My stomach dropped anxiously. I couldn't tell if I had upset her. She began to move forward, without acknowledging my apology. I followed a few steps behind her, reluctant to push too hard.

Her pace quickened and for the first time I was aware of her breath, swallowed by the silence. Abruptly she stopped and spun round to face me.

'Are you sorry for my husband too? For taking him away?' Her eyes blazed. She was close to tears. 'You keep coming to see me, trying to be kind, and I don't understand why. Do you expect me to be able to look at you without remembering that you took Matthew away from me?'

The tears overwhelmed her. Her bag fell to the ground as she pressed her hands against her face.

I wrapped my arms around her. She felt so small, the curve of her ribs shivering against my chest. But she didn't pull away. Instead she pressed her cheek against my shoulder.

'I was just doing my job, Lucia. I know it seems awful to you now, but you have to understand that people like me, we're here to protect you. We only arrest people as a last resort. And those people, they've done something bad. Matthew knew the rules when he started down this path. He chose to leave you; I didn't choose to take him away.'

She cried harder. 'I only want to know he's okay.'

I rubbed her back gently.

'It's better if you try to forget him. I know how hard it must be.'

She pulled back to glare at me. 'You don't know anything.' She scrambled to get away, grabbing for her bag. '*Why can't you leave me alone?*'

With a sob, she fled, catching her feet on the uneven ground. I let her go, my insides hollow. I was still watching her when she stumbled over something and fell, landing awkwardly. She didn't get up.

I hurried towards her. 'Are you hurt?'

She shook her head.

'Are you sure?'

'I… I don't think I can get up.'

I hauled her to her feet. She staggered against me, then quickly tried to step away, wincing as she moved. I reached out for her, but she pulled back.

'I'm fine, I just twisted my ankle.'

I sighed. 'Lucia, it's a long walk back to your flat. Let me help you. I can call my driver to come and get us.'

She stared at the ground. 'Fine.'

'I'll have to help you to the road. Here, lean against me.'

She had no option; she had to allow my arm to slide around her waist as we shuffled slowly towards the street.

I took a deep breath. 'I never meant to upset you. But you must realise that, with his crimes, Matthew can't be released. It would be too dangerous.'

Her whole body stiffened. She didn't reply.

I started to get annoyed. 'I wish you would see it from my point of view. What would happen if we let people carry on however they like?'

She stopped walking, standing awkwardly to save her injured ankle. 'Matthew's not a criminal! He teaches poetry and reads fiction with his students. He helps them understand art and meaning. He loves books, and that's all.'

I grasped her upper arms, meeting her gaze intently.

'In the right hands, a book can be a weapon. What has he done for any of those students, except fill their heads with pointless dreams? It's fiction alright; he lectures them on a different world, one that doesn't exist any more. And there's no place for him here. Not if he can't understand that.'

'But he's my husband,' she wept. 'He's a father. You've ripped my family apart.'

Gently, I cupped her chin in my fingers and made her look at me.

'*Matthew* did that. *Matthew* tore your family apart. I'm trying to help you pick up the pieces.'

She was beautiful. Her cheeks were flushed with colour. I kissed her angrily, my hand sliding to her neck. She resisted, her fists pushing against my shoulders. I wouldn't let her twist her face away. She bit my lip, hard. I felt a rush of blood from the broken skin. Shocked, I jerked away.

'What the hell…'

Her palm cracked across my cheek. The noise reverberated across the river. A flock of birds took fright, bursting skywards in a frenzy of beating wings. We stared at each other, her eyes searching mine, trying to find some kind of answer. I wished I knew what the question was.

I blinked and she was kissing me, her body pressed against mine. I staggered under the unexpected weight, my arms going around her waist, eyes still wide open in surprise. Her mouth was fierce, demanding something I desperately wanted to give. I found my footing, hands going back to her face, reaching up to pull at her hair. She moaned and every inch of my skin screamed at me. I lost myself in it.

But in that moment, I thought of her husband. How the fire

flickered in his eyes as he watched his books burn. How the light went out of him as the flames died.

I was buoyant the next morning, strutting into his cell, fit to burst with the knowledge that his wife had moved on. She had chosen me.

It made him seem all the more pitiful, slumped in his chair, hands cuffed behind him, securing him to a ring bolted deep into the floor. He didn't look up when I came in. My nose curled. He stank. His clothes were filthy. I could still smell the taint of the fire on him.

'Good morning, Professor Winter.' My voice was cheerful, too loud in the confines of the small room. He flinched at the sound, retreating further into himself.

I wanted to scream in his face, tell him to forget about his wife. I knew he was clinging on to her, picturing her in his mind. It provoked something in the pit of my stomach, to think of the things he had shared with her, the things they'd done. I wanted to be closer to her than anyone had ever been. If that meant I had to obliterate him, slowly, systematically, then so be it. He was nothing beside me. I puffed my chest out as I sneered down at his scrawny arms, the flesh purple and weeping.

He looked up at me and the sheer need in his face was unnerving.

'I thought of something I wanted to tell you today.' His voice was hoarse, little more than a whisper.

I folded my arms and waited.

'It's about a man who used to print pamphlets of poetry.' I looked bored. He hurried on, trying to win back my attention. 'But they were propaganda. He would hide codes in them too, in layers. Clever, really.'

I frowned and he tried to backpedal. 'Not that I ever...'

I held up a hand and he fell silent, lip trembling.

'Give me this man's name.'

He told me. It was so easy now; almost not worth bothering. I glanced up at the camera. Somewhere, that name would be noted in a file. Another one for the bag squad.

I nodded. 'Thank you, Professor. That's very useful. It's good to see that you're starting to come round to our way of thinking; to understand how important our work is.'

He nodded eagerly. 'Yes, yes. I'm sorry I didn't see it before. I just want to help.'

'Well, that certainly makes things easier for me.' A thought popped into my head. I had to fight the urge to smile. To cover the twitching at the corners of my mouth, I pushed up my sleeve and checked my watch. 'And as you've been so helpful, I think we can end today's session there.'

I could almost smell the relief coming off him in waves. His body relaxed visibly.

'Oh, *thank you*.' He closed his eyes.

I couldn't contain my smirk. 'You know...' I said, checking my watch again. 'I might have time to... no, perhaps not.' I pulled a sad face.

But I could see that I'd hooked him. 'What?' he asked.

'Oh, it's nothing.' I made a show of pretending that I shouldn't tell him. 'I've met a rather charming woman. Now that we've cut our session short, I might be able to meet her for lunch. Take her somewhere nice.'

He leaned forward a little. 'What's she like?'

My lips curved into a smile. 'Oh, she's beautiful.'

Sixteen

Her name had been on my lips all day. I'd wanted so badly to tell the professor that his wife was mine, that I'd been seeing her for weeks. That she'd been in my bed, while he'd been rotting in his cell, whispering her name just to make it through the night.

She'd been in my bed and I still couldn't get enough of her. She was in my blood. I pushed Matthew Winter further than I'd ever pushed a prisoner before, driving him to the brink of his sanity and then pulling him back inch by inch, until he relied on me; as though I was the one who had saved his life.

But it wasn't enough. His wife was mine, but there was something she held deep inside herself that I couldn't get close to. She would shutter it away, where my probing fingers couldn't reach. It was her heart. It was my obsession. It wasn't enough that I could possess her body; I wanted her to love me. I wanted to obliterate his memory so completely it would be as though he never existed.

When I went to visit her that night, I took a bouquet of delicate flowers that I had gathered from my own garden. It had taken me almost an hour of traipsing around the flowerbeds, through the long grass, trying to find enough. I cursed as I caught my hand on a thorn, a bubble of blood welling up from the skin. With a rush of annoyance I wiped it away, smearing it dark red against the pale flesh of my hand. I pictured blood streaking the white walls as the bag squad beat the professor. I stood in the observation room in near darkness, pupils dilating as they smashed his face against the wall.

The flowers were in my hand as I approached her front door, rubbing at my hair where it refused to lay flat. I knocked and the silence echoed around me.

It was the girl who opened the door. Expecting Lucia, I thrust the wild flowers forward with my most charming smile. The child stared at me blankly. I froze, the smile fixed on my face. I could feel it cracking as the muscles tightened. There was something unnatural about the girl. She turned my stomach.

I thought about pushing past her into the apartment, but that wouldn't give the right impression. And something about the idea of touching her gave me chills. So I waited. When she moved aside I slipped past her, the rictus grin dissolving in relief.

'Lucia!'

She sat on the bed, her back to me. 'Darius.' Her voice was a whisper. It always made me shiver when she said my name, but this was different.

I discarded the flowers that I had gathered so painstakingly; they fell to the floor somewhere with a rustle.

When I saw the bruises I thought I might hurt someone. Her eye was swollen and several shades of black, some I had never even seen before. Her soft lips were split. Livid finger marks and welts climbed her arms; she saw me taking in each injury and tugged her sleeves down to hide the wounds. I glared at the girl. She stared back at me, her eyes burning with challenge.

'Darius,' her voice pulled at the edges of my consciousness and I swam back from the depths of my rage. 'It's fine, it was an accident. I wasn't watching what I was doing at work and I fell down some stairs. It was my own stupid fault.'

The image of the welts on her arms was seared into my brain. I knew exactly what a strap mark looked like.

I felt wild. I grabbed her elbows and she gasped in pain. Her eyes widened as I dragged her closer and I could see my fury reflected there, burning through her fear.

'It wasn't an accident.'

It was the girl who spoke.

'Clara, no,' her mother tried to plead. I let go of her arms, my attention on the child.

'He hurt you, mama. I heard him.' Lucia began to cry, like an animal caught in a trap.

'Tell me who.' My voice was dangerously low. Clara met my eye and I could see it in her; she knew what her answer would mean. She wanted revenge.

The silence in the room stretched out so far I thought it would break. My nerves were taut. My fists balled up so tightly that my nails scraped the skin from my palms.

'It was the man from the theatre. Mama's boss.'

I couldn't look at Lucia. My voice threatened to shatter as I asked, 'Did he...?'

With a stricken sob she said, 'No.'

I closed my eyes and took a long breath, before I sat down beside her on the bed and opened my arms. I let her fold her body against my chest, unsure what other injuries I might find beneath her clothes. We sat together as she cried, the tears scarring my lapel.

Leaving us there alone, Clara slipped into her bedroom, her reprisal set in motion.

The street was quiet when we pulled up outside the theatre in a fleet of unmarked vans. The doors swung open as one, disgorging thirty members of the bag squad, their boots polished to a shine, hair cropped close. They melted into formation as they waited for me.

Slowly, I pulled the earphones from my ears, silencing the strains of Mozart. I took a long, deep breath, closing my eyes. Lucia's bruises were fresh in my mind. I pictured her flinching away from me as I touched her too hard, a pained noise caught in her throat.

I got out of the van and slammed the door. It wasn't a time for speeches or commands. I walked halfway up the theatre steps and turned to rake my eyes over my men.

'With me.'

They thundered up the stone stairs behind me as I blasted through reception, ignoring the girl behind the desk as she leapt to her feet. They followed me and she was swept away by the tide.

I burst through the STAFF ONLY door and ran up the narrow stairs two at a time, the sound of my steps muffled by the faded carpet, the pile stained and thinning. Lucia's office was at the back of the building. I'd visited her there once, when I took her out to lunch. That day the windows were wide open, light pouring in along with the stifling heat from the late summer streets. She stood up to greet me with a smile, the blue fabric of her skirt swirling around her legs.

This time she didn't stand. She was wearing thick black tights and a long-sleeved blouse, despite the lingering heat.

She'd done her best to cover the marks on her face, but nothing could hide the broken look that haunted her eyes.

As we exploded into that room, so much smaller now, she cast her gaze downwards, fingers hovering over the keyboard. I wondered what she had been about to type.

He leapt up from his seat, mouth dropping wide.

'What... what's the meaning of this?' His attempt at authority fell flat, somewhere in the air between us. I stared at him until he looked away, a slight cough marking his discomfort. The other women who shared the office were rigid in their seats.

I didn't speak. The bag squad were silent at my back, not so much as a squeak of leather from an errant boot or the rustle of clothes as their owner fidgeted impatiently.

I stared at him, taking in the grey stains beneath his arms, the rings on his shirt emphasising another day's sweat. There was a fat signet ring on his left hand, crushing the flesh of his finger, which swelled outwards around it. When I noticed a clump of shirt tail poking through his half-mast fly, I smirked.

'You need to come with us.'

His face paled. He glanced across at Lucia, still motionless at her machine. I could detect the urgency of a pulse at her throat. I had no idea if he knew about me, knew that she was mine. I knew all about him and his demands.

His tongue darted across his lips as he tried to decide what to do. I gave him time; I was content for him to try and hang himself.

'Surely you aren't here for me?' His voice was high. It pitched upwards as he spoke, disbelief and fear seeping from his pores. 'I know that, technically, I've employed the wife of a... dissenter... but she was never accused. I... please; I was only trying to help her. There's a child, you see, I felt sorry for them.'

Lucia's words cut across the room, so unexpected every head snapped in her direction. 'Were you sorry for me when you tried to fuck me, Donald? Were you helping me when you took off your belt?'

She rolled up her sleeves carefully, without another word. The other women stared at her arms, a sickness growing on their faces. One woman pressed a hand to her heart, as though she were the one in pain.

I hadn't noticed the door in the corner of the office. While we were distracted by Lucia's injuries, the theatre manager made a break for it, lumbering across the room in his shiny dress shoes, a streak of sweat like an exclamation in the small of his back.

He hit the fire door hard; it swung open and crashed into the wall as he staggered through, the alarm blaring.

I turned to scowl at one of the women. 'Shut that racket off.' She scurried for a row of switches on the wall.

The door had ricocheted back into the frame. I waved the bag squad forward. The first man shoved the door with the flat of his hand, but it didn't open. He leaned in, putting his weight to it. The door remained shut. Three of them couldn't get it open.

A knot of rage sat heavily in my stomach. My hands trembled.

'What the fuck are you waiting for? Get after him! Break the bloody door down if you have to.'

They divided seamlessly: half doubling back to trail the manager through the winding corridors of the theatre, while the others got to work on the heavy door.

Lucia had sunk back into her seat. Her colleagues hung back, afraid of us, but eager to offer some comfort.

'You should all leave,' I said quietly. 'Go home. You don't want to be here for this.'

They exchanged glances, uncertain.

'*Go.* Now.'

The darkness in my voice was enough. They snatched up their bags and cardigans, abandoning half-drunk cups of tea and the remnants of a late lunch. Their computer screens slowly dulled, until only a winking orange light remained.

Lucia was still at her desk.

'You should go too.'

She met my eyes with such fury that I was astonished. I'd never seen her so animated. 'No. I want to see.'

I studied her. I could feel the pain and shame and anger coming off her in waves. I recognised the smell.

'Fine. But stay behind me.'

With a shout, the bag squad had the door open. The hunt began. I trailed them, following the staccato rhythm of their boots, the sound echoing back at me from every direction. Lucia followed close behind me; her breath was hot on my neck.

For a big man, the theatre manager was surprisingly light on his feet. They caught up to him in the theatre, its Victorian splendour faded but still impressive. He was cowering in one of the boxes that would once have been reserved for wealthy patrons, high up in the gods.

I wouldn't let Lucia come with me. I told her I'd take care of things. I left two young soldiers to guard the stairs leading up to the box so she couldn't shadow me. I didn't want her to see.

I jogged up the steps, surprised at how high up we were.

The theatre manager was backed into the corner of the box, a chair clutched in both hands. He waved it in front of him, thrusting it towards anyone who moved towards him. But with each jab, he retreated a step further, until he found himself up against the wall. His arms began to droop, the chair swaying.

'Do you think that's going to help?'

He flinched at the harsh tone of my voice, his shoulders hunching up towards his ears. The distance between the chair and the floor lessened again.

I had a pair of leather driving gloves in my jacket pocket. I put them on carefully, flexing my hands until they clung like another skin.

'You never should have touched her.' I eyeballed him savagely. A flood of images overwhelmed me as I thought about what he'd done, what he must have felt. 'She's too good for you. Look at the state of you.'

He sagged further, the fight draining away. I stepped forward and snatched the chair away. His hands slid away, dropping uselessly at his sides. The bag squad formed a semicircle behind me; there was nowhere for him to go.

'I want to hear you say it.'

He looked at me. 'I don't...'

I slapped him. The sound of my leather-dressed palm striking his cheek sliced through the silence. He gasped.

'*Say it!* You're a pathetic fuck who could never get a woman like that. You couldn't even *take* what you wanted. I bet you couldn't get it up, could you, you dirty old pervert? So you took it out on her. What kind of a man are you? Nothing. You're nothing.'

His breath came in shallow gulps. When I saw the tears in his eyes I started to laugh. I couldn't believe it. 'I bet she didn't even cry like that when you were whipping her with your belt. You're a fucking disgrace.'

'Please... I'm sorry.'

I snorted. '*Sorry*. I'm sorry, but it's a bit fucking late for that. You don't think I'm going to forget about this do you?'

He wiped at his eyes with the cuff of his shirt. His snivels were grating on my nerves. I grabbed a baton from the grasp of the soldier closest to me. It nestled in my palm like it had always been there. I swung my arm up high, forming a beautiful arc as I brought it down across his face. His nose broke with a satisfying crunch. He tried to squeal, but he couldn't get the air into his lungs. Blood burbled from his nostrils as he clutched at his face, knees buckling.

'You... better... be... fucking... sorry.' With each word I hit him again, the baton striking hard against his loose flesh. He tried to curl into a ball on the floor, snuffling and weeping, not even trying to get away. I kicked him in the gut. 'Fucking bastard! Dare to touch *my woman* and think you're the one with the power.'

Adrenalin coursed through my body: I could see everything, hear his bones as they cracked and tore at the flesh. I felt it all. I felt myself growing taller, overtaken by the rage, by the power.

Flinging the baton down, I reached for his collar, trying to drag him off the floor.

'*Get up!*' I screamed. He didn't move.

I swivelled to face the bag squad. '*Get him up!*'

They sprang into action, hands hauling him up off the ground. And then I was on him. It happened so quickly, those few moments. I can't recall the words I screamed in his face, as my spit sprayed across his mottled skin. I remember my hands locked around his throat as though I was watching myself from afar, trying to force my fingers to meet around his neck. Somehow I manoeuvred him to the balcony. I pushed him up against the railing, his body leaning backwards, eyes wide in terror, arms windmilling uselessly; he tried to clutch at anything he could to save himself.

'I didn't know...'

I didn't care what he had to say. I was in no state to listen. All I could see was her pain. All caused by this disgusting animal who thought he had the right to touch something that belonged to me. He wasn't the first man I'd taken apart for her.

His fingers clawed at my face and, like that, I let go. His own weight carried him over the banister and down, down, down. His retched shriek filled the theatre. It only took a second for him to fall. When he hit the ground there was an almighty crash and then the echo of silence.

Lucia began to scream.

They took his body away in the back of a van. Half a dozen men had to haul the corpse out of the theatre, along narrow corridors, bouncing the body bag unceremoniously down the stairs.

The convoy of black vans pulled away with an urgent screech of tyres. They never were much for subtlety. Lucia and I waited on the street for my driver to collect us. She held herself anxiously, rubbing her arms as she stared off into the middle distance, a slick of tears drying on her cheeks, eyeliner seeping into the fine cracks under her eyes, making her look years older. She had that expression I often saw in new recruits, after their first interrogation, when the guilt still had a place to take hold.

I rested my hand on her shoulder and we stood there, waiting, each absorbed in our own thoughts. I suspected that we were thinking the same thing, but it meant something different to each of us.

'Is it always like that?'

She spoke so softly it took me a moment to process her words.

'Like what?'

She wrinkled her nose. 'Like... wild animals hunting down their prey. Do you kill them all?'

Her eyes shone. I knew that she was asking me about Matthew. I pulled my hand away, the pressure of her shoulder still tangible on my palm.

'No. Not all of them.'

'What happens to them? Do you let them go home?'

I looked at the floor; I couldn't bear the intensity of her gaze. There was a crust of dried blood on the toe of my shoe that I hadn't noticed earlier. I pulled a crumpled handkerchief out of my trouser pocket and bent down to scrub at the stain.

When I stood up, her attention had drifted away, caught by a couple who were walking slowly along the other side of the street, his arm around her shoulders. She grinned up at him, her face wide open, her fingers curled around the zipper on his top, gently tugging it up and down.

'We couldn't let them go home, not afterwards. But not many get to leave. We don't always kill them, but sometimes we don't need to.'

Her eyes followed the young couple as they drifted down the street and turned the corner. Their laughter floated towards us on a warm current of air.

'I used to be like that. Happy. Matthew would hold my hand when we were out walking. Whenever he smiled at me, he would squeeze my hand. I always loved that; it was like a heart-beat between us.' She looked at me over her shoulder, arms folded. 'I'm never going to see him again, am I?'

'No. Probably not.'

Her face was expressionless. 'I know he's not dead. I still feel him sometimes.' She put her hand to her chest and clenched it tightly against her heart. 'But he's gone all the same.' She spread her fingers, like leaves soaring away on the wind. Like letting go.

I took hold of her chin and she turned her body towards me. My thumb caressed her jaw. 'You know that I'll never let any-one hurt you, not again. Not ever.'

Her eyes were liquid, staring up at me. I felt myself falling.

'I love you, Lucia. And I want you to be mine. I'm not an idiot; I know you have to blame me for what happened to your husband. But that will fall away in time. I'll make you love me the way you loved him. More than that; I can give you so much more.'

I kissed her and she responded; her lips tasted like salt.

When we broke apart the driver had pulled smoothly to the kerb and was standing with the door open. Lucia gave the tiniest of smiles, touching the tips of her fingers to my cheek before she slid into the back seat. I climbed in beside her.

The driver accelerated away swiftly, merging easily into traffic. Lucia's hand was resting on the seat between us. I took hold of it and squeezed.

'I want to marry you.'

I caught a glimpse of the driver's eyes as they flicked up towards the mirror, then back to the road. He gave a small cough.

Lucia didn't meet my eye; instead she stared at our hands, fingers entwined. Delicately, she pulled her hand back. A pit wrenched open in my stomach. Her wedding rings caught the light, the diamonds flashing. She looked at me deliberately and began to twist the rings off her finger. Stretching her fingers, she slipped the jewellery into her bag and put her hand back in mine.

'I want to marry you too. I want Clara to have a father.'

My smile wavered at the mention of the girl. But I knew I couldn't separate them. In time perhaps, she might accept my presence in her life. And if she didn't, there was nothing to keep her in my house.

'I'll always look after you both.'

I leaned forward to kiss my fiancée.

Seventeen

I spent that night at Lucia's, for the first time. Instead of going straight home, I took her to one of the officers' clubs in the city. I wanted to celebrate our engagement and she wanted to drown out the image of the theatre manager falling to his death.

It was late when we finally went back to her flat. The lift was out of order so we staggered up the dozen flights of stairs. I don't remember falling into bed, other than a brief moment of satisfaction that this was another place where I had managed to replace her husband.

I woke in the morning to the weak rays of sunlight filtering through the gap in the curtains where we had failed to draw them shut. My head was pounding. I groaned, dragging an arm across my face to protect me from the light.

Lucia was still fast asleep next to me, curled up tightly on her side, her dark hair spread out across the pillowcase. Rolling over, I touched it, smoothing the ends between my fingertips. She moaned softly. I rolled onto my back, staring up at the ceiling, where a patch of damp festered above us.

I dozed for a while and was woken again by a noise from the next room. Clara was stirring. I listened to her getting out of bed and pottering around her room, opening and closing drawers as gently as she could.

When she crept out to use the bathroom, I pretended to be asleep. There was barely a whisper as she scurried by. The bathroom door clicked shut and I opened my eyes. My mouth tasted like death. As she turned on the water, I heaved myself out of bed and stumbled bare chested to the kitchen, switching on the kettle to make a coffee.

By the time the kettle shut off, I was sitting at the table, swallowing my drink as though my life depended on it. I could feel the liquid flooding my body, rehydrating the dried-out cells.

The bathroom door opened. She was wearing her school uniform, a white shirt tucked carefully into black trousers. Her feet were bare. She'd attempted to plaster her mother's make-up onto her face, apparently to cover a massive bruise that had blossomed on her cheek. Obviously she still had a lot to learn about painting her face.

'I made you a cup of tea,' I said, indicating the Mickey Mouse mug that sat on the table in front of me. 'Come and sit down.'

She looked as though she was considering making a break for it. But where would she go? The defeat on her face was stark when she sat down and picked up the cup.

'Who did that to your face?' I asked, keeping my voice low so Lucia could sleep.

Clara's hands curled around the mug. She stared into the murky depths of the tea. 'No one.'

'That didn't work when your mother tried it – do you think I'm going to fall for it from you? You're nowhere near the actress she is.'

The girl snuck a glance at me. I looked back levelly, took a sip of coffee.

'Do you want some breakfast? I can do toast.' There was half a loaf of white bread on the counter, wrapped up in plastic.

She nodded. 'Okay.'

I busied myself with the food, leaving her to her silence.

When the toast was ready, I returned to the table, a plate in each hand. She fell on hers like she hadn't eaten for a week. I nibbled at the crusts, feeling my stomach roil.

'So are you going to tell me about it then?'

She finished chewing and swallowed. Gave a shrug. 'Just some girls at school. They don't like me.'

'They don't like you, or they don't like that your dad was arrested?'

The girl put down her toast and looked me dead in the eye. 'What do you care?'

I glanced across at her mother, who was muttering in her sleep, the covers twisted around her legs.

'Look, we both know the reason I'm here is your mother; it has nothing to do with you. You might not be able to understand it yet, but when something affects her, it affects me too. And you're important to her.'

She studied me. I couldn't read her expression. With a small nod, she asked, 'What's that?'

I had a tattoo on my chest, above my heart. It had started life as an eagle, which was the crest of my unit in the military. But over time I'd added to it. The design had become more intricate, spreading down across my ribcage and under my left arm. It disappeared under the waistband of my trousers.

'I got it when I joined the army.'

She finished her toast. 'I should probably get ready for school.'

I reached out and caught her wrist as she went to get up. 'These girls, is this the first time they've hit you?'

She looked uncomfortable. 'Kind of. But it doesn't matter.'

I frowned. Like mother, like daughter.

'Is that the only bruise they gave you?'

She coloured, looking at her feet.

'It's not is it? Show me.'

Clara shook her head fiercely. 'No. It doesn't matter.'

'Show me.'

Blood burning in her cheeks, she untucked her shirt and hitched it up. She turned in a slow circle so that I could see the full extent of the damage. Bursts of blackness marred her milky skin, like storm clouds threatening. She tugged her shirt back down.

'What did they do to you?'

Her voice wobbled. 'They hit me with hockey sticks when I was getting dressed after PE.'

I felt a familiar anger spreading through my gut. 'Tell me their names.'

'No, no I can't.'

I put a hand on her shoulder. Standing next to her, I realised how small she was, although not quite as fine boned as her mother.

'Yes, you can. You're going to tell me.'

For a moment, I thought she would. But instead she cried, 'No!' and fled to her room, the door banging shut. I looked quickly at Lucia, but she was still lost, deep in her dreams.

On the way to work, I ordered the driver to take a detour. He pulled up outside Clara's school: an imposing red-brick building that looked as though it might once have been an orphanage, or some other kind of sterile Victorian institution.

Slamming the door, I straightened my jacket and marched inside, the medals on my chest all neatly in place. In the entrance foyer, a woman in heavy-rimmed spectacles sat behind a sliding glass window, vague office chatter filling the unseen space behind her.

As I approached, she slid the window open, hissing surreptitiously over her shoulder. The office fell silent. I caught sight of half a dozen women in dowdy blouses and skirts, all hunched over their desks or rummaging through filing cabinets. One of them glanced up in my direction, then quickly looked away.

'Can I help you, sir?' the receptionist asked.

I gave her my most charming smile. 'I'd like to speak with the head teacher please…' I paused to read the name badge pinned to her chest. '… Gloria.'

She smiled back. 'Can I tell him what it's regarding?'

'It's about my… daughter.' I stumbled over the word, unsure how else to refer to the girl. The school wouldn't speak to me if they thought I wasn't a relative. I suppose I would technically be responsible for her soon enough. 'She's been having problems with some of the other girls.'

The receptionist was flustered. 'Oh dear, I must say, we don't stand for that kind of thing here. I hope it isn't anything too serious?'

She gave me an inquisitive look, but didn't seem to expect an answer. I smiled thinly as she picked up the telephone to dial the head teacher's office, allowing my attention to wander so I didn't seem to be listening in.

'What's your daughter's name, sir?' Her hand was over the receiver.

'It's Clara. Clara Winter.'

The receptionist stared at me. I could almost see the question forming on her lips, but she held back. Instead she relayed the information to whoever was on the other end of the line.

When she hung up, her demeanour was serious. 'If you'd like to wait there, someone will be along shortly to take you through to the head's office.' She gestured to a row of leather chairs along one wall, beside a coffee table arrayed with old magazines. I thanked her and took a seat. She slid the glass panel shut sharply.

It wasn't long before the interior door opened and a dour man in a navy blue suit appeared. He held out a hand and introduced himself as the head teacher; I'd been expecting a secretary to collect me.

I followed him along the corridor, as teenagers in uniform darted around us, late for their lessons. He barked at a girl who was chewing gum and she paled, rushing to find the nearest bin.

A bell rang as he ushered me into his office and asked me to take a seat.

'So, Major Jackson, what is it I can do for you today?'

His grey eyes studied me; nothing got past a man like this.

'I want you to deal with the students who are bullying my daughter, before I'm forced to do something myself.'

Eighteen

Our interrogations had been going on for so long now that they'd slipped into a routine. Whenever I came into the room, our professor would rush to tell me something, anything that he thought I might want to hear.

Then I would pretend to huff and threaten, refusing to believe until he revealed something else, something that could be verified.

The saddest thing was he'd long since given up everything he could. Now he settled for rattling around in what parts of his memory I'd left untouched, striving for something new, someone he could incriminate. I knew that he always picked people who were beyond my reach in one way or another: this one was years dead, lost in a car accident; this one had a powerful uncle who wouldn't allow them to be touched; that one had already fled the country for safer climes.

But we clung to the dance. We played our roles. After it was complete, he would grin at me crookedly through his broken teeth and ask after my woman. I would laugh and tell him crude stories, all lads together.

I chose my moment carefully. I wanted to deliver my final

blow just when I was sure he relied on me; that he'd come to need me.

'I should thank you, Professor. If it wasn't for you, I'd never have met her.'

Uncertainty flickered across his face.

'I'm not sure what you mean…'

'Well, if you hadn't been scuttling around with your books and your secret classes, like a rodent, I'd never have been assigned to watch you. I'd never have been given permission to arrest you. And then I might never have met Lucia.'

He stared at me, the foolish smile stuck on his face, stretched a little too wide. I could see a nerve in his cheek twitching as he tried to process the words. He didn't want to believe them.

'I'm going to marry her.'

Slowly his lips tightened, the smile stripped away, his face falling apart. It was like looking at a real-life Picasso. I'd seen one of his paintings once, in a museum, on a school trip to France. I'd been more interested in spraying my friend with spit balls, as the other kids listened solemnly to the tour guide. The teacher dragged us outside by our arms, two writhing eleven-year-old boys in school uniform. My father tanned my arse when he found out about that incident.

'You can't,' the professor said. 'She's my wife.'

We were in one of the less secure interrogation rooms. He was seated at a table, his hands shackled as usual, chained to a metal ring in the floor. He banged his hands suddenly on the table.

'She's *my wife*.'

I shrugged, all at once tired of the game. 'Not for much longer.' I reached inside my jacket and pulled out a long envelope containing a sheaf of papers. His eyes fixed on me as I drew them out and placed them on the table in front of him.

I pulled out my fountain pen and slowly uncapped it, watching from the corner of my eye as he scanned the document.

'Annulment papers.' His shoulders stiffened. 'You want me to annul my marriage. How would that even be legal? We have a child for god's sake; we've been married for *fifteen years*.'

I curled my lip, dismissing him. 'But you're not a person any more. It's amazing the things that become possible when someone is arrested. You might be here, against all the odds, but you're not really *alive*. We've done our best to whitewash your existence. But it would be better if we had your signature.' I laid the pen carefully on the table. 'It would make it easier for Lucia; make it proper. There'd be no stain on her. Or on Clara.'

I knew that would provoke a reaction. 'Don't you say their names,' he cried, shoulders trembling. 'You don't get to say their names!'

I scratched my cheek innocently. 'I get to do more than that. Who do you think keeps me warm at night when you're tucked up in your little cell?'

He screamed, a guttural, animal sound that burned out through his chest, tearing open every wound the previous months had inflicted. I gave him time. I didn't try to soothe him or apologise. I couldn't make it better for him now.

But when he came down from the heights of his own pain, I held out my olive branch, the way I'd planned all along. 'I have something for you that I think you'll enjoy.'

His eyes were empty. I didn't know if he'd heard me. But I went out into the corridor anyway, to fetch my prize.

Lucia came into the room, her eyes wide and fearful. I watched her closely as she caught sight of him. She held herself well, but there was a twitch in her right cheek; I saw her eyelid flicker. Her hands were drawn in tight, fingernails digging into her palms.

'Hello Matthew.'

He didn't believe what he was seeing. All his dreams and his nightmares folded into one, standing in the corner of the room like a ghost in her white dress. The annulment papers lay on the table between them. He turned his face away to hide the tears.

'I won't sign.' He folded his arms across his chest, a stubborn tilt to his chin.

She stepped forward and pushed the pen towards him.

'You must.'

The agony in her voice drew his gaze. She swallowed. The raw knot in my stomach began to gnaw; it was all still there between them. Wavering, his hand slid towards the pen, grasped it. Her hand stuttered as though she was thinking of touching him.

It overwhelmed me. All the insecurities I kept buried rushed to the surface; I wanted him gone from our lives, from her memories. I swept her aside and raised my fist as though I might strike his face.

'Sign!' I roared.

He stared at me, defiance in his gaze. I thought I'd wrenched that out of him long ago, the night I burned his books to ash.

'She's my wife.'

I put my hand on her shoulder, my fingers digging into her flesh, claiming her. She didn't flinch, but I felt her body droop, ever so slightly.

'I haven't been your wife for a long time, Matthew. I don't love you.'

The words were whispered, her eyes on the floor. I squeezed her shoulder again and she slid her arm through mine, her body pressed against mine. I could feel her heat through the thin cotton of my shirt.

'Sign the papers. Let me go.'

I put my hand on her cheek and pulled her face to mine so

146

that I could kiss her. I forced my lips against hers, my hand sliding down to her throat.

He couldn't look at us. Instead he gripped the pen, his hands shaking. He stared at the paper, at her signature, stating she no longer wanted to be his.

With painful care, the professor scrawled his name beside hers; this woman who was his wife. He put down the pen and shoved the papers away.

'You got what you wanted. Now go, leave me alone.'

He turned his face away, but I could see the tears in his eyes as he strained to hide them.

I retrieved the paperwork, folded it carefully and tucked it back inside the jacket of my dress uniform. Still smiling, I picked up the pen. With a jerk, I brought it down onto Matthew's hand. The metal cut through flesh and sinew. He screamed, his hand speared to the table. A spurt of blood sprayed across my shirt, marring the pristine white of the collar. Lucia put her hands to her mouth in horror but she couldn't look away. His face was grey, coated in a fine sheen of sweat.

With a jerk, I pulled the pen free and he shrieked again. I tugged a handkerchief from my trouser pocket and began slowly wiping the blood away. No one said anything. There was only the sound of his laboured breathing.

I finished cleaning the pen and tucked it away with a smile. Turning to Lucia, I said brightly, 'Let's go darling, we've a wedding to arrange.'

When she looked at me, for a split second, every trace of artifice had fallen from her eyes. I could see that she hated me. But it was too late. With visible effort, she pulled herself together, but she couldn't hide the way her hands shook.

Gripping her wrist, I towed her towards the door. She paused, just long enough to look back. 'Goodbye, Matthew.' I pulled her out into the corridor.

When he started screaming her name, she quickened her pace until she was almost running. She burst through the exit before me as I lingered, satisfied that I had won.

Nineteen

For a time, after the wedding, I forgot about the professor. I was caught up in the bubble that we built around ourselves, in our little haven away from the city. I found an excuse to take time away from work whenever I could, to spend time with Lucia – even Clara.

We would gather in the family room to watch old movies, curling up on the sofa together with a bowl of popcorn. We'd switch off all the lights, so that the room was illuminated by nothing more than the flickering blue screen of the television.

But his presence would still niggle at me, especially at night, as my wife lay beside me in bed, sighing in her sleep. She would toss and turn and make these tiny little sounds of distress, like an animal whimpering. I would lie awake as she twisted around beneath the covers and wonder what dreams were troubling her.

Whenever I would ask, the next morning, as she wearily smeared face cream into the dark circles under her eyes, she would smile and shake her head.

'I don't remember, Darius. But I'm sure it was nothing important.'

I wanted to believe her. I wanted it so badly, but the doubt ate away at my insides. I would catch a faraway look in her eye sometimes, and I knew she was thinking of her first husband. I knew it with a certainty that frightened me.

But that knowledge only made me more determined to possess her. Some nights I refused to let her sleep at all, as I tried so hard to consume her, to erase the memories of the man who had her first.

So when she told me nervously that she was expecting a child, he was the first person I wanted to tell.

His interrogations had continued in my absence, more about routine than uncovering any new information. But still, I waited in the commander's office for a time, watching on the monitor as one of the younger interrogators brought Matthew into the room and sat him down in the chair. He was so cowed and physically weakened that they didn't even bother to secure his handcuffs to the metal ring bolted into the floor. They didn't consider him a threat.

His hand was still bandaged where I had stabbed him with the pen. He picked at the tattered fabric. Even on the monitor, it was clear that it was filthy, stained with so many layers of blood and dirt.

The knowledge that his former wife was carrying my child burned at my stomach. I could taste the words on my tongue. Leaving the wall of screens playing to the empty office, I bolted for the stairs, the urge to unburden myself too great.

When I burst into the room, the interrogator and the professor looked up at me, startled by my abrupt entrance.

'Professor,' I smiled, the desire to hurt itching away across my skin.

I gestured to the door, not taking my eyes from the prisoner. 'You can leave.'

There was a pause, and then the young interrogator left, mumbling something as he went. I didn't acknowledge him.

I stared at the professor, my breath still loud from dashing down the stairs. The silence hung between us.

'Did you want something?' he asked, his voice flat.

A bark of laughter escaped me. 'Well yes, I did actually.'

'There's nothing left.'

I tilted my head to one side. 'Excuse me?'

'If you wanted something else from me, you're out of luck. There's nothing left to take.'

A slow smile spread across my face. 'Oh, I wanted to tell you my news. I thought you'd like to know that Lucia and I are having a baby.'

He stared at me, his face completely blank. There was nothing behind his eyes. I wanted to laugh, to bray my triumph into his face.

He moved so quickly, I didn't register it until he was on me. His eyes burned into mine, his hands held out in front of him to grab my throat. His momentum sent me sprawling backwards, landing hard on the cold concrete floor of the cell.

The professor had been thin when we first arrested him, but now he was almost skeletal, head bulbous on his wasted body. But still, his strength was surprising. His breath was hot and rancid on my face as his hands closed around my neck and began to squeeze. I flailed at him, trying to break his grip as spots appeared in my peripheral vision.

The only thing in his eyes was the rage.

My head clattered against the floor, sending jarring shock waves through my bones. I could have laughed in disbelief; the moment was so ridiculously unreal. And through it all, he never said a word. He didn't need to. I thought I had broken him when I burned his books, when I took his wife.

I was about to pass into unconsciousness when they came rushing in. I saw half a dozen pairs of boots run past my head,

151

felt the release as they hauled him off me. I sucked the air into my heaving lungs hungrily, my throat burning.

But it was no use. I heard the dull thud of their fists as I slipped into oblivion.

I woke hours later to a cold house, an empty bed. My head swam as I struggled to sit up, my throat hot and painful. The curtains were open and the room was washed with silver light from the moon. I tried to call for Lucia, but my voice emerged nothing more than a croak. Shards of glass slid down my throat as I coughed hoarsely.

When the coughing fit subsided, I got out of bed, my feet like ice on the bare floorboards. The house was silent. I shuffled along the upstairs hallway, my head buzzing with a sense of unreality, of waking disorientated late at night, with no idea how I got home.

Clara's bedroom door was ajar. I pushed it open, thinking I might find my wife comforting the girl after a bad dream. But there was only the child, sleeping deeply sprawled on her back, her head tilted at an awkward angle, arms flung out wide. Something stirred in my chest. I crept into the room and half picked her up in my arms, moving her into a more comfortable position. A soft, fluttering breath hissed between her lips but she didn't wake.

I slipped quietly downstairs, desperate for a glass of water. But before I could reach the kitchen, a noise stopped me in my tracks. Lucia's hushed voice emanated from the living room.

I could almost make out the shape of the words, but not what she was saying. The door wasn't closed. I pressed myself against the lacquered wood and slid my head around the corner.

She was standing by the window, with her back to me. She moved and I could see something clutched tightly in her hands;

it glinted in the faint light. As I watched, she carefully positioned a photo frame on the window ledge, her hands shaking. She was crying.

'I'm so sorry, Matthew,' she whispered.

My whole body went cold. I could feel his hands around my throbbing neck.

She pressed her fingertips against the picture, the other hand flat on her stomach. 'It wasn't my choice... not really. It was for Clara, so she would be okay. I wish I could tell you how much I miss you.' Her voice broke.

I crept backwards out of the room, moving slowly to keep the floorboards from creaking. My heart was racing as I climbed the stairs and returned to bed, leaving my wife weeping over a photograph of her former husband.

Part Four

Twenty

His screams woke me in the night. I was torn from a violent dream, terrified that the soldiers had come back for us. The sheets were damp and twisted around my legs so tightly that I couldn't move and panic gripped me.

The baby was crying. I dropped back onto the bed, the fear rushing out of me in a wave. I felt limp. Ignoring my brother's cries, I tried to go back to sleep, but nothing happened.

With a groan, I rolled onto my stomach and buried my head under the pillows, but I couldn't drown out the sound of his distress. Dragging myself out of bed, I made my way towards his room.

I hated this house at night. It was too big and my footsteps echoed ominously, however quiet I tried to be. I missed our grotty flat and the views from the window, out across the city. I missed the noise of the children playing outside and the women chatting on their balconies. Here there was only silence. It didn't feel like home. The flat hadn't either, when I lived there, but I craved it now with a longing so intense it scared me. It wasn't really the place I wanted. It was the time, the family.

But I had a new family now. My brother's room was on the

other side of the house, beside my mother and the major's. I lingered in the hallway, unsure whether to go in.

I pushed the door open and beneath the baby's cries I could hear something else. My mother sat in a chair beside the window, the baby in her arms. She was weeping.

'Mama? Are you okay? What's wrong with Will?'

At first, I didn't think she'd heard me. Perhaps she chose not to answer; it wouldn't be the first time. After a moment, I turned to leave.

'He won't feed. I don't understand; he's obviously hungry.'

She cried harder, her breath coming in little sobs that merged with the baby's. The sound was a knife twisting in my stomach.

'Can I get you something?' I asked, hoping for a reason to get out of the nursery. The curtains were open and the tree branches outside cast eerie shadows across the floor, a cold light from the moon seeping in with them.

There was a noise behind me. The major appeared, tousled and gruff with sleep.

'Get back to bed, Clara.'

He didn't look at me.

I left the room, but I didn't go back to my own. I stood outside instead, listening. His voice was low and harsh.

'Can't you stop him crying? What's wrong with you?'

Her words were so soft I couldn't make out their shape. Only the sound of his anger as it swept over her.

In my room, I was glad that the only thing I could hear were my brother's cries.

The major was away a lot in the first few weeks of Will's life. It was never clear to me what he was doing and my mother never explained it. Without him, she struggled to cope.

Will spent much of the night screaming, so I spent much of it awake, lying in the dark willing him to be quiet. Sometimes my mother would get up and comfort him, but sometimes I could hear her shouting in frustration when he wouldn't be silenced.

It was hard to concentrate at school with so many interrupted nights. I never contributed much, but I became even more withdrawn. One morning, I almost fell asleep in Maths. The teacher was droning about hypotenuses and I could feel my eyes closing; there was nothing I could do to keep myself awake.

Someone kicked my chair and I jerked up, missing time.

Jasmine was needling me with a sideways glance from across the aisle. I must have made a noise – half the class had turned round to stare at me and the teacher paused in the middle of writing on the blackboard. She twisted her head, but didn't say anything. The room was silent. After a moment the scrape of chalk resumed.

What. Are. You. Doing? Jasmine mouthed the words, exaggerating each syllable.

I pulled a face and tried to mouth that I would speak to her after the lesson ended, but she frowned like she hadn't understood.

When the bell rang, she hung back, waiting for me to gather my books.

'What's wrong with you? You know Mason will put you in detention like that. You're lucky she didn't see.'

I tried to look contrite. 'Did I snore?'

Jasmine snorted. 'Er, yeah. Why d'you think everyone was staring?'

We left the classroom, trying to muffle our laughter. It was lunchtime and we went to the dining hall to collect something to eat. The selection wasn't exactly great.

'Another delicious dinner.' I dipped a ladle in a bowl of brown mush and examined it, before letting the goop slide back into the pot, one lump at a time. Behind the counter, one of the dinner ladies frowned at me, her hairnet slipping a little too low over her forehead.

Jasmine gagged. 'Gross.'

She spooned some plain white rice onto her plate, adding a side of shrivelled peas and a small carton of juice. I wasn't really hungry; the smell in the canteen always made me nauseous. I grabbed a packet of crackers and an apple. We handed our cards to the stern-faced dinner lady to stamp.

Jasmine and I always took our food outside, away from the other kids. Neither of us was exactly popular. We were the only two kids still in school with a relative who had been spirited away by the Authorisation Bureau: my dad, her brother. Jasmine had never been sure what he'd done, but she suspected it was something to do with a march he'd once been on, campaigning against forced detention.

I knew she missed him, but we didn't talk about it much. We ate our lunch and talked about a geography test we had that afternoon and whether we felt prepared. She did, I didn't.

'It's impossible to study when Will's always crying,' I complained. 'And he's awake half the night; I can never get anything done. When he does go to sleep, I can usually hear my mother crying, or arguing with my stepfather.'

Jasmine nodded. 'My mum cries a lot too. She doesn't think we hear her, but we do.'

I immediately felt awful. While I lived in the major's enormous house, slept in my own bedroom and had space to escape from my family troubles, Jasmine lived in a small flat with her parents and grandparents. There was no privacy or quiet there, yet she still managed to study more diligently than I did. But I always enjoyed visiting; Jasmine's grandparents were German and would tell us stories about growing up in Munich and the extended family members who still lived there.

The canteen door opened and a burst of chatter escaped as three older boys came outside to eat. We finished our lunch in silence and trailed inside before the bell rang, when it began to drizzle.

My mother was unusually quiet that evening, her face pale and drawn. The major was away and we ate dinner in the dining room, where it was cold. Mary the housekeeper silently placed the plates in front of us. Ice clinked in my mother's glass as she took a sip of her drink, ignoring the food. Mary patted my hand when my mother wasn't looking and left the room.

I began to eat.

A sudden wash of light swept across the window as a car made its way up the drive. My mother's glass banged against the table. There were loud voices outside and the front door burst open. I stopped eating, knife and fork poised in mid-air.

'Mrs Jackson! Mrs Jackson!'

The major's driver was shouting. My mother stared at the door for a moment, frozen to her seat. Upstairs, the baby began to cry. Mary came running along the hall and my mother finally got up, knocking over her chair, pristine napkin falling to the floor. She hurried to the door and I was left alone in the room.

Putting my cutlery down carefully, I got up and followed the sound of raised voices into the living room. From the hall-way, I heard the driver say something about an ambush. I crept into the room. The major was slumped in a chair in front of the fire, blood gushing from a cut on his cheek. His uniform was torn and covered in dirt. I hovered in the doorway, my eyes wide. No one noticed me standing there.

'Mary, we need to call for the doctor,' my mother wailed, her hands fluttering as she tried to decide whether to remove the major's jacket or touch his face. 'He's going to need stitches.'

'Don't bother,' the major grunted. 'The roads are hell; it'll take him hours to get through. Hunt will do it.' He gestured at the driver, wincing as he tried to raise his arm.

My mother gasped in horror. 'But Darius, no, your face.'

'Shut up and get some thread. One of you must have a sewing kit.'

Mary backed away. 'I'll get it, and some hot water and towels.'

'And bring the vodka,' barked the major.

They all seemed oblivious to Will screaming upstairs in the dark. I slipped out of the room and fled upstairs, my heart thundering.

Twenty-one

Sometimes after school I'd go with Jasmine to the café where her parents worked. Her mum inhabited the narrow space behind the counter, taking orders, making change and fixing drinks. Jasmine's dad worked in the kitchen, preparing ingredients. He had been a lawyer, once.

They both worked long hours and we went there to study. Jasmine's mum would let us have a table in the corner for the price of two cups of tea and we would spend the late afternoon gossiping and sharing notes from that day's classes.

I wasn't keen to go home after last night's drama. The house was quiet when I got up for school that morning. Mary made my breakfast and helped me get my things together, but she was unusually subdued and wouldn't be drawn on what had happened to the major.

At school, I'd heard a group of kids whispering about an attack, but their voices rose and fell as other students came close and I couldn't make out the details of their conversation. I listened all day, but didn't learn anything else.

We walked along echoing streets to the café. A sense of unease followed us there; on every corner was an armed soldier, a pair, a group, guns strapped across their chests, fingers tight to the trigger as they watched the people passing by with piercing eyes.

The bell rang as Jasmine opened the door. There were only a few customers in – the lull before dinner. A couple sat in a booth, him intent on the newspaper, her much younger, eyes flitting around the room as he ignored her. She smiled at us as we walked to the counter.

'Clara!' Jasmine's mum smiled when she saw me, her whole face brightening. 'You want some brownies, girls? Made fresh today.'

'Yes please, Mrs Beck.'

We laughed, letting Jasmine's mum find us a table and fuss around us, bringing us tea and cakes as we opened our school books. When we were settled she patted my hand and kissed Jasmine on the head. On her way back to the counter she stopped to clean another table, brushing away crumbs with her cloth and gathering empty plates together.

She looked up with a smile when the bell rang again. I watched as it drained from her face and the rag she was holding fluttered to the ground.

The soldiers rushed inside, their voices loud in the small space. I shrank back into the booth as they surged forward to grab at Jasmine's mum, forcing her into the seat beside her daughter.

One of the men marched through the café, waving his gun at the diners and ordering them to leave. They fled. The only one who looked back was the young woman, as her partner dragged her by the wrist towards the door. The bell chimed again as the door swung shut behind them.

'What's going on out here?' Jasmine's dad appeared from the kitchen, his eyes growing wide as he took in the scene before him. He yelled, putting his hands up to protect his face as the men charged forward to grab him. They dragged him towards

164

our table, forcing him to the floor as Jasmine screamed. One of the soldiers slapped her across the face. She clutched her cheek, voice silenced, redness blooming across her skin. I couldn't move, couldn't find my voice. I shouldn't have been there.

'Please, tell us what's happening,' Mr Beck begged.

A soldier glared down at him, but didn't speak. Slowly, he spat on the floor at Mr Beck's feet.

'Your son is a terrorist. He's responsible for the deaths of a lot of people. We know you were working with him.'

Mrs Beck let out a wail of grief.

'Silence.' The soldier pulled out a handgun and pointed it at her face. She couldn't control her tears, her shoulders quaking. With a mean smile, he turned the gun on Jasmine. Her parents both let out animal noises, as Jasmine's mother reached for her, pulling her against her own body. Jasmine's eyes were screwed shut and her lips moved as she whispered a prayer.

'Tell us what you know, or we'll take the girl.'

I pressed my back against the wall, willing them not to look at me, not to ask for my name.

'We don't know what you want,' Mr Beck cried. 'Our son hasn't done anything. You took him! He's gone!'

The soldier dropped the gun to his side.

'No. Your son is a terrorist. He was responsible for the Whitehall bombing. We want to know who he was working with.'

Fear swelled in my stomach. I didn't remember the bombing itself, I was too young then, in the time before. But we'd learned about it at school. It was the final attack, the turning point that inspired the First General to take control and save us from the grip of the terror groups.

In Whitehall, a teenage boy strapped a bomb to his chest and waited on Parliament Street. He stepped out in front of the Prime Minister's car, but he didn't detonate the explosives fast enough. The driver swerved, accelerating along a side street as the bomb went off, the explosion engulfing the car behind, which carried two Cabinet ministers, as well as several other vehicles. A young family on their way home to Wales were all killed in the blast, as were two police protection officers, a journalist heading to the Houses of Parliament in a taxi and a passing cyclist. The facades of the buildings on that street still bore the scars.

For weeks afterwards, the faces of the victims were plastered everywhere, their names on all our tongues. They were feted as martyrs, whose deaths ushered in a new era.

But it happened years ago. How could Jasmine's brother have been involved?

Mr Beck wept.

'Please, my son did not do this. He's a good boy.'

The soldier sneered. With a wave of his hand, he sent the other men on a whirlwind of destruction. They smashed the glass case that sat on top of the counter, hurling the food to the floor. They slammed rifle butts against mirrors, windows, tore pictures from the walls. We listened as they rampaged through the kitchen, the sound of metal reverberating through the air.

'Tell us what you did!'

The soldier grabbed at Jasmine, his fist twisting in her hair. She screamed as he dragged her out of the booth, across her mother, who clutched at her child's flailing limbs but couldn't hold on.

My body shook furiously. I couldn't process what was happening. It was all too much. I remember the room in snapshots, still frames of fear that are seared on my heart.

And then it stopped. There was a burst of gunfire somewhere outside, the echo carried to us on the wind. Everyone stopped. The soldier let go of Jasmine as his radio crackled. He reached for it, his whole body tense.

In a moment they were gone. I didn't know if they would be back, but I couldn't move. Mr Beck was shouting at me but there was a ringing in my ears and I couldn't hear what he was saying.

He pulled me up, out of the booth. Jasmine was sobbing into her mother's chest, as they clung to each other.

'Clara, you've got to run. You must get home. Be careful, child.' He ushered me to the door, my school bag trailing on the ground behind me, strap clutched awkwardly in my hand. I didn't have a chance to say goodbye to Jasmine, to ask if she was okay. As Mr Beck pushed me gently onto the street, I saw Jasmine turn to watch me go, her face streaked with tears.

The next morning, Jasmine wasn't in registration. She normally arrived at school early, but her desk was empty. I picked at my nails as the other students filed in and sat down, still full of whispered secrets. The teacher arrived and closed the door behind her. Everyone fell silent.

Then, just as the bell rang, the classroom door burst open and Jasmine dashed inside. She mumbled an apology to the teacher and then scuttled to her seat, chin tucked firmly into her chest, hair falling over her face. As the teacher began calling out names I tried to catch Jasmine's eye, but her gaze was locked on the desk in front of her.

Once the register was marked, the teacher launched into that day's announcements. There would be no outdoor physical education classes that day and students were not to leave the school grounds during breaks. No one was to go home unaccompanied after lessons. The air of tension in the room increased.

The clang of the second bell startled me, but before I could say anything to Jasmine, she bolted from the room without looking back.

She was waiting for me at lunch, her face pale and drawn. I took my tray outside, where she was sitting alone, the table empty in front of her.

'Are you okay?' I asked, fighting back tears. 'I was so scared all night that something had happened to you.'

A single tear slid down Jasmine's cheek. It glistened in the cold autumn light.

'We're leaving. I have to say goodbye.' Her hands shook.

My throat was tight, my voice pitched too high. 'What do you mean, you're leaving? When?'

'Shh!' She pressed a finger to her lips, glancing quickly through the window to the other students who laughed and chatted in the warmth of the canteen. I followed her gaze, my own face reflected back to me in the glass.

'We're leaving tonight. My dad knows someone who can get us to France. We're going to stay with his cousins in Munich.'

My mind whirred, trying to process what she was saying. 'By boat? You're going in a boat?'

She shrugged. 'Is there another way?'

The Channel Tunnel had been blocked for years. It was closely guarded by the Authorisation Bureau, who shot anyone trying to sneak through on sight. Even on the French side, it was rumoured the entrance to the tunnel had been destroyed. In the early years France struggled to cope with the influx of people trying to escape, often bloody and broken.

But a boat. I hadn't heard of anyone brave enough to venture out into the open water, exposed. I pictured Jasmine standing on the deck of a fishing boat, her hair blowing around her face as she stared out to sea, the lights of the French shoreline twinkling in the distance. My chest contracted.

Jasmine squeezed my hand. 'Please Clara, you can't say anything. Dad said I had to come to school, to be normal, so no one would suspect. But we have to go.' She hung her head, her fingers loosening. 'Mum didn't want to leave Christopher, but Dad says he's probably been dead for a long time. Or if he is still alive, there's no hope for him now. Not when they're calling him a terrorist.'

I didn't know what to say. All I could feel was the swell of my own pain at the thought of losing Jasmine.

'I don't want you to go,' I whispered, my voice raw with unshed tears.

She looked at me.

'I'm going to miss you so much, Clara. I hope, one day, we can see each other again.'

We sat together until the bell rang to announce the end of lunch, staring out across the field, letting the rain hide our tears, my food left uneaten.

When our final class finished, I couldn't look at Jasmine. We went to our lockers in silence, collecting our bags and coats. She closed her locker door firmly, leaving behind a pile of books and school work.

It was raining outside. We stood together outside the gates, neither of us wanting this final moment to be over. When Jasmine took my hand, I started to cry.

'I'll miss you.'

She squeezed her fingers around mine and then they slipped away. I stood for a long time watching her grow smaller as she moved towards the end of the street. At the corner she paused, looked back at me. I lifted my hand and she was gone.

I walked home, not caring as my clothes grew heavy with rain and clung to my skin. My hair was plastered across my

forehead, water running cold over my face and down the back
of my neck. A fierce knot of emotion burned inside me.

I could hear Will crying before I even got inside the house.
He lay on his back in the Moses basket, waving his arms angrily
in the air. Water dripped from my hair onto the pale carpet,
leaving a dark stain. There was no one else in the room. I wandered through the house, looking for my mother.

She was in her room, curled up on the bed, staring off into
the distance. An almost-empty bottle of vodka lay discarded on
the rug. Rain lashed against the window.

'Mama? Will's crying.'

She didn't turn to look at me.

'I can hear him.'

'Aren't you going to see what he wants?'

She sighed. 'You do it, Clara. You're a good girl.'

I hated her, then. I'd never felt so alone. Furious, I stormed
downstairs and picked up my brother, basket and all, and
hauled him up the stairs, where I deposited him on the bed
beside our mother. He never once stopped crying.

She turned to me, her eyes blank and watery.

'I thought you were going to take care of him for me?'

I snapped. 'He's *your* son! You do it. I just hope you can look
after him better than you looked after me.'

Before she could reply I rushed from the room, almost col-
liding with the major as he appeared in the doorway. He
grabbed my arm and forced me to stop.

'What the hell is going on?' he yelled. 'Can't you stop Will
from bloody crying?'

My mother raised her voice in response. I listened to them
arguing, the knot in my stomach growing tighter. 'You expect
me to do everything. Why don't you deal with him for once,
he's your son too.'

The major stalked across the room to pick up his son, awkwardly cradling the baby against his chest. His foot knocked the vodka bottle and sent it clattering across the floor.

'What the fuck is this?' he asked, his face growing tight. 'Are you drunk, when you're supposed to be looking after our child?'

He thrust Will into my arms and pushed me out of the room. 'Take him downstairs.'

He slammed the door in my face so hard it bounced open again. I couldn't move. I stood there watching as the major advanced across the room, cursing my mother for being a drunk.

With a crack, he brought his palm across her face. Her head snapped to one side and she cried out. Blood welled on her split lip. The baby was staring into the bedroom and I took a step away towards the stairs, then another. He murmured and reached out, but for the first time he didn't cry, eyes wide, taking it all in. I walked part-way down the stairs and sat, listening to my mother whimpering and the dull thuds of the major's fists on her flesh.

It was late and I couldn't sleep. The rain hadn't stopped all night. I lay in bed with the curtains open, listening to the sound of the storm striking the glass. I wondered if Jasmine was out there somewhere, in a boat on the open ocean.

My throat was dry. I wanted my mother. I pulled back the covers, shuddering as the cold air wrapped itself around me. Wrapping my arms across my chest, I went to her room.

From the landing, I heard the major's voice. I hadn't heard him come home; after their argument earlier he'd summoned the driver and he was still out when I went to bed. The door was ajar and the blue light of the television flickered. He was watching the government channel, with its endless propaganda cycle masquerading as news. My mother was in bed beside him. I could hear her faint snores.

Tonight there were raids on properties across the city, where associates of those responsible for the Whitehall bombing were taken into custody. In total, thirty-seven people were arrested.

My stomach dropped. I crept closer to the door, just enough so I could peek into the room and see the screen. A young man was standing in front of a block of flats, a blaze of light behind him as three men and a girl were dragged outside in handcuffs and shoved into the back of unmarked cars, blue lights strobing on their roofs. The caption in the corner of the screen read: *David G. Tubby reporting live.* Uneasiness prickled across my skin. This wasn't how the Authorisation Bureau usually operated. They arrested people in silence and secrecy; there were no light shows or television cameras to record the moment for posterity. But they wanted people to see this.

I focused on the family, being dragged away in the back of the shot, praying it wasn't Jasmine or her parents. The girl looked even younger than we were. Two of the men weren't even men at all, just teenage boys. The third man might have been their grandfather. He was stooped, his shoulders slumped, refusing to acknowledge the camera.

When the major spoke, I jumped. For a horrible moment I thought he was talking to me.

'I'm watching now. It looks like the raids went well. Hmm. Well that's a pity.'

He was on the phone. There was a long pause.

'Look, I know these people have nothing to do with the bombings, but it wouldn't be the first time a few nobodies had to disappear to strengthen our hand.'

I stopped breathing.

'No, no. Of course, sir. That's right, it was my plan. We

managed to round up all those who took part in the bombing campaign last month, but I didn't feel it was enough. We've caught three of these groups in the last six months, all trying to rebel against us. What if they start banding together next? There are enough of them out there.'

He fell silent again.

'That's exactly what I'm saying, sir. We have to do something public. There has to be a deterrent. And what can we connect it to? The Whitehall bombing is still one of the worst atrocities to happen in this country. Even now, people are still furious about it. Can you imagine if they ever found out we did it ourselves, so we could step in and take control? They'd rise up in the streets.'

It took me a moment to realise what he meant. All those people: the ones who died in the bombing and those who were lost afterwards, in its name; Jasmine's brother, her whole family. The major did this.

I couldn't contain myself. As he finished his conversation and hung up the phone, I launched myself into the room.

'How could you? You killed those people!'

He turned in surprise, eyes widening as I flung myself at him, arms flailing and clad in flannel pyjamas. I struck him on the side of the head. A shock of pain rushed through my hand and into my wrist, but he barely flinched. He tried to grab my hands, pull my arms down to my sides. We struggled for a minute, but I couldn't match his strength. As he wrapped his body around mine, making me small, the reporter on the television carried on talking, praising the brave men who had broken up this terror cell before they could do further harm. As he spoke, photos of the Whitehall victims flashed onto the screen.

'Clara, calm down please,' he said in my ear, like he was settling an animal. 'You need to stop this.'

I screamed at him, jerking my head back instinctively, but

it bounced off his chin and I only dazed myself. 'You did this! You killed them and blamed Jasmine's brother.'

My mother stirred and let out a grumble. But she didn't wake, didn't say anything. She'd been drinking again. Anything to numb the pain from her bruises. I didn't know whether it was the physical scars or the emotional ones that troubled her most.

The fight went out of me in a rush and the major let go. I flopped onto the sofa, my arms and legs trembling, head spinning. Bile threatened to rush up my throat. The whole world was falling out from underneath me and the major started to laugh. He laughed so hard that he had to bend over, hands on his knees and tears in his eyes.

'Oh Clara, if you only knew the half of it.'

'Why?' I asked quietly.

His laughter faded and he stood straight, his face growing serious.

'How else would we have taken control?'

I stared at him and my heart turned to ice.

Twenty-two

The next morning the major told my mother he was sending me away to school. She didn't ask him why, didn't even fight for me to stay. She didn't seem to feel strongly about the situation at all.

The major's driver was assigned the task of delivering me to my Scottish boarding school. When we set off, there was snow on the ground and the sky was thick with clouds. My mother embraced me in the hallway, the smell of alcohol on her breath.

She touched my face softly, 'I'll miss you, Clara.' She kissed both my cheeks carefully, in her old-fashioned European way.

I did not reply.

The major had left early for work. As he slid into the car, the driver informed me that my stepfather wanted to see me before I left. He took me to the Authorisation Bureau headquarters, a place I'd never been. As we drove through the heavy gates, past walls lined with razor wire, a sense of dread overwhelmed me.

We parked underground, where the major was waiting alone. It was still early and the place was quiet, the only sound a dripping water pipe somewhere in the shadows.

'Come with me,' he said abruptly, walking away so quickly I was forced into an awkward half-run to keep up with him. The driver didn't move, just stayed where he was, leaning against the car, a cigarette in his mouth. I looked back as the major led me through a metal door into the building to see him watching us.

I followed the major along narrow corridors with no windows, only harsh strip lights unsteady above us. The further we went into the building, the more I lost my sense of direction. The smell of bleach burned my nostrils.

Eventually the major stopped and unlocked a heavy metal door. He stood aside to let me go first into the room. It was an empty cell, a camera blinking in the corner. I couldn't take my eyes off a dark stain in the corner, afraid it might be blood.

'This is where we brought your father.'

It was a cruel thing to say and my mind didn't know how to cope with the sudden flood of images, as I imagined the man I loved in this room. I realised that I'd always held a lingering hope that I might see him again. But standing here, that light was extinguished.

The major stepped closer, his expression never changing.

'You know a secret now, Clara. One you shouldn't know. If you ever tell a soul about it, there's a room just like this waiting for you.'

The drive to Scotland took most of the day; nine hours spent in silence in the back of the car, staring out of the window as the rest of the country flashed by. I had barely ever been outside London, not since the days before the military government, when we were still a family.

I was used to the checkpoints; the bus had to stop at them each day as I travelled from the village where the major's house was to my school in the city. Usually the guards would board the bus, guns strapped to their chests, and glance quickly at the passengers.

But out here it was different. There were roadblocks every-where. Each large town had rows of soldiers who stopped every car, whether coming or going, and waved the occupants out onto the side of the road. Cocooned inside the major's offi-cial car, we coasted past the checkpoints, my nose pressed to the glass as I watched the other drivers hand over their ID cards and submit to a rough search.

The faces of the people were blank as the guards manhandled them. At a checkpoint somewhere in the north, half a dozen guards suddenly descended on one man and hauled him to the ground even as he struggled, his wife and child beside him. We had already passed by when the gunshots rang out. I sat back in my seat, feeling nauseous. In the rear-view mirror, I caught the driver watching me.

'It happens,' he said quietly. 'More than you'd think.'

Then he turned his gaze back to the road and I allowed my head to loll back against the headrest, slowly drifting into a troubled sleep.

I woke as the car came to a stop, the engine dying. It was growing dark. We were in a shadowy forecourt surrounded by a chain-link fence. Barbed wire ran around the top.

'Where are we?'

It was a fuel stop; the old-fashioned kind, with half a dozen petrol pumps at the front and an abandoned building that might once have been a family restaurant. The driver got out of the car and began filling it with petrol. I climbed out behind him and stretched carefully as I took a look around.

There were a handful of other cars inside the gates, but most looked as though they had been parked there a while. On one side of the building was a small shop; someone was moving around inside. As the driver busied himself with the fuel, I started to wander towards the building. The radio buzzed inside.

On the pavement outside stood a rickety metal carousel, filled with postcards of Scottish landscapes. On the floor beside it was a pile of newspapers, bundled together with twine. A couple were loose on top of the rest; I picked one up and unfolded it so I could scan the front page. It was dominated by a picture of the First General. I'd heard a rumour at school that he was sickening, in the grip of a degenerative disease that slowed his body and withered his mind. But the picture the paper had chosen to print was old. It showed the general at one of his early rallies, shortly after the junta came to power. He stood proud behind a podium as he gave a famous speech proclaiming freedom for the people. His hands pumped the air in celebration as the audience cheered wildly. A woman at the front was crying ecstatically.

I didn't read the headline; looking at the newspaper made me feel sick. I dropped it, the First General's face falling flat on the dusty concrete.

'You ain't a fan then?'

I jumped violently. The man was watching me from the doorway of the shop, leaning against the frame as he smoked a cigarette.

'Sorry, I… I was just looking…'

He took a heavy pull on the cigarette, letting my words hang awkwardly between us. With a thick cough, he stubbed it out against the wall and flicked the end away, the embers dying away to nothing.

He was young, no more than twenty-five. At some point his hairline had begun to recede and he had responded by shaving his head, so that only a soft black fuzz remained. It suited him though. He had an angular jaw and sharp cheekbones, stubble heavy across his cheeks. He dug the cigarette packet out of the pocket of his jeans and as he did so his sleeve rode up. I glimpsed the bright swirl of tattoos on his arm.

He saw me looking and pushed his sleeves up further. The design covered his forearms. My eyes traced the different colours. On his right arm was an anchor, surrounded by intricate patterns. There was a heart on his left arm, with a sun emerging above it. A scroll twisted across it, with a single word printed in black script. Marianne.

He smiled wryly as he drew a cigarette from the packet and lit it. I noticed his fingers were yellow with nicotine, his nails cracked and dirty. He held the packet out towards me. 'Smoke?'

I shook my head quickly. 'No, thanks.'

He shrugged. The fuel pump clicked as the driver finished filling up the car.

'You're not from round here.' He said it plainly, a fact rather than a question.

'No.'

He looked away, his eyes finding some point in the distance as he smoked slowly. 'Not many are now.'

I didn't know how to answer him. My feet shifted uncomfortably. I wanted to say something profound; I wanted him to think me older, more worldly, not just a sheltered schoolgirl. But I was wearing my new uniform.

The moment stretched to breaking point and then the driver appeared at my shoulder. The younger man tossed his cigarette away.

'Fuel?'

The driver inclined his head. 'And some water. Do you have any food?'

'In the back.'

I followed them inside. The shop was dimly lit and the faint smell of mould assailed my nostrils. I wandered the aisles as the driver went in search of sustenance. The shelves were almost bare, occasional items punctuating the emptiness. The radio was tuned to the approved station; a newscaster was reading the headlines in a monotone voice. There had been a series of attacks on off-duty officers, but those responsible had been apprehended. A rash of graffiti had sprung up in the centre of London, but had been quickly dealt with. There was a rice shortage thanks to restrictions put in place by overseas suppliers.

The young man drifted towards the till, where he sat, one booted foot propped up against the counter. The radio continued to drone in the background. A noticeboard in the corner caught my attention. I moved closer so that I could study the things that were posted there. There was a flyer advertising an old car for sale. A photograph of a lost cat. A poster listing the names and pictures of criminals thought to be in the area.

I continued reading as the driver dumped a small loaf of bread and a tin of corned beef on the counter, along with two bottles of water. He paid for them, and for his petrol. The young man put everything in a brown paper bag and handed it to the driver.

'Let's go,' he said as he walked past me.

I looked back at the young man, alone behind the counter. It seemed right to raise my hand in farewell. His mouth seemed to twitch, and then he too lifted his hand.

The last thing I read on the noticeboard was a 'missing' poster, with a black and white photograph of a beautiful girl with long pale hair. Her name was Marianne.

When I woke again it was dark. I was dazzled briefly by a car heading in the other direction, the full beam of its headlights raking across my face.

'Not long to go now,' the driver told me. I could hear the tiredness in his voice and knew he would be looking forward to his bed, in a small guesthouse close to the school. There was no way he could make the return drive that night.

I'd never spoken much to the driver; I always associated him too closely with the major. But I was glad that there would be someone I knew nearby for that first night, when I was alone in an unfamiliar place.

I squinted out of the window at the black bulk of a row of Scottish mountains that ran alongside the road. I could see their silhouette out through the windscreen as the road twisted and began to climb. As we neared the highest point of the road, I could make out a row of lights in the distance. My stomach tightened.

We drove through the village first, past the hotel where the driver would spend the night. He turned his head to look. The building was old and rundown, with layers of mesh barring the windows. The sign above the door was peeling and the car park was empty, but for an old Citroen with the exhaust hanging off.

The village was little more than one main street, with a dozen houses lining either side of the road, their gardens overgrown. Bags of rubbish were piled up on the pavement, their guts spilling out onto the tarmac.

I was relieved when the village was behind us, until I caught sight of a sign looming out of the darkness, proclaiming that this was the way to the Fairfields School for Elite Girls.

The driver slowed the car and we turned onto a narrow road that disappeared into the middle of a thick wood, so dense that tree branches scraped across the windows of the car. Something burst out of the undergrowth on one side and bolted across the road, forcing the driver to curse and slam on the brakes. I was jolted forward, the seatbelt cutting into my chest.

As he accelerated again, the driver muttered, 'I wouldn't much fancy being stuck out here in the back of beyond. Creepy, this is.'

I didn't know how to reply, so I kept quiet, picking at the skin around my fingernails. After what felt like an eternity, we emerged from the woods and the school came into view. It had once been a grand Gothic manor house but, like the village, it had fallen into disrepair. It was difficult to tell in the dark, but I could make out the shadow of loose guttering and missing roof tiles. Weeds had begun to creep among the paving slabs.

Gravel crunched as the driver pulled up at the front entrance and a security light flashed on. They must have been watching for us, because the front door opened immediately and two women emerged.

The first was smartly dressed and even at this late hour was neatly made up and wearing heels. The second woman I assumed was a housekeeper of some kind. She was bundled up in an old cardigan that she pulled about her expanding waistline, as she hurried down the steps.

They waited as the driver got out and opened the door for me. I emerged into the sharp night air and accepted the hand that was offered.

'You must be Clara. I'm Mrs McGreevy, the headmistress here. Welcome to Fairfields, it's a pleasure to have you.' She smiled warmly, leaning forwards to say, 'I met your father once, years ago. He's a great man.'

I shook her hand, wondering which father she meant.

The building's interior betrayed its roots: the decor was heavy and dated, and no doubt hadn't been altered in over a century.

Oil paintings hung on the walls, depicting various members of the family who had once called this place home.

They probably had no right to it now, if there were any of them left. The disappearances didn't always happen this far north, the government didn't have the resources at first, but exceptions could easily be made for prominent figures: former ministers or those from wealthy and historic families.

The matron, Maggie, headed for the stairs, tugging my case up behind her. She turned left at the top and we began to walk along a lengthy corridor. Stopping at the third door, she pulled an old-fashioned brass key from her pocket and unlocked the door, beckoning me to follow her inside.

The room was small, with two beds. A second door led into a small washroom.

'This is my room,' Maggie informed me. 'You'll stay in here with me tonight, and then tomorrow we'll get you settled into your own room. You'll be sharing with three of the other girls, but they're all in bed now as it's so late.'

She pointed to a narrow single bed. 'You can sleep there. We keep a spare bed in here in case one of the girls is sick in the night and I need to keep an eye on them.'

I stood quietly in the doorway taking everything in. I could feel my bottom lip trembling.

Maggie must have noticed because her voice softened. 'Now, now pet, it'll be fine, you'll see. They're a good bunch here. And with a father like yours, you'll be part of the crowd in no time. These girls all have families who are important members of the government and they're all destined for government jobs too, just like you. We're like the beating heart of things here, preparing the next generation to keep things running right. Now, you get washed and your nightie on, while I go and fetch your dinner. Then when you come back we'll see about unpacking your stuff, eh?'

She closed the door on the way out of the room and locked me inside. Feeling afraid, I went to the window, in time to see the car drive slowly away. I watched until I could no longer see the headlights in the distance and I was left alone.

I ate my supper from a tray on my lap while Maggie went through the contents of my suitcase. She touched my things almost apologetically, as though she wasn't used to having the owner there watching her.

All of my clothes, my shoes, my underwear, were regulation. I hadn't brought any make-up and only basic toiletries, as most things would be provided by the school. The only things outside the list were my books and a framed photograph of my mother, the major and Will that she had insisted on packing. When she came across it, Maggie nodded approvingly, giving me a look that was surely reserved for the other dutiful daughters.

She closed the lid of the suitcase with a satisfied click. 'That's all fine, sweetheart. That's a lovely family you have there. A bonny lad.'

I nodded, my mouth full of potatoes.

'I've got a few things to do down in the kitchen, but you finish up your dinner and feel free to get into bed. I'll be sure not to disturb you when I come back up.'

This time I was ready for the metallic twist of the key in the lock. I knew there was nowhere I could go.

I finished the food and placed the tray carefully on the floor, where it wouldn't be in the way when Maggie returned. I took my time in the bathroom, examining my face in the mirror until my features blurred and grew undefined. I left my clothes folded neatly on the chair at the end of the bed.

When I went to pull back the covers and climb into bed, I

noticed that Maggie had left the photograph out on the bed-side table. Perhaps she thought I might be missing my family. I picked up the picture in its simple silver frame and went to chuck it back into the case, but a thought crossed my mind. She would expect me to have the photo close by. With a sigh, I stood it up on the bedside table.

Despite the long journey, I didn't feel tired. Too many con-flicting emotions were flooding my body, stirring my mind into action. I wondered where Jasmine was, what she was doing. I hoped desperately that she hadn't been locked behind one of the steel doors in the major's building. Instead I pre-ferred to picture her in France, in a small cottage with her par-ents, eating dinner together. Either way, she was lost to me forever.

I rummaged through my meagre possessions until I found one of the novels I had packed. I didn't bother to look at the cover, simply grabbed the first one that came to hand. I slipped between the scratchy sheets and settled against the pillows to read.

I frowned at the book. It wasn't one of mine; in fact, it was years since I had seen it. I ran my fingers across the cracks on the binding and pressed it to my face, breathing in the scent of old paper and ink.

It was a book of poetry that my father had owned, before he met my mother. He always said that his favourite poem from the collection reminded him of her. They had a friend read it out at their wedding. I hadn't seen it for years, since the rest of his collection was sold.

When I opened the front cover, my father's scratchy hand-writing was large on the page, the ink faded but still legible. He had dedicated the book to my mother, with promises of love and eternal happiness. She must have kept it, hidden it away somewhere, even after she married the major.

I began flicking through the pages when something caught my attention. There was a piece of paper tucked inside the book. I drew it out carefully and felt something swell within my chest.

It was a photograph: the one that she had meant me to have. A picture of my parents and me, grinning excitedly at the camera on a day out at the beach. My mother was sitting on a colourful picnic blanket on the sand, my tiny child's body pulled onto her lap. Beside her my father was gazing at us with open admiration, his arm resting against my mother's back. I must have only been about three or four. I could vaguely remember the day, a trip we had taken to the coast with my grandmother. She must have been the one behind the camera.

This was the family picture I should have framed beside my bed. But my mother had kept it with her all these years. I slipped the photo carefully back between the pages of the novel and slid it under my pillow. When I lay down to sleep, I let my hand rest there, touching the pages, a reminder that I wasn't quite as alone as I had thought.

Part Five

Twenty-three

The air was thick with smoke and the cloying scent of perfume. The commander sat across the table from me, a cigar gripped in his teeth and a glass of cognac in his hand. He was laughing uproariously at something Major Donovan had said.

I sawed angrily at my porterhouse steak, staring at the blood as it slowly pooled on the plate, staining the delicate crushed potatoes red. Lucia sat beside me, sipping from a champagne flute. I could see her swaying gently from the corner of my eye.

The commander clapped Donovan on the shoulder and roared at his wife, 'Did you hear that? Not only is he the best man in my command, but a bloody comedian as well. Brilliant, bloody brilliant!'

The commander's wife smiled, eyeing the young major through false lashes. She was the latest in an ever-growing line of barely adult brides, none of whom lasted past the age of twenty-seven. The commander liked them fresh and blonde and wide eyed. He liked them, until he didn't. I couldn't even remember this one's name.

Across the table, Donovan was smirking. The commander pulled out a second cigar and gave it to him. They leaned towards each other for a brief moment while Donovan sucked on the cigar, until it flared into life. I hunched more tightly over my meal, the din of the restaurant rattling my nerves. Lucia's face was flushed from the champagne, her food barely touched. The tendons in her forearm were taut as she clutched her glass so tightly I expected it would shatter. A picture of her in tears with bloody hands flashed through my mind. I felt a surge of excitement.

She looked frail tonight. Naturally her face was painted so that she would blend into this crowd of elegant wives and mistresses. Her lipstick was the right shade of red and her dress was expensive, the appropriate designer label sewn into the neckline. But her cheeks were growing hollow, the bones starting to jut. A ripple of disgust disrupted my digestion as she finished the champagne and beckoned for the waiter to refill her glass.

I was pulled back into the conversation as the commander crowed, 'Mark my words, Donovan here is set for big things. Hell, he might even fill my shoes one day.'

Twenty years ago, that was me. I had sat beside the commander in a restaurant much like this, short-skirted waitresses hurrying past us carrying trays laden with drinks. He clapped me on the shoulder with his meaty palm, fed me expensive brandy and cigars until I felt like I would vomit. He told me then I was the one.

The restaurant was full of them: all those people who knew how to rise to the heights of power and influence, no matter how many backs they had to trample across to get there. At the table across from us sat a well-known business leader and his wife. He'd been inconsequential before the First General took over, but had made a fortune during the transition. Rumour had it he wasn't afraid to get his hands dirty, for a price. Across the room was a famous newsreader, who appeared on our screens each night with the latest updates, straight from the pen of the Propaganda Department. But he wasn't with his wife and co-presenter – instead he was surrounded by much younger women, all of them hanging on his every word, their eyes glassy and bright. One of them slipped from her seat and headed towards the bathroom. She didn't even wait until she was out of sight before pulling a small sachet of powder from her bag.

I stuffed a forkful of steak into my mouth and chewed, look-ing at my plate and avoiding the growing bulge of stomach spilling over my belt. I remembered how the theatre manager had sickened me, all those years ago. And I was slowly adopt-ing his corpulent form, consoling myself with expensive food and fine wine. I looked at Donovan and the sleek line of his shirt, the way his jaw was pulled tight and the muscles in his upper arms flexed. I hated him.

In the car on the way home, the back seat was a wasteland between my wife and me. She hunched in her seat, arms folded, staring out of the window as the streets flashed by. The diamonds in her ears glinted in the dim light. I could see the ghostly reflection of her face in the glass. For a brief moment she was the woman I had longed for; I put my hand down on the leather seat and thought about sliding it towards her. But as we paused at a junction the car flooded with harsh light. She turned to look at me and I saw that her make-up was gaudy and overdone; I saw every line on her face and the yellow tinge of her eyes. And I remembered how much she repulsed me.

There was a certain stage she reached when she had been drinking for some time, but hadn't yet consumed enough to slip into unconsciousness. She became brazen. She stared at me now, seeing the way my lip curled as I glared at her.

She tilted her chin defiantly. 'What?'

My brows drew closer. 'What do you mean *what*?'

'You're staring at me.'

She slurred her words slightly. When she was drunk, the old

lilt of her family accent re-emerged. The car pulled away again and we fell back into darkness.

I looked away. 'I'd forgotten, for a moment...' My voice trailed away.

'You'd forgotten what? How ugly your wife is? How much she despises you?'

'Be quiet.'

'No. I won't be quiet.' Her voice rose, the shrill sound like nails on glass. 'I won't be quiet Darius. I've been quiet for years. And where did it get me? Well?'

She began to sob. I couldn't look at her. The driver's shoulders were resolute as he drove us home, set apart from our domestic drama. Lucia's weeping intensified and I couldn't stand it.

'Shut up.' My words cut across the back seat of the car. But still she cried. '*Shut up!*'

It was the crack of my hand across her face that silenced her.

She pressed trembling fingers to her cheek. Her shattered profile was an accusation.

The second the car slowed to a stop outside the house I was out, leaving the door flung open wide. I didn't stop to help her; I left that for the driver. He was making his way around the car as I ran inside, catching Lucia as she stumbled out.

A photograph from our wedding day confronted me as I fled to my study. With a shout I picked it up and flung it across the room, the glass smashing against the wall. I was full of rage. I couldn't look at my own face, because I'd have to acknowledge my own failure. I'd been so desperate to fuck this woman, to fuck the professor's wife, that I'd fucked myself in the process.

I thought of Donovan driving home to his city apartment, high up in a luxury apartment block. The young officers lived in the city now, where there was more life to be had. I knew he would take a woman home, perhaps not one from the restaurant – not the commander's pert wife as he might have preferred. No, he would go on to a bar and find someone there. Someone beautiful but disposable, who would warm his bed enthusiastically and then disappear from his life forever.

Hands shaking, I poured myself a drink. I threw it back and poured another, settling down into my chair to work through the bottle so that I might pass out here and escape another cold night in bed with my wife.

It was worse the next day in the office, a raging hangover sickening my spirit. The interrogations I performed were brutal yet perfunctory. They were over quickly. I knew now how to take someone apart at speed. It was an art I'd perfected over the years.

I might have struggled with Matthew Winter, but now I devoured men like him. I ruined them and they never troubled me for a second. I'd whittled my heart to nothing.

But he still haunted me. I'd taken his wife and daughter, burned his books and broken his body, but I couldn't shake the feeling that I'd never touched him. I tried for a long time until we reached a stalemate. He'd been in this prison longer than anyone else. It had been so long since he saw the sun that his skin had grown pale and transparent.

I should have killed him. I tried more than once. I stood in the corridor outside his cell with a gun in my hand, the other on the door handle, trying to summon up the will to go inside and put a bullet in his brain. But there was always something that made me hold back.

In the end, the commander made the decision for me. After twenty years of the new regime, there was a period of amnesty, where the government agreed to release a number of political prisoners. They weren't permitted to return to their homes –

if they still existed. Instead they were sent abroad, into exile. We banished them to sympathetic regimes in Africa or South America, where they would work and die in the shadows.

I think it was then that I lost the commander's respect. He had indulged my obsession with Matthew Winter, although he never understood it. But by that time, when it had burrowed under my skin and weakened my heart, he had grown tired. Instead of directing my feelings into the system, where they could be of some help, I'd turned them too far inward. I'd lost sight of the cause. I don't think he ever forgave me, although he kept me around out of some kind of loyalty. My misery gave me a brutality that he found useful.

I sat in the guard room, filling out a sheaf of paperwork before the bank of monitors. A dozen interrogations were happening in front of me, but it was like nothing more than some late-night film playing on a loop.

The paperwork absorbed my attention for a long time. My hand scrawled across the forms, filling out endless details that would be filed away somewhere, a record that no one would ever see.

My wrist was growing tired when a flicker of movement caught my eye. It was Donovan. The young major had a particular talent: he was adept in the interrogation of women. I think it was the reason he appealed so much to the commander.

I'd heard the talk of course, the whispers, but I'd never paid much attention, too busy with my own desperation. There had been rumours for a couple of years of women who had been brutalised to the point of suicide. They were found occasionally, hanging in their cells, the bruises still fresh. One girl had somehow managed to break a piece of metal off the bedframe and use it to slit her wrists. But she must have changed her mind at the last minute, when it was already too late. The scene

194

when she was discovered the following morning had lingered in the imaginations of some of the more squeamish men.

Now it was all there on the screen. I saw exactly what it was that made these women crack. I watched for a long time, the light flickering across my face as I leaned into the monitor, holding my breath. I watched, a fierce heat burning low in my gut. I watched and thought of her, the woman I had wanted so badly, all those years ago.

As two of the bureau's best interrogators, it fell to Donovan and me to teach occasional classes with students from the Authorisation Bureau academy. Sometimes we would be invited to give a guest lecture, where we would talk about our technique and the approved methods for information gathering. And sometimes the students would come to us, to watch us at work. They were always shocked at first, by the reality of the interrogation room. The smell was the first thing to affect them, as they laughed among themselves and pretended to retch. But by the end of the session, with blood and violence, it was no longer funny.

When the students came to observe an interrogation, they did so in small groups. We would take them to the interrogation room before the detainee and let them look around. The room felt claustrophobic, even with a small group there. Then they would go into the observation room, where they could look through the glass as the prisoner was brought in.

When it was Will's turn for observation, Donovan carried out the interrogation. I stood behind the glass with the students and commented on his technique, offering my own thoughts and advice as some of them scribbled notes and others simply stared at the action.

The woman he was questioning was very young, barely

older than the students who were in the room with me. She had been arrested earlier that week, caught in the act of vandalising a public mural depicting the First General and his lieutenants.

She had been a pretty girl, but it was hard to tell now, beneath the broken nose and swollen eyes. She had to breathe through her mouth, and when she sucked in a lungful of air, the gaps in her white teeth were visible.

Donovan was screaming at her. I could feel the tension in the students around me. You could always tell the ones that would make the grade as interrogators and the ones that were destined for the bag squad. The interrogators pushed forward, so close to the glass they were almost touching it. The rest would hang back, averting their eyes, shocked by the brutality. At least in the bag squad they could hide behind their team; in the interrogation room you were alone. I wondered if they were already regretting their career choice.

I was pleased to see Will at the front of the group, his breath hot on the glass as he watched Donovan intently. The girl was crying, but I could tell it wasn't her that held his attention, even when the interrogator ripped her shirt away, leaving her exposed. I felt the teenagers around me shift awkwardly.

Then Donovan looked up, directly into the observation room.

'How about we get someone else involved?' he said, his voice heavy with menace. 'Any volunteers?'

It seemed only natural that Will would turn to look at me. I nodded and he pushed through the door to join the interrogation. Under the harsh lights he looked younger, his eyes wide, nostrils flared.

'How do you want to begin?' Donovan asked.

'Sir?' For a moment, Will looked overwhelmed to be in the room, with this girl and the man who had inflicted so much pain on her already. Then he looked around with a focus that made me smile. But as he paused, then took off his belt, I felt something else, something I couldn't quite identify. As he stalked behind the girl and brought the lash down across her bare shoulders, as she screamed again, I had to look away.

Twenty-four

After Clara left school, we rarely saw her from one month to the next. I knew her mother would meet her sometimes, but she didn't often come to the house.

I hadn't been thrilled when she decided to pursue a career in academia; even less so when I realised she intended to teach literature, as her father had done. It felt like a slap in the face. She'd been a bookish child, so I shouldn't have been surprised, but I was disappointed that she didn't know better. After a while I began to suspect that she did, that she'd chosen her career to spite me.

It was another mark against me. I had enough of a reputation that she was permitted to hold a job at the university, but her presence didn't go unnoticed. I don't think she realised it, but they watched her. Her and that boyfriend she insisted on parading around with.

From the day she brought him home I was suspicious of his motives. It didn't help that he was so much older, near enough my own age. It was clear from the way that Clara acted around him that she was smitten. She would follow close at his side, her face wide open and smiling, always looking up for his approval.

I felt that he was watching me. I never managed to catch

him; I would sense his eyes on the back of my neck and turn sharply, only to find him chatting to Lucia, or examining one of the pictures on the wall.

Despite my suspicions, when I was confronted with the evidence of Simon's betrayal, I couldn't believe it. It was Donovan who told me. He came to my house, late in the evening, after dinner had been cleared away and Lucia had retreated to bed with a bottle of gin.

I brought him into the study, closing the door firmly behind us. I mixed him a drink slowly, to hide my unease. He'd never been to the house before and his presence made me nervous. I feared there was an unmarked van waiting somewhere in the darkness, the bag squad ready to burst through the door at Donovan's signal.

But instead he sat back in the chair, one foot slung casually over the other knee, and tossed a folder onto my desk. I picked it up as though it might burn me. It was full of photographs. Surveillance photographs of Simon, talking to a man I vaguely recognised.

'That's Caleb Morris,' Donovan said. 'He's the leader of a group we've been watching for some time, Lumière.'

I nodded. 'I'm familiar with them. They've been around for years, here and there.'

Donovan's dark eyes examined me closely. 'They've been ramping up their activities over the last year or so. That bombing outside Manchester over the summer? That was them. And the kidnapping of the security minister. We managed to keep that quiet, but we were forced to pay his ransom, money that can only have strengthened the group's infrastructure.'

I flicked slowly through the photos. They'd clearly been taken over the course of several weeks.

'And you want me to know that my daughter's boyfriend is involved with them.'

The corner of his mouth twitched into a smile. 'But she's not your daughter, is she? Her father was the rebel professor, Matthew Winter.'

I returned his gaze, my mind working quickly through the problem. Should I push the point that I had raised Clara and risk being implicated in this, or deny all knowledge and throw her to the wolves?

'That's true. But Clara hasn't seen him since she was eleven. Too young to have absorbed any of his ideals.' I thrust the folder at him. 'And I notice you don't have any pictures of her meeting Caleb Morris. Only her boyfriend, who I must admit, I have never approved of.'

Donovan's eyes narrowed. 'So you've had your own suspicions?'

I tapped my fingers on the desk. 'I've always had the sense that there was something more to the relationship for Simon. I suppose he could have been attracted to Clara by her father's reputation. I'm told he's quite famous in certain circles.'

Donovan nodded thoughtfully. 'It's true; we've never come across your stepdaughter during our surveillance. But that doesn't mean she's not involved.' He gathered the folder and its contents back together. 'And we know that Simon has been teaching classes at the university, off the books if you like. We don't know what he's preaching, but it won't be long before we get a worm into the group. One way or another.'

I paused, my heart thundering.

'Let me look into Clara. I'll find out if she's been doing anything she shouldn't.'

The young major raised his eyebrows. 'And if she has?'

I stood up, scraping my chair back to announce that this meeting was over.

'Then I'll arrest her myself.'

It wasn't difficult to find out more about Simon's activities. The photographs Donovan showed me were only a small part of the intelligence that had been gathered. It amazed me that such an intelligent man could have been so stupid.

It was clear that he'd been teaching a number of students unofficially. They'd all been captured on film and identified. They in turn had people watching them. I made the order to arrest one of them.

We chose a young man whose family had a questionable background. He had an uncle who had been killed in the early days of the regime; an uncle who had undesirable friends that this boy had attempted to contact.

I hadn't joined the bag squad on a raid for years. I was above that now, my work taking me out of the field and into the squalid cells of headquarters, where I was most effective.

But this time I joined them. I sat in the front of the van, blood singing in my veins. I'd forgotten this sensation, the excitement. I felt like a predator, prowling through the streets at night, a pack of hyenas at my back.

It was late when we arrived at the halls of residence. Despite the curfews there were usually some students who stayed out late – partying, studying, fornicating – and we didn't want to risk them stumbling upon the scene.

A lone night porter was at a desk in the entrance foyer of the building. I had to buzz for him to admit us. He'd been reading a newspaper, but he put it down at the sound of visitors. His face stiffened when he saw who it was, but he opened the door without comment.

'It might be best if you took a short break,' I told him, as the bag squad marched past towards the stairs. 'You look tired; get yourself a cup of coffee.'

He spun away wordlessly, almost sprinting towards a door marked Staff Only, the newspaper forgotten.

Whistling softly, I followed the boys upstairs. They moved carefully in sync, through the door and along the corridor in near silence. It was only when they kicked the boy's bedroom door in that the disturbance began.

I waited outside, listening to the shouts and muffled thumps from inside the room. In a matter of moments, the bag squad had their prisoner outside with a hood over his head and his hands zip-tied behind his back. He was wearing nothing more than a pair of boxer shorts and his feet clawed clumsily at the carpet. A fierce bruise was already blooming over one of his kidneys.

The brief assault must have woken most of the residents on the corridor, but only one door opened. A Chinese boy appeared in the doorway, drowsily trying to straighten his glasses.

'What's going on?' he called. 'Jerome!'

Without missing a beat, the two soldiers who were dragging the prisoner away dropped him abruptly and stepped menacingly towards the interloper. He shrank back away from them.

'Keep your nose out, mate,' one of them said.

He blinked quickly behind his thick lenses. 'But…'

The other soldier punched him in the face. While he was dealing with the shock, they shoved him back into his room and pulled the door shut.

'Right, lads,' I said. 'Let's get this one in the van.'

I started Jerome's interrogation as soon as we got him back to base. It didn't take much work to make him talk. He was young and soft, more so than he could have imagined, the tears flowing long before the pain began.

He told me all about Simon's classes and the things they discussed. And later, he told me about Lumière. But the thing that shocked me the most was when he told me about Clara.

That she had attended an underground meeting wasn't proof of much. But it was the first sign of betrayal. The one I'd been waiting almost twenty years for. I had given her a chance at life despite everything, and this was what she had decided to do with it.

Part Six

Twenty-five

I was alone in the apartment, in darkness. I sat on the floor, back against the wall, my knees pulled up to my chest. I watched the door, waiting for a sign that they might come here, for me. I had convinced myself that they hadn't seen me out there, in the street. Grabbing Simon and leaving me behind was an oversight; a mistake that would be quickly rectified.

I stayed in the street for a long time after the car vanished. The sun finally disappeared between two buildings, leaving behind a flaming orange glow that seared the sky, before that too faded.

It was a quiet street, which didn't lead anywhere important. So it was a long time before another car appeared, headlights flashing, forcing me to snap out of my reverie and get out of the middle of the road. It roared past me, horn honking, and sped into the underground car park around the corner. I could hear music blaring even after the car was out of sight.

Shaking, I stood on the pavement, unsure of what to do. My life had altered course brutally, here in this tiny corner of the city. I had entered a new reality, one that seemed to float around the recesses of my consciousness, trying to force its way inside. I waited for someone to come and tell me what I should do, but no one appeared.

It was then, as I stood on the pavement with my world crumbling around me, that I noticed the carrier bag. It was lying on the floor, the contents spilling out into the street. Simon must have dropped it there as he was forced into the car.

I bent to examine it. There was a bottle of red wine, smashed now, the contents seeping through the cracks in the tarmac. There were a couple of mundane household items: tissues and a tube of toothpaste. And there, beneath a copy of today's newspaper, was a tiny packet of jelly sweets, all set in the shape of a diamond ring.

I jerked awake, to find myself on the floor, curled into an awkward foetal position, still wearing yesterday's clothes. Someone was banging on the front door. A rush of nerves flooded my body.

'Clara,' my mother's voice called. 'Are you in there?'

The realisation hit me. It was Sunday and Simon and I were due to meet her for brunch. 'Oh shit,' I muttered.

Stiffly, I clambered to my feet and staggered for the door, rolling my shoulders to work out the knots. I took a deep breath. My mother stood in the corridor, knuckles poised to knock again. Her dark hair was still long, although it was tinged with grey. Her petite frame was encased in a designer wrap dress and knee-length boots, an expensive handbag hooked over her arm.

She saw me and raised her eyebrows. 'Where on Earth have you been? I sat and waited for you for half an hour!'

'Sorry.' I moved aside to let her in. She marched past me and began surveying the apartment.

'Where's Simon?'

I had planned to make up an excuse, to lie and claim that he had to work today or had been called away to a sick relative. Apart from the monthly brunches, I rarely had any contact with my mother, so she wouldn't know any different.

I opened my mouth but nothing came out. Instead I burst into huge, shuddering sobs. My legs failed and I collapsed onto the carpet. My mother looked horrified.

'Goodness, Clara! Whatever is the matter?'

She eased herself down beside me, took hold of my hands and forced them away from my face. I gulped, trying to hold back the torrent of emotion. 'Tell me what's wrong, darling.'

'It… it's Simon,' I managed to croak. 'They took him.'

She tried to hide it, but the shock flashed across her face. She knew the answer, but she asked anyway. 'Who took him?'

'They were in a black car. Four men got out and dragged him inside. They were… they were…'

She took my hand. 'It's alright; you don't need to say it. I understand.'

'What should I do?' I wailed, the tears intensifying again.

She sighed. 'What can you do, Clara? When your father was arrested I wanted to go to the police station, go to every prison and bang on the door until they let me visit him. I wanted to go out into the streets and ask people if they'd seen him, if they knew where he was. But that would only have made more trouble. It probably would have made things worse for your father too.'

'So, what? I'm supposed to pretend that Simon never existed? Get up and go to work with a smile on my face, like you did?' I shook my head furiously. 'No, I can't do it.'

Her face was grave. 'It doesn't matter what you want. Do you think anybody else cares? They all have their own problems. Don't make things worse for yourself.'

'Thanks for your support, mother. So basically, I have to shut up and pretend everything is normal, or else I'll be in trouble too.'

'Clara, I hate to be harsh with you, but you've been through this before. You know exactly how it works. I was in exactly this situation with your father.'

I got to my feet and walked away from her, gazing out of the window at the people on the street, going about their daily lives. A young woman with bright red hair and a stylish mustard coat was passing the building, chatting to the man beside her, a huge smile on her face. In that moment, every atom in my body longed to be her; to be happy.

'Yeah I remember,' I said softly. 'But I'm not like you; I won't marry the first man who comes along and forget about the person I claimed to love.'

She didn't reply and I didn't want to face her. I knew the comment would hurt, but I said it anyway. When I eventually turned around, the apartment was empty. My mother had left without a word.

Twenty-six

Arriving at the university on Monday morning was a surreal experience. Unsure whether I should seek out Simon's boss and tell him what had happened, I went to the History department. It was early and there weren't many people around. When I walked by Simon's office, the door was open. Stomach churning, I poked my head around the corner.

His desk had been completely cleared. His papers, his books, his computer, even the photograph of us together had been removed. The shelves assigned to him were empty too. Not even the fleece jumper he left hanging over the back of his chair remained.

A soft moan escaped my lips. I didn't know if the university was responsible for this comprehensive elimination of one of their most prized employees, or if there was a more sinister explanation. If I went to Simon's boss and asked him to return the photograph, would he help or would the black van be waiting for me when I left that day?

In the lobby along the corridor, a ping indicated that the lift had arrived. There was a low whoosh as the doors opened. Before anyone could disembark, I backed away from the room that had been Simon's office and fled for the stairs.

Fortunately my Monday schedule was sparse; I don't think I would have coped otherwise. I had a two-hour seminar in the morning that wasn't running, as the class had an independent study week to enable them to work on their latest assignment, which was approaching deadline. In the afternoon I had to give a lecture on the work of the current Poet Laureate, whose odes to the First General were required reading.

I had given the same lecture many times before, yet I struggled to focus without using my notes. I stammered over my words, unable to meet the gaze of my students as I usually would. I referred back to my slides frequently and kept my eyes locked on my note cards.

As I talked, I was sensitive to them watching me, their eyes following my every move, noting each time I stumbled over a phrase. I imagined what they must be thinking; surely by now everyone would know about Simon. Even in the shadows, gossip travelled fast. I remembered how I was treated at school after my father disappeared and wondered how long it would be before the students began abandoning my classes.

The final slide in my presentation contained a list of recommended reading. I went through the books one by one, briefly explaining how they related to the subject.

'This brings us to the next assignment for this module. I want you all to select two of the collections from this list and critique them, based on one of the essay questions.' I picked up a stack of photocopies and held them up for everyone to see. Moving to the front row, I handed the papers to the girl sitting on the end and gestured for her to pass them along. She took one sheet and handed the stack to the boy beside her.

'Choose one question to answer, and make sure you write about both of your texts. I also want to see references to some of the secondary texts included on the list, but you can also use books that I haven't mentioned.'

I walked back to the front of the lecture hall as the students scribbled down my instructions and waited for a copy of the essay questions. 'Once you've got the questions you can go. Thank you everyone.'

There was a shuffling of feet and bags and the sound of chairs slamming upright as the students at the front made their way to the exit. I looked up to smile, but the expression froze halfway, my face contorted.

A movement at the back of the room had caught my eye. It was the major, seated apart from the class in the last row. As I watched, he got to his feet and tucked his hat under his arm. He began to descend the stairs towards me.

'Do we have to write about the books on the slideshow?'

I was jolted back to the classroom, to find a young girl with unnaturally red hair standing in front of me, paper in hand.

'Excuse me?' I asked, trying to pull my attention back to her.

'Do we have to write about the poetry collections on your list? I want to write about Thomas Elkin's book, *The Sun Kings*. It's about the First General's success in building trade partnerships, so it would fit the topic.'

I thought hard, trying to remember the book. I hadn't read it, but it had received good reviews when it came out. And so it should, as the author was a retired member of the government. I focused on the girl's face, mentally recording her as a possible party member. I'd be careful what ideas I discussed when she was in class.

'Um yes, I think I can make an exception. But you'll have to make sure that the second book is one from my list, okay?'

She nodded, pleased with her victory. 'Thanks.'

As she left the room I glanced towards the stairs, seeking out the major, but he had already gone.

I made my way home slowly, waiting until the other staff in my department had left so that I wouldn't have to talk to them on the way out of the building. I'd seen most of them in passing, but had avoided engaging in conversation. A couple had given me tentative smiles, but most had pretended to be busy whenever I walked by.

I'd used my free time to catch up on some of the marking I needed to do, so I didn't have a lot of work to take home with me. I couldn't have faced it even if I did.

I slipped my coat on and pulled on my favourite bobble hat, which Simon had given me as a gift one year on my birthday. I pulled the fabric low over my eyes, as though it would protect me from the stares of people on the street.

Outside it was cold; the beginnings of a frost made the pavement sparkle. I made my way carefully across the deserted campus to the bus stop, walking more quickly when I saw that a bus had pulled up, brake lights flaring.

The bus was quieter than the one I usually caught. I glanced at the other passengers from beneath the shelter of my hat, careful not to let them catch me looking. At the front of the bus sat a young man, dressed in uniform. Everyone else had kept their distance, as though he might be harmful somehow. He was running the brim of his hat through his fingers, round and round. As though he sensed my eyes on him, he looked back over his shoulder, straight at me. I looked away sharply.

When I dared to glance back at him, he was still staring at me. He smiled and my cheeks flamed. I turned away, hunching into my overcoat and staring resolutely out of the window for the rest of the journey, seeing nothing beyond my own reflection.

I jumped up when the bus arrived at my stop, hurried past the soldier at the front and down the steps onto the street. I walked quickly towards our apartment block as running foot-steps quickened behind me.

I stared straight ahead and walked faster. The footsteps came closer and the soldier from the bus appeared alongside me, slightly out of breath.

'Can I walk you home?' he asked, smiling.

I stopped, not wanting him to know which building I lived in. 'No thank you, I'm fine,' I said stiffly, looking around for someone who might help me.

I started walking again, intending to keep going past my flat. He followed me. 'Have we met before? I'm sure I know you from somewhere.'

I shook my head, not looking at him. 'No, I don't think so, sorry.'

He tried again. 'You do look awfully familiar.'

My heart was racing as I looked over my shoulder, stepping out into the road in the hope that he wouldn't follow. Apparently he didn't get the message as he stuck to my side, ignoring my attempt to shake him off.

As we approached my building, I walked even quicker, being careful to keep my gaze fixed straight ahead. I reached the end of the street and began to panic, unsure of which way to go now. How long would he keep following me? Some of the streets around our apartment were practically deserted; I didn't want to end up alone and cornered by an unknown man.

Abruptly, I turned left, remembering there was a pub some-where along this road. Perhaps I could duck in there and hide until he went away. I'd climb out of the damn bathroom win-dow if it meant losing him. But I didn't get that far.

I'd pulled ahead of him slightly and was praying that he would leave me alone. Instead, his hand reached for my arm, arresting my momentum. I came to a halt, forced to look at him, eyes wide beneath the brim of my knitted hat.

'What the hell are you doing?' I cried, shrugging his hand away. 'Get off me!'

His hand dropped away, his face suddenly serious. He leaned towards me and said in a low voice, 'Don't you live back there, Clara?'

I turned to ice. Before I could collect myself, he gave a cheery smile and jogged off in the other direction. I stood there, alone on the street, staring into the distance long after he had gone.

My hands were shaking as I struggled to get the key into the front door of my apartment. It scraped against the metal, jangling my nerves.

'Come on, come on,' I muttered to myself, checking over my shoulder.

The door opened and I fell inside, spinning round to slam it shut and twist the deadbolt in place. I collapsed against the door, breathing heavily.

It took a few minutes for my heart rate to slow and my eyes to adjust to the darkness inside the apartment. The bed, which I had left in disarray that morning, was now neatly made. One of Simon's work shirts, in need of stitching, was hanging from the cupboard door on a coat hanger when it had been over the back of a dining chair for at least three weeks.

I flipped on the light, flooding the room with a bright glare. Squinting, I ran to the kitchen and grabbed a knife from the block on the counter, holding it out in front of me shakily. I rushed to the bathroom, yanking the cord to turn on the light and checking that the room was empty. I shut the door and circled the main room, checking behind the counter, in the cupboard, under the bed, my blood rushing louder in my ears with each step.

There was no one else in the apartment. Realising that I'd been holding my breath throughout my search, I flopped on the bed, letting the air out in a rush. I shook my head at my stupidity. My mother must have come round during the day and tidied up in a bid to make amends after our disagreement. I ignored the fact that she had rarely ever cleaned in her life, even when she was married to my father. The major certainly never permitted her to pick up a dishcloth; they had a small army of household staff who took care of everything while she drank the day away.

Putting the knife on the bed, I sank back onto the covers, my head on Simon's pillow. Underneath, something crackled. I sat up, a sense of apprehension gnawing at the pit of my stomach.

On the pillow was a piece of paper folded in half. I stared at it, unable to understand how it could be there. I abandoned the pretence that my mother had been in the apartment. I reached out my hand painfully slowly for the sheet of paper, as though touching it might hurt me.

It was good-quality paper stock, thick and expensive. My name curled across the front in blue ink. It looked alien, like something that did not belong to me. Taking a deep breath I unfolded the paper. There were two lines of text printed there, nine words in total. I couldn't breathe.

We know where Simon is.
They are watching you.

I let the paper fall from my fingers and glide to the floor, like a dead leaf falling from a tree. The curtains were open, the outside world a gaping black void that could be concealing any number of prying eyes. I jumped up from the bed and ripped the curtains closed, the material quivering under the ferocity of my touch.

I didn't bother to undress. I lay on the bed, burying myself in the duvet, as though it might protect me. I lay down, but I did not sleep. Instead I lay awake all night, my eyes searching the darkness for monsters.

Twenty-seven

I was in my office when the major came to see me. I was staring blankly at my computer monitor as the radio played quietly, eyes heavy from days without sleep. My hair was shoved back into a messy bun, lank and unwashed. I hadn't bothered with make-up or clean clothes. I jumped at the slightest unexpected sound.

He came into the room without knocking. On the radio they were talking about a terrorist bomb that had exploded at a roadblock, killing three soldiers and the young mother whose car they were searching. I turned, expecting to see my boss, poised to deliver another lecture on the importance of maintaining a professional appearance.

'Clara,' the major said.

I silenced the radio, waved a hand at the mess around me. The spare chair that I reserved for my students to use during office hours was barely visible beneath a pile of textbooks and stray notepaper.

'I'd offer you a seat but… well.' I shrugged.

He looked around disdainfully. 'Do you always work like this, or is this chaos a symptom of your situation?'

I glowered at him. 'What do you know about my situation?'

He sighed. 'Clara, do you honestly think anything happens in this city that I'm not aware of? Especially to my own... family.' He hesitated over the word.

I forced myself not to break down in tears. 'What do you want?'

He leaned against the edge of my desk, crossing his arms. 'I know you think I don't care about you, that I've never treated you like a daughter, and I suppose that's true. When I married your mum, I found it difficult to know how to treat you. I had never had any experience of children and you'd been through a traumatic experience, with your father going missing.'

The major rarely ever addressed the issue of my father, preferring to consign him to the depths of our collective memory, a ghost flitting around the edges of our consciousness. But when he was forced to talk about him, about what had happened, this was the term he always used: 'went missing.' As though my dad decided to get up and walk out of the house one day, leaving his entire life behind.

I always wondered if it was a lesson they gave to the Authorisation Bureau during their training; never directly refer to the arrests of our citizens. If we don't mention it, the people won't even realise it's happening. They're too stupid, like cows, chewing on the cud we provide for them.

'And now this thing with Simon.' He sighed. 'I always hoped you'd find someone reliable who would care for you, Clara.' I scowled. Read: someone who would take you off my hands. 'But I guess he wasn't the one.'

I looked at him in disbelief, but if he noticed, he chose to ignore it.

'I know it's hard when someone you love leaves like that, out of the blue. But you have to be strong. You'll find someone else and all this will end up a distant memory.'

I couldn't take it any more, him looking down on me, lying like this. I stood up.

'Are you fucking kidding?'

He frowned. 'Clara, please.'

I held up a hand. 'No, you're in my office now, you can hear me out. I'm not some child who you can keep under the thumb any more. We both know exactly what happened to Simon. I stood there in the street and watched it happen.'

His eye twitched; he hadn't known I was there. He opened his mouth but I carried on. 'I'm not going to stand here and listen to you tell me that the solution is for me to get a new boyfriend. That's bullshit, and you know it.' I folded my arms. 'If you don't have anything else to say, I suggest you get out of my office.'

He stood up straight again, placing his hat carefully on the desk amongst my dirty coffee cups and half-marked essays. He looked contrite.

'I'm sorry, Clara.' He rubbed his forehead, where the hair was receding. 'It's been so long since... since I actually had a real conversation. My life is all about second guessing people and subterfuge, working out who will stab you in the back if they get the chance.'

He took a step forward and put his hands on my shoulders in an almost fatherly gesture. 'We don't live in a world that knows how to tell the truth any more. It's far too dangerous. But I know... the reality of things. It's what I do. And I know what happened to Simon. That he was arrested.'

I started to quiver, digging my nails into the palm of my hand in an effort to stop the impending tears. 'Oh Clara,' he sighed.

Then he did something that he had never done before. He pulled me towards him, wrapping his arms around me tightly. My body tensed at this unexpected affection. I couldn't bring myself to return the embrace, so I stood there stiffly and allowed him to hug me. I was too shocked to cry.

When he released me, he looked at my face earnestly. 'I can help you, if you want me to. I can find out why they took Simon, where he is. It might be possible for me to see him, give him a message from you. If you want?'

I wanted to clutch at this offer like it was the only real thing in a desert mirage. But eighteen years of distrust wouldn't be easy to abandon.

Still, I found myself nodding, my desire for knowledge of Simon overwhelming me. 'Yes, please; find out where he is.'

And I started crying weakly, my face twisted in pain, although there were few tears left to fall. Drained, I collapsed into my chair and buried my face in my hands.

The major patted me gently on the shoulder, retrieved his hat and strode from my office, closing the door softly behind him. I was so exhausted I wondered if that had really happened, or if it was a figment of my imagination.

After my encounter with the soldier, I was afraid to take the bus home from work. I walked a mile out of my way to the nearest underground station instead, figuring there would be more people around, should anyone try to approach me.

Descending the stairs into the station, I was jostled by the crowd. My chest felt tight; I remembered why I always hated taking the underground. It was always crammed full of people, surreptitious groups of pickpockets circulating through the mob. A popular urban legend recalled the tale of a woman who caught a thief sneaking her purse from her bag. Before she could cry out for help, he shoved her in front of a train. The police ruled it a suicide.

Stories like these had been whispered about for years; I'd

grown up with them and never believed that they were true. But whenever I entered the underground, the possibility of their truth would strike me.

I clutched my bag to my chest and made my way towards the front of the platform to wait for the train. When it arrived, I was carried forward by the swell of passengers all struggling to get on board. I was caught in the aisle, my back pressed painfully against the upright metal pole. I tried to shift position as the train pulled away.

At each stop more people crowded forward, trying to board the train. A flutter of panic settled in my chest as I was crushed more tightly into the mass of people. I could no longer see the doors and worried that I wouldn't manage to get off at my stop.

After almost half an hour struggling to breathe, the train arrived at the station nearest my flat. Following in the wake of three burly men in construction boots, I managed to elbow my way to the platform, narrowly escaping the doors as they slid shut with a hiss of air.

The platform here was much quieter, the rush hour almost past. I stood and caught my breath as the builders clomped towards the exit in their steel-toed boots. The train disappeared into the tunnel, pushing on towards its next destination. As it pulled away and the sound of rushing metal subsided, the air was full of hushed yet excited chatter.

Trailing after the builders in their dirty work clothes, I turned the corner into the foot tunnel that ran around the station and up onto the street outside. A crowd had gathered at the bottom of the stairs, all focused on something that I couldn't make out. They whispered to each other, looking around nervously.

As I got closer, the sea of people parted and I caught a glimpse of what was causing such consternation. On the wall, almost ten feet high, was a painting. It looked familiar and I searched my memory, trying to figure out where I had seen it before.

It was a replica of a photograph that I'd seen in one of Simon's books and, years before, it had been infamous across the world. It showed a young girl, on her knees, screaming into the camera, as behind her stood two soldiers with automatic rifles, poised to shoot. In the original photograph, the background of the shot was littered with debris: bodies broken and bleeding, men being dragged away, hope dying.

In this painting, the background had been stripped away, instead focusing on the girl and the two soldiers in that moment before her death. Above the image, in bold letters, it said:

FREEDOM WILL BE OURS

I couldn't help myself, I gasped, my hand flying to my mouth. But no one took any notice. They were too busy staring at the graffiti, powerful in its simplicity, the imagery subverting the common message that had always accompanied it: *we will destroy all who fight against us.*

In the bottom corner of the painting, like a signature, was a symbol I had seen before. It had begun to mark walls around the city, briefly, before the authorities had it removed. It was the symbol I remembered seeing a few weeks earlier, being painted out of existence by the station caretaker: a heart with the word Lumière scrolling across it. It was the symbol that always returned.

The murmuring of the crowd was silenced as two pairs of feet clad in army boots descended the stairs from the street. The soldiers stopped two steps from the bottom, eyeballing the people gathered there, who avoided their gaze.

They were young, with broad shoulders and bullish expressions. Like all the patrols, they carried guns. A young boy close to the front, holding his mother's hand, couldn't tear his eyes away. The first soldier noticed and smiled at him. Perhaps he meant to be kind, but there was something chilling about the way he looked at the child. The boy's mother picked him up and hurried up the steps away from them. They didn't bother to move aside and let her pass easily.

With the soldiers blocking the stairway, the crowd couldn't disperse. The first soldier, still smiling, took the final two steps and turned to see what had captured all the attention.

He saw the graffiti and stared at it for a long time, his jaw tightening. Slowly, he turned back to the crowd, nodding to his companion, who lifted his gun to point at them.

'You need to leave,' the soldier said loudly, gesturing to the stairs. Without raising their heads, the people began to filter past, beginning the slow climb to the surface.

As I waited for my turn, he took out his radio and pressed a button. It crackled: three short bursts of static. 'Level one graffiti in sector nine, over.'

A response erupted from the handset, but I couldn't make it out. 'Repeat, over.'

I reached the stairs and started up. As I walked past him, the second soldier looked me full in the eye. I fixed my gaze on my feet, not daring to look back at him.

Somewhere at the top of the stairs, where the first passengers were emerging onto the street, there was a commotion. A shout came ringing out of the darkness, echoing down the stairway and along the tunnel, causing everyone in it to stop moving and stare upwards.

'Freedom will be ours!'

As the shout fell away, the soldiers looked at each other

and the remaining passengers resumed their ascent, a new sensation burning in their chests. I was filled with anger; I knew it wasn't enough to worry about Simon, to wonder what had happened to him. I had to do something to get him back.

Twenty-eight

After that first portrait announced itself, brazen on the wall of the underground station, others began to appear. There was one painted on the corner shop, in an underground car park, on bus shelters, even on the pavement itself.

As quickly as the authorities could remove one, another would appear to replace it, somewhere even more prominent. There was a current in the air, whenever you took to the streets. It was like people were waking up from whatever dream they'd submitted to, years ago.

Wherever you went, people would catch your eye, boldly tilting their chins and daring you to judge them. If you nodded in greeting, they would smile. People began to find their voices; on public transport, conversations were carried out in regular tones, where before they had always been conducted in whispers. Confidence was growing.

But as the people became more daring, the attitude of the soldiers who patrolled the streets also changed. They were freer with their weapons, more intimidating. More on edge. They became pack animals, beating men with their rifle butts at the slightest excuse.

In classes, the students were more open with their questions. We touched on subjects that violated the curriculum.

But it was me who chose to take it further. I was home alone one night, going through my bookshelf, when my eye fell on the novels that I had saved from my father's collection. One of them was more worn than the others; I slid it carefully from its place on the shelf. *Nineteen Eighty-Four.* I remembered how Simon had referred to it during his class and something stirred in me. I opened the book and began flicking through it.

My eye landed on a particular page and I began to read.

The next day I arrived at the university early, so I could have the staff office to myself. My first class was a small postgraduate literature group. It was only the most dedicated students who pursued their education to this level, as a degree didn't guarantee a respectable job if your face, or your family name, didn't fit.

When I walked into the classroom, they were all seated, chatting amongst themselves. I shut the door firmly and marched to the front, dropping my bag onto the floor. In my arms, I carried a stack of photocopies.

The students turned to me expectantly. 'Today we're going to do something a little different.' I held out the papers. 'Who here has heard of a novel called *Nineteen Eighty-Four*, by George Orwell?'

A deathly hush fell over the room. The students looked at each other nervously. Our lessons were carefully structured to ensure they never strayed from the curriculum. Several raised their hands. After a pause, the rest did too.

'Have any of you read it?'

They looked shocked. 'It's banned,' one girl said confidentially, leaning towards me.

I slapped the pile of paper onto my desk and placed a hand on top of it. 'Literature is not something that should be banned. Why do we read? Why do we write? It's not simply for entertainment. We want to be able to understand something profound about ourselves, about the human condition. We want to connect emotionally with people and situations we will never be able to encounter in our own lives.

'Our stories are how we grow and understand our place in the world. They give us a voice. They are fundamental to our being. We shouldn't have to live without them.'

I lifted the photocopies and began to circle the group, placing a small pile, stapled in the corner, on each desk. There was a benign title on the cover, and then a blank page.

'In this document, you will find the first eight chapters of the novel *Nineteen Eighty-Four*. We're going to read them and discuss the concept, the themes, the message the author wanted to convey.'

I circled back to the front of the room and perched on the edge of my desk. 'You all know the status of this book; it's been mentioned here. If you don't want to participate in this, I fully understand. If that is the case, you may leave now. This won't count against your final grade. But I ask all of you not to discuss this outside of the classroom.'

I looked around the room, focusing on each of my students. 'Now, who would like to begin reading?'

They looked at each other, their expressions worried. I gave them a few moments to make a decision. I didn't take this lightly. No one got up to leave.

There was a cough, the scraping of chairs. One girl raised her hand. 'I'll start,' she offered tentatively.

She began to read, stumbling at first over the words, but quickly gaining fluency. After each chapter was complete, another student would take over. The power of each forbidden word reverberated around the room.

We came to the end of the eight chapters surprisingly quickly. As the last reader fell silent, everyone in the room exhaled. I watched them as they digested what they had read and heard.

'So.' I looked around. 'What did you think?'

They stared at me and then all began talking at once, their voices excited. I could barely make out a single comment, but I grinned, exhilarated by the passion flooding the room. At that moment, there was a lot of noise in the hallway. I checked my watch; it was time for the lesson to end.

'That's all the time we have for today, but listen guys, we will pick up this discussion on Thursday. Go home, think about what you've read here today and we'll come back and discuss it. Next class, I'll give you the next set of pages.'

They got to their feet, still talking animatedly.

'And remember,' I called out. 'Keep this quiet, okay?'

As the others left, one girl rushed to the front of the room. She smiled nervously. 'I just want to say, I think that was amazing. You're so brave.'

I shook my head. 'I'm a teacher. It's my job to introduce you to literature that means something, that will help you to think independently.'

'Well, I think you're doing something special.'

With a quick wave, she hurried after the other students, her eyes shining.

Despite his unexpected kindness, I never expected the major to search for Simon. It was an empty promise, like so many I'd received over the years.

After my students left, I was careful to collect every copy of the text I'd made, tucking them inside a folder where no one would see. I scanned the room, searching for anything that I might have missed.

When I was satisfied the room was clean, I turned to leave. The major was standing in the doorway, watching me. I jumped and almost dropped the folder. Half a dozen copies of *Nineteen Eighty-Four* fell out and slid across the floor. Cheeks burning, I dropped to my knees and hurried to shove them away before he noticed.

'I didn't mean to startle you.'

He came into the room, taking care to close the door behind him. The chatting voices of the students in the corridor faded.

'Do you have time to talk?' he asked. 'It's about Simon.'

I nodded, unable to speak, clutching my things to my chest. The major pulled out a chair and sat down. Uncertainly, I placed my books and the illicit folder on the desk and went to sit across from him.

He reached into his pocket and pulled out a piece of paper.

'This won't be easy to read, Clara,' he said, handing it to me.

I took it wordlessly. The sheet had been folded twice; I smoothed out the creases and began to read, the paper trembling almost imperceptibly. He waited until I'd finished before he spoke.

'I did what I could for him, but these are serious charges.'

I stared at the paper, trying to process the words, accusations against Simon. It was a copy of his arrest report. His name and ID number were printed at the top of the page in bold letters. I read them three times to be sure they didn't belong to someone else.

'No. This can't be right. Simon isn't a terrorist; this is ridiculous.'

But it was there in twelve-point type: conspiracy to commit acts of terrorism.

'What exactly are they accusing him of?' I asked, my voice close to breaking.

The major shifted in his seat. 'The full details are classified. All I can tell you is that Simon was involved in a number of serious incidents, including one where four people were killed.'

I stared at him. 'You can't expect me to believe that?'

He gestured to the paper that was still clutched in my hand. 'It's there in black and white, Clara. I know it's not the truth you were looking for, but that doesn't make it any less so.'

I got to my feet. 'This isn't the truth. I refuse to believe it. He's a teacher, for god's sake! He would never, ever hurt anyone. Not like this.' The piece of paper crumpled as my hand closed into a fist.

'I don't know what else I can tell you. I went through the proper channels to find this report; this is what we have on file.'

'Did you speak with him? Is he okay? What did he say?' My voice wavered at the thought of Simon, locked up in a cell somewhere.

The major shook his head. 'I'm sorry, he's been transferred out of the city, to one of the facilities where we keep prisoners suspected of terrorism. They're extremely high security; no visitors allowed. Not even me.'

'Can't you try? Surely you know someone who works there?'

He got up and walked around the desk to stand in front of me. He placed his hands on my shoulders. 'It wouldn't work, Clara. I am sorry, you must believe that.'

I nodded, dropping my eyes to the floor. He squeezed my shoulders, pulling me against him in an awkward half hug.

'You can keep the report,' he said. 'But if anyone asks, it didn't come from me.'

I shoved the paper into the pocket of my jeans as he straightened his jacket and headed for the door. 'Take care, Clara.'

I waited until he was gone before I slumped into a chair, my eyes glazed. I didn't want to believe any of this. The more I thought about it, the more I knew that Simon wouldn't be involved with people who weren't honourable. And if they were fighting against the government, then maybe they would help me to find Simon.

I took a chance on the only person I knew who might be involved in Simon's group. Elizabeth looked pale. I watched from a distance as she emerged from a late-afternoon seminar, waiting until she was alone.

'We need to talk.'

She looked around, surprised to see me there. But there was something else in her expression; something that might have been fear. After a brief pause, she nodded.

'Not here.'

She set off through the campus, with me walking silently at her side. We passed by the students' meeting hall and out onto the old playing fields, behind what used to be the gym, back in the days when team sports were still allowed.

When we were a safe distance away, Elizabeth dropped her bag onto the grass and plopped down beside it. She rummaged around, pulling a plastic-wrapped sandwich out. I sat down beside her.

'I want to know if you're involved in this... group... that Simon belonged to.'

She took a bite of the sandwich. I waited while she chewed carefully and swallowed.

'I might be.'

'I need to get a message to them. I need them to help me to find Simon.'

She took another bite of the sandwich, shaking her head.

'It's not as easy as that...'

I cut her off. 'I don't care. I need them to help me.' I got to my feet, brushing grass off my trousers. I looked her square in the eye. 'They owe me that.'

This time the message was waiting in my office. After class was over I retreated to my sanctuary, some paperwork to fill out, and photocopies to shred. It was a dull afternoon and I had to flick on the light as I went in.

Something crackled under my foot; there was a piece of notepaper on the floor, shoved under the door. I stooped to pick it up, tossing my bag down.

We should meet.

I crumpled the paper in my fist, squeezing my eyes closed. I could picture Simon, so earnest in his desire to help Jerome. I had been so dismissive, so afraid. With a frustrated noise I hurled the paper across the room, where it hit the window and fell behind my desk.

There was no decision to make; the note didn't say anything about when or where to meet. It just said that we should. And I didn't even know who 'we' was. For all I knew, some member of the Authorisation Bureau was bored and had made it his mission to toy with me. I remembered the soldier on the bus and a cold feeling settled in the pit of my stomach.

My reflection stared back at me from the blank monitor of the computer. I studied this blurred version of myself: the gaunt cheeks, eyes bruised from lack of sleep.

A flicker of movement made me spin round. I inhaled sharply. There was another sheet of paper, carefully folded, pushed under the office door. I got up, moving tentatively towards it, holding my breath. I pressed my hand against the door, listening, but could hear nothing in the corridor outside.

I yanked the door open, heart racing, but there was no one in sight. The note demanded my attention. Hurriedly I closed the door and locked it. The handwriting was the same as in the other notes I'd received.

Penny Crescent.
Wait outside the entrance to the gardens,
away from the street.
Tomorrow. 10pm.
Come alone.

Twenty-nine

I don't know how I managed to get through my classes that day; they passed by in a blur of anticipation and nervous energy.

A little before 10pm I found myself standing alone in an unfamiliar neighbourhood, a scarf positioned so it obscured the lower half of my face. It was a freezing cold night; whenever I exhaled my breath fogged the air. Crystals of frost were beginning to quicken on the pavement beneath my feet.

It took me longer than I had anticipated to find Penny Crescent. It was one of those grand old streets lined with Edwardian town houses, the kind with five floors and metal railings running parallel to the street. Once they would have been home to wealthy families with servants, owned by bankers and businessmen, whose genteel wives took afternoon tea and attended balls.

Now it showed little sign of life. These were the kind of houses appropriated by the military junta after they took power. They didn't believe individuals should own such valuable property. Instead they became offices, or barracks, or sites for all the unmentionable things that went on in a society undergoing such a dramatic change.

236

But they were expensive to maintain and many fell empty, left to disintegrate, as their original owners were shipped off to shared accommodation – or worse.

Even the street lights in Penny Crescent were barely functional. Two of the remaining lamp posts at one end of the street offered a dirty yellow glow; I shied away from them, preferring to stay in the shadows. As per my instructions, I skirted the houses and found an alleyway behind them that led to what might once have been a private garden for the surrounding residents. Who knew what secrets it guarded now?

I made my way along the alley in the dark, barely able to see where I was putting my feet. The passageway was cobbled and my feet slid over the frosty stones, catching on piles of rubbish and broken glass. I made slow progress, staying close to the wrought-iron fence, my hand tracing the bars for guidance. Eventually, about halfway along the alley, I found a gate, barely noticeable under the overgrown vegetation.

I waited, the blank windows at the rear of the houses staring down at me. My eyes scanned each pane of glass; I was certain for a moment that there was a face, but when I looked again it was gone. It could have been my imagination; I had no way to know.

My hands shook, but not from the cold. I touched the crumpled note in my coat pocket, telling me to come here. My hands clenched and the crush of paper filled my fist. Somewhere nearby there was the sound of breaking glass and a high-pitched, animal shriek.

I didn't know why I had chosen to come here, alone.

I was poised to turn around and leave when there was a rustling in the gardens behind me. I edged away from the gate, but it didn't feel safe to stand in the middle of the alley, even in the darkness. Quickly I scurried towards the nearest house, pressing myself against the wall, in the shadows. I trained my eyes on the gate.

The rustling grew louder and the plants swayed violently. I held my breath as a hand emerged, not daring to look away.

And then he appeared from the night, as though he had materialised from another plane of existence. The gate swung open with a rusty cry. He stood beneath its ornate archway, his face hidden under a hooded sweatshirt.

'I know you're there.' His voice was low.

I tried to melt into the brickwork of the house behind me, unsure if he had seen me.

'I know you got my message, Clara. It's pointless trying to hide. We can help you.'

Who knew how long he would stand there, waiting for me. Taking a deep breath, I took a step forward. He didn't move. I took another step.

'Who are you? How do you know my name?'

Instead of answering, the faceless figure said, 'Follow me,' and disappeared back into the gardens, leaving the gate open behind him.

I took one last look around the alley and plunged into the darkness after him. Unsure whether to close the gate, I left it open; I might need to make a quick escape. Hopefully no one would notice an old garden gate standing ajar in an abandoned alley and decide to investigate.

I couldn't see him ahead of me, but I could hear him moving through the undergrowth. I followed as quickly as I could, the wild plants clawing at my face. I pushed them away, feeling them snag my clothes as I passed by.

Then the trees gave way and I emerged into a clearing, which must have been the garden proper, years ago. I could make out little of anything in the darkness.

A voice at my ear spoke. 'We can talk here. No one knows about this place but us.'

I spun round with a gasp, pressing my hand to my chest. He had pulled down the hood and I caught the glint of his eyes, but still the rest of his face was hidden.

'Who are you?' I asked again. 'Why did you bring me here?'

He gave a low whistle and all around us there was the faint sound of movement as people began to appear from the bushes. A few of them carried old-fashioned storm lanterns that they held up to ward off the darkness. They closed in around me, until the light filled the circle.

He stood at the front, the rest of the group gathered around him. The lanterns illuminated his face and for the first time I could make out his features. He was handsome, in an edgy kind of way. The lines of his face were sharp and the metal glint of piercings gave him an air of otherworldliness. His hair was buzzed close to his skull and a jagged scar ran along one side of his face, curving under his jaw and down his neck.

'For too long, the people in this country have lived their lives in darkness; it's our mission to bring light back into the world.'

I frowned at the religious undertones in this statement. Organised religion had been driven underground years earlier; no one went to church any more. He must have sensed my confusion.

'This isn't about religion, Clara. It's about freedom. Freedom will be ours.'

The graffiti from the wall of the underground flashed across my memory. 'Are you the ones who have been painting that picture everywhere, of the woman and the soldiers?'

He nodded. 'We wanted to use that image to subvert the message that the government have always forced on us. We want them to know that they cannot control us, not forever.' He paused to light a cigarette. I watched as it flared at his lips.

He inhaled and let his hand drop to his side, looking me in the eye. 'Simon knew that.'

At the mention of his name, I gave a start. 'Simon? What does Simon have to do with this?'

The cigarette rose to his lips again. 'Much more than you know, Clara.' He gestured to the people surrounding him. 'Simon was one of us.'

The world around me shifted and my vision began to blur. 'I don't understand.'

'He was working for us. He had been for a while. When he decided to start teaching his students outside the government curriculum, he came to us first. He knew we could offer a certain amount of... protection.'

I shook my head vehemently. 'No, no that can't be true. Simon wasn't working with you, you're lying. Why would he do that and not tell me?' My voice began to rise.

He took a final drag on the cigarette and flicked it away. The orange flame was extinguished somewhere in the shadows. 'We were friends, Simon and I, years ago. We grew up together. We both studied History at Oxford, back when it was still a university. We were in the final year of our degree when the coup took place. The military were especially careful to enforce their rule in universities, where they feared large groups of young people might band together in order to rebel against them. All the students were forced to submit to a re-education programme. Those that refused were taken away and forcibly detained, until the military could be sure they weren't a threat.' He gazed off into the distance. 'It was three years before I got out and saw what the world had become, with them in charge.'

I stared at him. 'What about Simon? They didn't...'

He shook his head. 'No, Simon agreed to their programme. It was years before I saw him again and he was teaching by then. As a subject of forcible re-education, I couldn't hold any position of influence. When Simon heard I'd been released and found me again, I was living in a shelter, doing odd jobs wherever I could find them.

'Eventually I met some other *like-minded* people, and we began to talk about how we could fight back. And that's how Lumière came to be formed.'

The name aroused a stab of recognition. I remembered the symbol on our roof. Something clicked and I realised it was the same one I'd seen at the station. My cheeks were wet with tears. 'No, it can't be true. He would have told me.'

A girl stepped forward; I hadn't noticed her before. It was Elizabeth. 'It's true, Clara. When Jerome disappeared, he told me that he had friends who could help us find him.' She came closer and took my hand. 'He didn't tell you because he didn't want to put you in danger.'

'I guess it's too late for that now though.'

I began to cry in earnest. 'Is that why they took him? Because of you? Is it your fault they have Simon? I thought it was the classes, and I blamed myself. I never knew it went further than that.' I reached into my pocket and pulled out the crumpled arrest report. I waved it under his nose. 'This says they arrested him for terrorism. Is that what you are? *Terrorists?*'

'It's not our goal to terrorise; we want to free people, to wake them up from this world they've allowed themselves to sleep-walk into.'

'But you do use violence?' Anger swelled in my gut. He didn't need to answer; the look on his face was enough.

I pushed past Elizabeth and reached for him, scratching at his face. 'You're the reason they took him, it's your fault. I'm alone because of you!'

A dozen hands restrained me as he said, 'It's okay, Clara. It's okay.' He signalled them and they let go of my arms. I didn't try to fight any more. I was exhausted.

'Do you know where he is? My stepfather told me… my stepfather is… part of the regime. He told me Simon is in a facility for those suspected of terrorism. It's high security.'

His face grew serious. 'We know who your stepfather is, Clara. Major Jackson is an important man, with a lot of power. He was tipped for greatness, a rising star with some powerful friends, although he never progressed further up the ladder. He's one of the key figures in the Authorisation Bureau.' He looked at me earnestly. 'But you can't believe a word he says.'

'I never did…' I whispered. 'But I thought… I hoped he might be able to help.'

'He lied to you, Clara. No doubt he has his reasons. But you can trust us; we can help you.'

I wiped my eyes. 'So you know where he really is?'

'We think so. There's a place where they take all the ones who disappear, at first. Simon was asking too many questions about Jerome and we couldn't protect him. That's why they took him.'

He stepped forward and gave me a hug, pressing my face into his neck. 'I'm sorry,' he whispered in my ear. Elizabeth was still standing beside me; she reached out and put her hand on my back.

I pulled away and looked him in the eye, my tears drying. 'What's your name?'

The corners of his mouth twitched into a smile. 'My name is Caleb.'

I nodded. 'Okay Caleb. So, are you going to help me get Simon back?'

He studied me for a long time. 'There might be a way, but we'll need you to help us.' He raised his eyebrows.

I held out my hand. 'I'm willing if you are.'

He grasped my hand in his and the agreement was made.

It was after midnight when I arrived back at my apartment, the thrill of nerves still rushing through me as I climbed the stairs to my floor. I opened the stairwell door to find a man slumped on the floor outside my apartment. I paused in the doorway, about to turn and retreat downstairs.

'Clara!' He scrambled to his feet; it was my brother. He looked a lot thinner than the last time I had seen him, months earlier.

I stepped out of the stairwell, letting the door click shut behind me. I fumbled in my pocket for the keys as I approached him. He shifted from one foot to the other as he waited for me, tousling his hair with both hands.

I unlocked the front door to the apartment and Will followed me inside. Flicking on the light, I tossed my keys on the table and began unravelling my scarf.

I waited for him to speak but he carried on fidgeting, unable to meet my eye.

'So, what prompted this visit?' I asked my brother.

'Oh, er…' he fixed his gaze on the wall, as though he was examining a crack in the plaster intently. 'It's a while since I saw you. I was passing and decided to say hi.'

'Hi,' I said. He stared at me. I took off my coat and folded it over the back of the chair, resting my hands on top of it. 'What do you really want?'

His face darkened. 'Why do I have to *want* something? Can't I visit my sister? It's not a crime.'

I folded my arms and threw him a knowing look. 'No, but you never bother coming to see me. When was the last time?'

He shrugged and didn't answer. I bet he couldn't even remember.

'It's late, Will. I can make you a cup of tea or something and then I'm going to have to go to bed.' I went into the kitchen and put the kettle on without waiting for his reply.

He pulled out a chair and sat down. 'You're right, it is late. It's after midnight and you're only just coming home.'

I turned around slowly, hands gripping the edge of the kitchen counter behind me.

'Where have you been, Clara?' He didn't look so nervous any more. His eyes were bright and fixed on my face. He had a scar above his eye, the skin puckered and white. I forced myself not to look away.

'I haven't been sleeping well lately.' That, at least, was the truth. 'I thought I'd go out for a walk and get some air.'

He studied me carefully. There was a tremor in his hands as he laid them on the table in front of him. 'You shouldn't be walking about on your own so late at night; it isn't safe. What would Mum say if she knew?'

Behind me the kettle hissed, giving me an excuse to turn away. It wasn't against the rules to go out late at night, but it wasn't exactly encouraged. I took my time finding two cups and making the tea.

'Where were you really, Clara?' I jumped. Will had come up behind me so quietly I hadn't heard him. I faced him, holding the two mugs of tea between us like a barrier.

'I told you, I went for a walk.' I tilted my chin defiantly, daring him to challenge me further.

'I don't believe you.' He didn't take the drink. 'I know that Simon was arrested.'

I glared up at him. 'Who told you that?' He hadn't lived at home for several months now. He was enrolled at the military academy for his Authorisation Bureau training.

'That's not important.' He leaned closer, his pupils painfully dilated. 'I won't tell anyone what you've been up to. But you have to do something for me; I need some money.'

Bile rose in my throat. I pushed away from him, sloshing the scalding tea onto his arm. He cursed loudly. I slid the cups onto the kitchen unit and backed away from my brother. 'I don't know what you think it is I've been doing, but I'm not going to give you money.' I gestured at the tiny apartment. 'Do you think I've got anything to give?'

I marched to the front door and opened it. 'It's late, Will. I think you should leave.'

His lip curled, but he didn't say anything. 'Get out!' I said forcefully.

He complied, shoving past me to get to the door. He turned back to look at me, pointing his finger. 'I won't forget about this, you know.'

Thirty

The next time I saw Lumière, I was again summoned. I left my office late after classes; with Simon gone there was little incentive to go home to the empty apartment, so I would stay in my office after my colleagues had gone. Sometimes I even stayed later than the cleaning crew, a faceless group of people who were ignored by most of the staff.

I left the building via a side entrance; the only one that remained open past 7pm. As I came down the stone steps, I slid my shivering hands into woollen gloves, rubbing them together to generate a little bit of warmth.

Elizabeth was sitting on the wall opposite, swinging her legs as she waited. When she saw me emerge from the building she jumped up, stamping her feet.

'Can I talk to you?' she asked.

I looked around quickly, but there was nobody else in sight. 'Sure. What can I help you with, Elizabeth?' I smiled at her warmly as though she was any other student.

She inclined her head and we started to walk towards the street, winding through the tree-lined paths of the university campus.

When she spoke, she kept her voice low. 'You need to come with me. Caleb wants to speak to you, in person.'

I looked at her out of the corner of my eye. She was staring straight ahead. 'Now?'

She nodded. 'He'll meet you at the same place as before.'

As we approached the street, she slowed her pace. 'We probably shouldn't be seen going there together. Let's split up; I'll meet you there.'

'Okay.' I paused on the pavement as she thanked me like a good student and turned to leave. She didn't look back.

I walked slowly through the darkness of the city streets, down barely lit roads lined with broken street lights, where the only things that functioned were the security cameras that watched us going about our lives.

My bag was heavy; by the time I reached my destination I was exhausted. I made my way along the alley, dragging my feet over the uneven cobblestones. I found the gate, locked, and waited for Caleb to come and find me.

His voice, when it came, was behind me. I spun round but couldn't make out his figure in the darkness.

'Here!' his voice hissed again. There was a flutter of movement on the periphery of my vision. I turned my head until I could make him out, standing at the bottom of a flight of steps in front of some yawning basement doorway that belonged to one of the grand old houses.

I hurried towards him, down the stone steps, my feet slipping slightly on their damp surface. He stepped aside and ushered me into the house, locking the door behind us. My heart pounded as my eyes strained to see in the pitch-black corridor.

'This way,' he said, touching my hand as he passed.

I followed him into oblivion, concentrating on the wooden floor beneath my feet as it creaked with each step. We entered another room; I paused, sensing the change in space. Somewhere to one side there was a rustling and the strike of a match.

Soft light illuminated Caleb as he worked his way around the room, lighting candles and storm lanterns to chase away the dark. When he finished we were encircled by the flickering of many flames, each one alive somehow.

We stood there, neither speaking. I let my bag fall to the ground with a thud, my eyes drifting around the room. We were in what must once have been a study. Bookshelves lined the walls, climbing high to the ceiling. Most of the books were long gone; I could make out the thick haze of dust that had settled along the wood. I let my mind wander, picturing the room as it must have been years ago, full of heavy leather-bound volumes, perhaps with prints on the walls.

Caleb didn't interrupt my reverie, only stood and waited. Eventually I turned back to him. 'So, you wanted me to come here?'

He gave a nod. 'We know where Simon is, for definite.'

I stared at him, a strange sensation rising in my chest. 'How do you know?'

He examined my face. 'We have people, on the inside. They tell us things when they can, although it's incredibly dangerous for them.'

'Where is he?' I couldn't breathe.

Caleb tucked his hands into the pockets of his jeans. 'It's as we thought. The Authorisation Bureau have him at their headquarters.'

'No, no, that can't be right. My stepfather, he told me...' I trailed off, the long years of my life with the major stretching out in front of me. I could picture the conversations we'd had about his work. I always knew that he lied, but I didn't realise how naive I was in my understanding of the truth.

Caleb came closer and laid a hand on my shoulder. 'We

248

know all about your stepfather, Clara. Of course, it's natural that he wouldn't tell you the truth about his work. Especially because of your father.'

I pulled away from him. 'Why would he care about my father after so long? The major got everything he wanted – he knew my father was dead and would never trouble him again.'

Silence hung between us. His brow furrowed. 'Your father isn't dead, Clara.'

The ground beneath my feet was suddenly unstable. It came rushing up to meet me as my legs went weak. When I came to my senses, Caleb was crouching beside me, his face concerned.

My eyes flickered. 'Are you alright?' He touched my cheek.

I struggled to sit up, the room spinning. 'I'm sorry, I… I don't understand.'

He sighed. 'If I'd known, I wouldn't have told you like this, Clara. I thought your mother would have told you the truth about what happened.'

Nausea quickened in my throat. 'What does my mother have to do with this? Please, just tell me.'

He sat carefully beside me, folding his legs in front of him. I waited for him to speak.

'Your father was in prison for a long, long time. He had a difficult experience. They weren't… easy on him.'

Tears pricked my eyes as I remembered the kind man who would read me poetry before bed. I remembered how his hands always seemed so large as he held the book reverently.

'Go on.' My voice cracked; the words barely audible.

Caleb looked away. 'After so many years had gone by, it was decided that your father no longer served a purpose for the Authorisation Bureau. For whatever reason, they decided it wouldn't be appropriate to simply execute him. Instead, they decided to send him into exile.'

Blood thundered in my ears. 'I don't… exile?'

249

'Perhaps it was some act of kindness on the part of your stepfather. He couldn't kill the man who he had become so attached to, in a perverse way. So he sent him away.'

My hands shook. 'Are you saying that the major knew, all these years, where he was?'

Caleb looked at me sadly. 'Your stepfather is the one who handled his case. He oversaw the interrogations, decided on the punishments, carried out the investigations. It was only after they had held your father for over a decade that he was released. You must have been beginning your academic career at the time.'

I couldn't process his words. 'You mean, all that time when I was growing up, he was alive? Every day my stepfather went to work, he was seeing my father and he never breathed a word of it?'

'I'm not sure of the specifics, Clara. But yes, he knew. I think he kept your father alive to torment him, at first, as he built a relationship with your mother. But somehow, he was afraid of him. Afraid that he was still the one thing in your mother's heart; the one thing he wanted to break down until he could be sure of her feelings for him. In the end, it went on for so long that it didn't matter. When they released your father, he wasn't the same man you knew. And they didn't just let him go. As a condition of his release, he was transported to Ireland. From there, they took him to America. They still have contacts there who will watch people if they consider them a threat.'

My face was wet with tears. I struggled to hold on, to hear the rest of the story.

'That's where I met him. There are others like us around the world, who left Britain to escape the junta and haven't been able to return for fear of their own safety. But they make plans and they take action, quietly, in the hope that things will change and they can come back.

'When he heard that I was returning to the country, your father asked me to bring a message. To your mother. He wanted his family to know that he was still alive. That he was free.'

I couldn't take any more. Scrambling to my feet, I vomited in the corner of the room, my body heaving. When there was no more, I pressed my forehead against the cool wall, trying to steady myself as what was left of my world tumbled around me.

'Why wouldn't she tell me that he was alive?' I couldn't stop myself from wailing. 'Why?'

Caleb carried on. 'I came to your house, when I knew that your stepfather was away. I sat in the living room and spoke to your mother, told her that her husband was alive. That he still thought of her, and you, after everything. She thanked me and asked me to leave. That's the only time I ever saw her.'

A wave of anger swept through me. I clenched my fists and banged them hard against the wall, the shock reverberating through my skull.

Caleb grasped my shoulders and pulled me away. I let him draw me in against his chest. We stood for a long time, quietly, as I battled with my emotions.

'What about Simon? What are you going to do?'

He stared at me, his expression serious. 'We're going to get him back.'

When we emerged from the old study and made our way deeper into the house, we found Elizabeth. I looked at her in surprise; I had forgotten that she was coming here.

She sat at the kitchen table, with a lantern glowing beside her.

'I thought I'd leave you alone,' she said softly.

I flushed, conscious of how I must look, my face tear stained and puffy, my clothes marked with vomit.

Caleb bustled past me and rummaged in a cupboard under the sink. He pulled out two cans of Coke and handed one to me. I stared at it; I hadn't seen any for years, not since the factories closed and most of the manufacturing moved abroad. Noticing my amazement, he said, 'We get supplies from a few places. There are warehouses still full of stuff that you can't buy any more since they restricted imports. When was the last time you had a Twix?'

I popped open the can and took a sip. The drink fizzed across my tongue in a shock of sweetness. I gulped it down, savouring the way the sugar clung to my teeth. It reminded me of childhood.

We sat at the table beside Elizabeth. 'Tell me what happens next.'

They exchanged a glance. 'We need to find out more information first,' Caleb said. 'I've already left a message for one of our contacts; he's going to report back as soon as he can find out where Simon is being held.'

'But I thought you said he was at the Authorisation Bureau headquarters?'

Caleb gave a dark smile. 'Have you ever been there, Clara?'

I remembered the day I was sent away to school. I hadn't thought about it in a long time. 'Yes. My stepfather brought me there once, to scare me. I knew a secret he didn't want me to share.' Anger surged through me. 'Did you know they were responsible for the Whitehall bombing?'

His reaction was a disappointment. I'd expected shock, but there was only resignation. 'Sure. That's something we found out many years ago. It's an open secret in some circles.'

'So I was afraid for years and everyone knew anyway?' It

hurt to think about how much I'd lost because of the regime, because of my stepfather.

Caleb and Elizabeth exchanged a look. She continued to discuss the Authorisation Bureau's headquarters, her gaze somewhere to one side, allowing me to compose myself as she talked.

'It's got floor after floor built underground. That's where they keep the prisoners, the ones they think will be useful in some way.'

I shuddered. Caleb continued, 'There are tunnels there too. Some of them are ancient, over two hundred years old. There are modern ones, which provide secret ways in and out of the building, should it come under attack.'

I looked from Caleb to Elizabeth. 'And you're planning to use these tunnels to access the building?'

They nodded. 'We've been working for years to build a map of the tunnels, but it's proved incredibly difficult as there are no comprehensive plans. Most were created here and there and never officially recorded. We've had to go on hearsay and the reports of our undercover people. But we're getting close.'

Caleb leaned towards me. 'It won't be long now and we'll be able to go in and get Simon back. You can bring him home.'

Thirty-one

The news that my father was still alive overwhelmed me. For days I could think of nothing else; it haunted my dreams. I pictured him as he might look now, the man he could have become. I created elaborate fantasy lives in my mind, none of which felt real.

The truth was, my father, my real dad, was so far back in the depths of my memory that he had ceased to be a part of my real life. I thought about him every single day, had done for years, but somewhere along the line he had become nothing more than a construct that I crafted my carefully curated memories onto.

I couldn't admit it to myself, but I was afraid. I didn't know what he had endured, locked away with the Authorisation Bureau. But he had spent so long with them – with the major – that he had to have been through so much pain. And pain like that, it changes you. He wouldn't be the same restless dreamer with his love of poetry. He would be older, harder, the edges sharp around something fundamentally broken. He wouldn't be the man I knew.

After lying awake into the early hours for the fifth night in a row, I decided to confront my mother. I'd been distracted at work for days; it would be easy to claim sickness and take the day off.

It was a convoluted journey to my mother's house, using the chaotic public transport system. I didn't bother to wait for morning; instead I clambered out of bed, the icy night air biting at my ankles as I moved around the apartment getting dressed, the only light seeping into the room from the street lights outside.

The streets were empty, bathed in the silence of the early hours. I swaddled myself in my winter clothes, drifting unseen through the city.

By the time I reached my mother's house, a watery light had broken over the horizon. I waited in a narrow grove of oak trees at the end of their driveway, watching the uniformed neighbours as they emerged from their homes, climbed into their cars and left for the day. It was only when the major's car rolled away, with him in the back seat, immersed in paperwork, that I approached the house.

I rang the doorbell and waited, rubbing my hands together. My breath emerged in bursts of mist. Eventually the door opened behind me and I turned, expecting to see the housekeeper, a sour-faced woman who had replaced Mary after she retired to live with her sister on the south coast. My mother stood in the doorway, in her expensive silk dressing gown and slippers; her eyebrows rose when she saw me.

'Clara! What are you doing here?'

I ignored the question, craning my neck to see past her into the house. 'What, no housekeeper? It's not like you to answer the door yourself.'

I took a step forward and she opened the door enough to let me into the house. I peeled off my boots and heavy coat in the hallway while she waited. In a small act of rebellion, I left the boots in the middle of the floor, one shoe toppled over, scattering grains of dirt across the expensive hardwood boards.

Tossing my coat over the newel post on the banister, I strode along the hall and into the living room, my mother behind me. I didn't sit down. Instead I turned to fix her with my gaze, arms folded across my chest. She settled on the edge of the sofa, hands folded primly on her knees, eyes darting around the room.

'So,' I said. 'My father's alive then.'

Her mouth opened then closed, lips pressed together in a tight line.

'Aren't you going to say anything?'

She reached up a delicately manicured hand to smooth her hair. 'I don't know what you're talking about, Clara. And I think it's cruel of you to come here and blurt something like that out when you know that your father has been dead for years.' She sniffed.

I snorted. 'Oh, okay. So you're telling me someone didn't come to this house, what, two, three years ago, and tell you that they'd met Dad in America?' She stared straight ahead, chin aloft, refusing to meet my eye. 'Are you that fucking evil that you pretend it didn't happen? That your own husband isn't still alive?'

I jabbed my finger at her. 'Because he is still your husband, you know. All this,' I waved a hand at the expensive furnishings and glossy wallpaper that decorated the room, 'It's all bollocks. It's not yours, it's *his*. And you're not even married to him.'

She looked at me coldly. 'You want the truth? Fine.'

She stood up, head still held high, and left the room. Suddenly deflated, I didn't know what to do. I went to the window and gazed out across the gardens, still thick with early morning haze.

Several minutes passed before my mother returned, a piece of yellowed paper clutched in her hand. She held it out to me.

'Darius arranged this before we were married.'

Her hand trembled slightly as I took the sheet of paper. I stared at it for a long time, unable to decipher what I was seeing. It was a certificate of annulment.

My father's name was there in bold type, his stunted signature – so familiar even after all this time – struck me a vicious blow to the heart. My mother's name sat beside it, her longhand letters curling across the page.

My hand dropped to my side, the paper fluttering to the ground, face down. 'He knew you were getting married to someone else?'

She nodded, her eyes glistening with tears. 'Darius told him. He forced your father to sign the paperwork so that he could marry me.'

My voice cracked. 'How could you do that to him? Don't tell me you didn't know; your signature is on that certificate. The marriage wouldn't have been legal without it.'

She sat on the sofa with a sigh, curling her legs underneath her body. She wasn't the polished woman I had always known: even in the dim early morning light there were lines deepening around her eyes, the soft sag of the skin at her throat, the stray hairs left untouched around the arch of her brow. For the first time I saw her as a woman, not just my mother.

'I knew. Darius came to me a few days before the wedding with some documents. He had me sign before he went to your father. He knew that would hurt him more, to have the wedding confirmed on paper, in my own writing. It would be a betrayal. In the end, he went one better. He took me to the prison so I could tell your father I wanted to end our marriage.'

'You *saw* him. You saw Dad, and you didn't tell me?' My

voice was pained. 'You didn't have to marry the major you know. Maybe if you hadn't, Dad would be here with us now.'

She fixed me with a fierce stare. 'But I did, Clara. Don't you see that? Without your stepfather, where would we be now? Do you think that you would have gone to such a good school and become an academic?' She shook her head. 'They wouldn't have touched you. Not after what happened to your father. I did it for you.'

I started to weep. 'Don't tell me you betrayed my dad for me, for a man I've always hated. You did everything for yourself. Why else would you let me think he was dead for all these years? You didn't want to stir up the past, disrupt your comfortable little life here.'

Her voice rose. 'Comfortable? You call my life comfortable? Well yes, if all you care about are possessions, then I suppose it is. No Clara, this place is a prison.'

'A prison? You're comparing your life to my dad's again, as though you've had it harder.' I sneered. 'You disgust me.'

I stormed past her into the hall and began struggling with my boots, trying to force my feet inside. The laces were still too tight and they wouldn't go. She ran out and caught my arm as I was yanking my coat on, the front door half open, cold air flooding in.

'Please, Clara! Don't leave – we can talk about this!'

I shoved her away. 'I don't want to talk to you ever again. You're not my mother.'

She let go and I burst outside into the frigid air, my lungs burning with cold as I gasped through my tears. I broke into a sprint, trying to get away from the house as fast as I could, my feet leaving hasty prints on the frost-covered driveway.

When I reached the street, I couldn't breathe. I stopped for a moment. She was standing in the doorway, watching me. I turned my back on her and walked away, jagged breaths rattling in my ears.

I didn't go home. A fire possessed me and I needed to do something; I couldn't cope with another night staring at the walls of my empty apartment, imagining Simon's voice echoing through them.

I found myself returning to the abandoned houses on Penny Crescent, to the house where Caleb had told me about my father. I crept down the basement steps and tried the back door, heart pounding. The handle was icy against my skin.

The door swung open with a creak. The room beyond it was a black mouth; my senses were screaming, but I placed one foot over the threshold and then the other, feeling my way into the darkness with one hand pressed against the wall.

'Hello,' I called, as loudly as I dared. 'Is someone here? Caleb?'

My voice disappeared into the void. I could hear my own breathing, too loud, as though someone was standing right behind me. I tried to hold the air in my lungs, until black specks flickered at the corner of my eyes. There was no answer.

I crept further into the old house, aware of every scrape of my shoes on the tiled floor. 'Hello,' I called again.

Somewhere above me, a floorboard squeaked. I froze, ears straining through the darkness, heart racing. Another squeak, slightly to the left of the first one. I thought about calling out once more, but my voice stuck in my throat.

'You shouldn't have come here.'

The voice came from an empty doorway. I shrieked and leapt forward, ricocheting off the wall with a crack. Hands grasped my arms as I stumbled, trying to recover. I fought them but they pulled me out of the hallway. Behind me slow feet climbed the wooden stairs.

The hands released me and I staggered back, trying to reach the door, but the other person was already behind me, coming into the room. There was the flare of a match and the outline of a man hunched over the fireplace, lighting a storm lantern. He turned as a soft light filled the room. I vaguely recognised him as part of the group in the park that first night.

Behind me, Caleb said, 'Clara, we weren't expecting you so soon.'

He came into the room. 'I don't think you met Zeke the last time you were here?' He gestured to the man on the other side of the room, whose hands had grabbed me so furiously. I rubbed my arms.

'No. We haven't met.'

'Zeke is one of my lieutenants. We were working on our plans to infiltrate the Authorisation Bureau headquarters when we heard someone come in.'

I nodded. 'Good. That's what I came to talk to you about.'

Zeke glowered at me. He was tall, with dark skin and a shaved head. I watched as the soft light reflected on the planes of his skull, giving him a ghastly air. When he spoke, I noticed a slight accent that I couldn't place.

'She doesn't belong here. There will be trouble, Caleb, you'll see.'

Caleb laughed. 'Of course she belongs here. Clara has lost as much as any of us have; we need her.'

Zeke scowled, the muscles of his upper arms bulging as he folded them across his chest. My eyes shifted from one to the other. Neither looked away.

I spoke softly. 'I went to see my mother. To confront her, about my father still being alive.'

They both turned to look at me. I could sense their interest.

'She told me that the major had my parents' marriage annulled. He had my mother sign the papers first, before he took them to my father. He wanted him to see, that she had already left him.' I blinked quickly, looking at the floor. 'She said it was for me.'

'Clara...' Caleb took a step towards me, holding out his hands as though to offer some kind of comfort.

I raised my own hand, palm outwards. 'No. That's why I'm here.' I looked Zeke in the eye, taking in the impassive details of his face, the way his eyes looked hollow in the light. 'If she destroyed my father because of me, then I want to do something to make amends. It's too late for me to help him, but maybe I can help Simon, or the others who are trapped in that place. There *are* others?'

Zeke raised an eyebrow. 'There are always others. It never stops.'

I nodded slowly, thinking about all the people who had disappeared from the fringes of my life over the years: a teacher, a friend's brother, a boy from my university study group. 'You need to tell me the plan. I can't stand this waiting. It feels, all the time, like something bad is about to happen. I walk down the street and it feels like there are eyes everywhere.'

They exchanged a glance. Zeke gave a curt nod and I knew they would tell me their secrets. Caleb beckoned me to follow him. 'Come upstairs. We have the plans there.' I shadowed him as he left the room, with Zeke close behind.

'You must understand,' Caleb said as we climbed upwards, 'that this incursion, rescuing Simon, it's part of something bigger.'

'Bigger how?' I asked.

He laughed. 'We're going to bring them down. The government. We're going to stop this.'

I stopped abruptly. 'You're going to *overthrow the government.*

And how do you propose to do that? It's not as though you have an army at your disposal.'

He turned back to smile at me. 'Oh there are more of us than you realise. Lumière is made up of groups all across the country. There were a dozen of us originally, until we split off and travelled to different corners of the country, recruiting others and quietly spreading our message. There's Leanna, with her pack of young fighters who live out in the wilds of Exmoor, periodically attacking the prison camp there. And Fraser on the Scottish borders. He never got over what happened to his fiancée, Marianne, who disappeared when they were young.'

I stared at him, trying to wrap my head around the scale of this operation. I wasn't entirely sure I believed him. He seemed to see it in my eyes.

'Come on.'

They took me to one of the rooms on the first floor, which must have been the master bedroom, once. The windows were lined with heavy blackout curtains, so the room could be fully lit. A grand fireplace dominated one side of the room, but there was no fire in the grate. I wondered if the chimney was blocked after years of disuse, or if they were afraid that the smoke might bring them to the wrong people's attention. In the centre of the room was a huge table, covered in rolls of paper and photographs.

Caleb stood back so I could examine the contents of those papers for myself. He watched from the doorway as I ran my hands over the plans, which showed layer upon layer of prison cells, driving down into the earth. The scale of the building made my head spin.

But the photographs were worse. I don't know who had taken them, why, or how old they were, but my heart froze. Men and women – some barely old enough to be acknowledged adult – were shackled on mattresses weighed down with filth, their eyes staring blankly at the camera. They were bloody and emaciated, their clothes torn or covered in bodily fluids. Some of the pictures depicted scenes of torture. There were women being raped by gangs of men, wearing balaclavas to shield their identities from the camera. There were people strapped to tables or hanging from chains; masked doctors with syringes and scalpels, poised to inflict damage even as they saluted the camera; there were even executions. A boy with a spade crying as he dug his own grave. As I handled the photos I came across a series that captured a mass execution. A dozen people knelt before the trench that would become their final place of rest, a trench that they had no doubt been forced to dig, before they were forced to their knees in the dirt. I flicked through the images as the soldiers lined up, automatic rifles in hand. They towered over the prisoners, who slumped, awaiting that final moment. There were pictures of the soldier who had given the order, his arm raised; of the bullets slicing through the air; of the people as they fell, heaped together on the ground. The final picture showed a seemingly empty field, its wretched secret buried beneath the soil.

'Why are you showing these to me?' My voice shook, but I didn't mean it as a reproach. I needed to know. All those years of imagining had left their own scar. The reality couldn't be worse than the scenarios I had spent my whole life visualising.

It was hard-faced Zeke who stepped forward from the shadows to answer me. 'We need to know what we might find when we get there. It won't do any good for us to collapse in horror at the state of the people there. We need to try and get them out. Then we need to make sure the world knows what the Authorisation Bureau did, so that they can pay.'

I nodded. I understood. 'Is this what they do... to everyone?' I thought of my father and of Simon. He'd been gone so long already. My mind couldn't handle the implications and I squeezed my eyes closed, trying to force away the images as they threatened to emerge.

Zeke's voice was much softer when he answered. 'The things they do... depend... it's different for each person. It depends on what their *crimes* are...' He almost spat out the word, heavy with sarcasm. '... and who they were before, who they know. What secrets they might be able to reveal.'

I could tell then, that he had lost somebody too. It was etched in every line on his face. But I couldn't bear to ask, so instead I said, 'Does anyone ever get out?'

He gave me a smile so twisted that I feared this question was worse. 'Some do. The lucky ones.' He started to laugh. It chilled me so profoundly that I couldn't move or speak or do anything beyond stare at his face, examining it for some kind of madness.

My father had been trapped in that place for over a decade. There was a kind of madness in that too. I recognised it in myself.

Caleb walked to the table and swept the photographs into a tidy stack, placed them into a folder and closed it. Even though we could no longer see the images, our eyes followed the folder as he carried it away and onto a shelf in the far corner of the room.

'We should concentrate on the plans,' Caleb told us firmly.

We all sat around the table as he spread out the copies for us to see. He pointed to a network of dotted lines that circled the main building. 'These are the hidden tunnels. The ones that are marked anyway.'

I focused my attention on these tiny pathways, such an insignificant detail; an afterthought for the planners. Yet my entire life might depend on them. Clarity descended on me as I examined the outline of the building, trying to commit every corner to memory.

The secret tunnels were intricate; they zigzagged across my retinas, the hope of freedom. I screwed my eyelids shut, trying to sear them into my brain.

When I opened my eyes again, they were watching me. I took a deep breath.

'I need you to tell me the plan.'

'We will,' Zeke said. 'But we need you to do something for us first.'

I left the house via the back door, emerging again into the alley. I rattled the handle to make sure the door had closed behind me and turned to climb the steps.

Before I could move, there was a rustling noise and a figure emerged from the darkness.

'What are you doing down there? Those houses are empty.'

I flinched as a bright light shone into my face, exposing me. I raised my arm to shield my eyes, but there was nowhere for me to go.

He repeated the question, louder this time. 'Well, what do you think you're doing?' The light came closer. 'I ought to turn you in – you were robbing that house.'

'No! I...'

A hand grabbed my arm. 'No please, let me go. You don't understand.' He pulled me up the steps and into the alleyway. The soft click of the door unlocking was barely audible.

I was trying to wrest my arm free when Caleb emerged from the shadows.

'Let her go!'

'What the hell...' the man began, trying to swing his torch around so that it illuminated Caleb. He didn't get the chance.

There was a sudden movement and a popping sound. Something sprayed across the side of my face. The grip on my arm loosened as the man fell to the floor.

'Caleb,' I cried, my voice verging on hysteria, 'what did you do?'

He tried to hush me, taking hold of my arms and shaking me gently. 'I had to. He saw you coming out of the house. He was going to turn you in to the authorities. We couldn't let that happen. He's probably a spy; he must have followed you here.'

'You killed him. You *killed* him.'

'Clara, calm down. The man was a spy. I stopped him from taking you away. But you have to help me; we have to hide him.'

I began to shake my head. 'No, no. I can't.'

Caleb tried to reason with me, his voice low and urgent.

'What the hell is going on out here?' Zeke materialised out of the night.

I suppressed a shriek. 'Caleb shot someone.' I began to panic. 'Oh God, I've got blood all over my face. That was his blood wasn't it?'

I flapped at my face, trying to rub away the wetness that felt as though it was burning into my skin.

'Probably some brain too,' Zeke said. I gave a small wail.

'Shut the fuck up,' Caleb ordered. 'This guy obviously followed Clara here. That means *they know where we are.* We've got to get rid of the body and get out of here. It isn't safe.'

Before Zeke could respond, there was movement in the bushes beside us. Caleb sprang into a crouch, his gun aimed. Something slithered through the fence and brushed against my legs, heading towards the dead body. There was a snuffling sound and a low whine.

'It's just a dog.'

A cold sensation flooded my body. 'A dog? Where did it come from?' Full of foreboding, I crouched and felt around on the ground until I found the torch, which had been extinguished when it fell. I switched it on.

'Clara!' Zeke hissed, 'Turn that off!'

I swung it around so the beam of light broke across his face. 'No. I need to check something.'

I turned back to the body. It was a middle-aged man, wearing narrow-rimmed glasses. His eyes looked unusually wide behind the lenses, as they stared up at the stars. Half his head was missing.

I fought the urge to vomit. The dog was lying on the floor beside him, its face pressed into its paws. It lifted its head when I shone the torch in that direction, the light catching on a name tag dangling around its neck.

Taking a deep breath, I leaned forward and began methodically going through the man's pockets. Slowly, I pulled my hand out and turned so that the others could see what I was holding.

'Shit,' Zeke said. Caleb kept quiet.

'He was walking his dog.' I waved the lead at them. 'His fucking dog! And you shot him. He was an ordinary guy; he's probably got a family somewhere waiting for him to come home.'

Caleb's face was expressionless under the light of the torch. The shadows gave him a sinister aspect. He looked me in the eye.

'It doesn't matter. He saw you coming out of this house. He would have told someone and that would have been it for us.'

'But you didn't have to kill him!'

Caleb shook his head. 'The only thing that matters is the mission. He isn't important.'

I couldn't believe what I was hearing. For a minute, no one spoke. My head was spinning. The dog pressed its warm body against my legs.

'We have to move the body.'

I stared at Caleb in disgust. 'Clean up your own mess.' I flung the dog lead at him and walked away, rubbing hard at the side of my face until my skin felt raw, trying to ignore the animal as it followed in my wake.

Thirty-two

I would have stayed away from my mother, if it were up to me. I would have ignored the messages that waited for me when I returned home from work each day, imploring me to talk to her. I had nothing left to say.

I couldn't forget what had happened in the alley. The look on Caleb's face when he told me the man he killed didn't matter. I never wanted to see him again.

But I knew that would mean giving up on Simon. There was no one else who could help. And Caleb wanted me to visit my mother.

I put my feelings aside and grudgingly accepted an invitation to have a family dinner with her and the major. I tried to think of myself as a soldier, doing my duty by following orders, no matter how distasteful.

I arrived late, anxious in my best dress and low-heeled shoes. It seemed right to make the effort, to consign my jeans and ratty sweatshirt to the back of the drawer for one night. I even brought a bottle of wine, a heady red recommended by the man in the village shop. When he rang it up I winced at the price. But he had the grace to smile as I counted out the coppers from the bottom of my purse and handed them over to make sure I had enough.

When I arrived at the house, it was Will who answered the door. He was sullen in tracksuit bottoms and an old t-shirt with some forgotten comic-book hero on the front. He looked so much younger without his uniform. I gave him an awkward hug and felt his hands press lightly against my back.

'I didn't know you were going to be here. How's the academy?'

He shrugged and rubbed his nose. 'Yeah, fine. I'm just taking a few days off.' He avoided my eyes so I didn't question him further.

My mother was waiting for me in the lounge, sipping a cocktail. She stood by the fireplace, glass in one hand, the other fiddling with the rope of pearls around her neck. When I came in she started forward as though to embrace me, then stopped, suddenly self-conscious. She tossed back what was left of her drink and waggled the glass towards me.

'Martini, darling?'

I nodded, 'Okay.' Remembering myself, I held out the bottle of wine. 'Or red, if you prefer? I brought you this.'

She took it from me carefully and scrutinised the label. 'Lovely. We'll have this with dinner, shall we?'

I didn't reply and she turned to the sideboard, where an array of liquor bottles and crystal decanters were on display. I watched as she mixed two martinis, the tremor in her hand almost imperceptible. Over her shoulder she called, 'Will, darling, do you want one of these?'

My brother was lurking in the doorway; I'd forgotten he was there.

'Yeah, okay.'

She brought us each a drink and we sipped them slowly. The martinis were strong; the alcohol burned its way along my throat and my eyes watered. Will tried not to grimace. She collected her glass and took a gulp. None of us sat down.

We were hovering around each other uncertainly when the major came into the room. 'Clara! I didn't hear the doorbell.'

He turned to my mother, with a nod at her martini glass. 'Make me one of those would you, Lucia.' She hurried to the bar as the major eased himself into his expensive leather armchair, crossing his legs.

'Sit, sit!' He waved us in the direction of the matching sofas.

'So Clara, how's life at the university? What are you teaching at the moment?'

I gave him a brief rundown of what I'd been doing recently, which books and writers were currently on the syllabus. He nodded along, interested in what I had to say, although he must already have known the answers.

'Do you have any plans for the holidays?' he asked.

My mother appeared at his shoulder, clutching the martini. 'You could come to us for a few days; we'd love to have you.'

Her face was so full of hope, her eyes so desperate, that I had to look away. I focused on the major as he took the cocktail from her.

'Oh, I haven't thought about it. I'll have plenty of work to do over the holidays, marking and such. But I'm sure I'll have time to do something before the new semester starts.'

'Well make sure you fit us in, your mother always enjoys your visits.' He took a sip of his drink. Before I could promise anything, the housekeeper came in to announce that dinner was waiting.

After the meal, the family retired to the lounge. My mother was animated once more, flush with red wine and morsels of food. She hung from Will's arm as they wound along the hallway, regaling him with some story, her heels echoing on the parquet flooring.

I hung back, waiting for the major, who was giving the housekeeper a series of orders in hushed tones. I couldn't make out what they were discussing, but it seemed to be something to do with the food.

When he saw me lingering in the hall, he raised his eyebrows.

'Can I talk to you?' I asked. 'In private.'

He scrutinised my face. 'I was going to have a brandy in my office. I've no interest in hearing about the latest goings on at the country club.' He turned and began to walk towards his study.

I was about to follow my mother and Will into the lounge, heart sinking, when he glanced back.

'Aren't you coming?'

His office was tucked away at the back of the house, away from the family rooms. The walls were lined with photographs of important officials, some from the government, others notable in different ways. In most of them the major was shaking hands, or receiving a pat on the back. A few even depicted him in receipt of a medal, on stage at some awards dinner.

I closed the door as the major sat behind his desk.

'I wanted to talk to you about Simon.'

I was sure to keep my voice soft. The servants were all carefully vetted, but you never really knew. And working in a house like this, they'd have certain political leanings.

The major bent to open his desk drawer, pulling out two glasses and a bottle of liquor. 'You'll have a brandy, won't you?'

I nodded, my mouth dry. He poured two generous measures and passed one to me. I took a gulp, then another. It didn't burn as badly as the martini.

'I know you told me... that Simon had been transferred to a

prison in another part of the country. But...' My voice cracked and I had to take another swig of brandy.

'But...' he said ominously.

I shoved my hand into my pocket and pulled out a crumpled piece of paper. I thrust it towards him.

'This says otherwise and I... I needed to know if it was true.'

I didn't have to fake the tears that welled in my eyes.

The major took the paper and studied it, frowning. It was a note. A note that Caleb had given me, scrawled in a heavy hand, which told me where Simon was being kept. Where he really was.

'Where did you get this?' the major demanded.

'I found it, shoved in my pigeonhole at work. Is it true?'

He glared at the piece of paper. 'I showed you the arrest report I pulled for Simon.' He screwed up the note and forced it into his trouser pocket.

I allowed my voice to waver. 'I... I... I don't want to... but we both know that things aren't always... the truth. How do you know that's where he is?'

The major looked furious, his brow drawn heavily over his eyes, which seemed almost black in the dim light. He got up from his desk and stomped to the window, where he stared out into the night as he drained his brandy glass. 'I don't like this, Clara. I never thought he was good enough for you. And now...'

I crossed the room and laid a hand gently on his arm.

'Please. I know it isn't you, but I... I need to know where he is, if he's close by. I can't take this.' I began to cry.

When he turned his head to look at me, the major's expression was softer. He sighed heavily. 'What I told you was true, Clara. I don't know where he is. But I suppose, what it says in that note, it could be true. We do have buildings in the city where we keep prisoners sometimes, especially those who are considered high value.'

He must have remembered taking me to that building, all those years earlier. But he wasn't going to acknowledge it. I played along with the pretence.

'But why would he be there? What could he possibly know?'

The major kept quiet.

I looked up at him, eyes glistening. 'Do you think – if I went there – they would let me see him?'

'No. Don't do that,' he said abruptly. He forced a laugh, as though trying to lift the mood. 'Here, let me get you another brandy.' I handed over my glass.

As he poured two even larger measures of liquor, he said, 'I'm sorry, I didn't mean to sound harsh. But you can't just turn up at a place like that, you'd be at risk. These facilities are heavily guarded and they're not the kind of places that accept visitors. They'd shoot you as soon as look at you. Do you understand?'

I accepted the brandy. 'But there must be a way? Someone I could speak to?'

'No. These places aren't for families. You're not even supposed to know about them.' He lowered his voice. 'You mustn't discuss this with anyone. It's an offence to share information about government facilities. I shouldn't even be discussing this with you.'

'I won't say anything.'

He squeezed my shoulder. 'Good girl, I know you wouldn't want to get me in trouble.'

I sipped the brandy, savouring its bite across my tongue. 'Do they ever transport the prisoners? Perhaps if we knew Simon was going to be moved, I could wait somewhere, I could *see* him…'

He cut me off. 'Absolutely not. Prisoner transports are rare and they're carefully managed to avoid drawing attention. Not to mention the level of security. No I'm sorry, there's no possible way you could get to Simon.'

He put his glass down and took me by the shoulders, looking me square in the eyes. 'If I were you, I'd give up on him. It's admirable that you care so deeply, but don't ruin your life for him. Consign him to the past and move on. I'm sure your mother and I know of any number of young men who'd be suitable for you, if that's what you want.'

I gave him a weak smile. 'That's kind of you, but no, I don't think so. Not yet anyway.'

He gave me a hug. I clutched the brandy glass awkwardly between us.

'I should probably leave you to your work. Mama will be wondering where I've got to.'

He smirked. 'Yes, go and save your brother, or he'll be in a mood for days.'

'Goodnight. And thank you.'

As I left the room, he was settling into his chair, pulling a cigar from the pocket of his jacket. I had what I needed.

Thirty-three

I stood at the bus stop in the rain, not caring that it soaked my hair, plastering it against my scalp. It was mid-afternoon and growing dark, but it had barely been light all day, the city shrouded in mist. Two girls in school uniform stood beside me, huddled under an umbrella, giggling quietly to themselves as they talked about a boy. Half a dozen others waited for the bus, all absorbed in their thoughts, shoulders stiff against the cold.

A group of soldiers were walking along the street in our direction. They passed a parked car where three men were smoking, talking amongst themselves, hats pulled low and scarves tight around their necks. The bus came around the corner in the opposite direction. One of the teenagers held out her hand to signal it.

As the bus pulled to a stop, the passengers began shuffling into a queue, the two girls at the front. There was a shout.

'Hey! Hold the bus!'

One of the soldiers ran towards us, waving his hand in the air. He was holding a gun. Shoving past the waiting passengers, he jumped onto the bus and barked at the driver, 'We're requisitioning this bus on Authorisation Bureau business.' He started to laugh.

The other soldiers followed more slowly. One of them carried a bottle of whisky. He turned to us and yelled, 'Who wants to come for a ride?'

I felt uneasy. The passengers glanced at each other, but nobody spoke. Nobody moved. Along the street, the three men stepped away from their car, flicking their cigarettes into the gutter.

The soldiers were off duty, but still dressed in their uniforms. None of them carried radios and only the first had his gun. Two of them jumped onto the bus and went to sit down. I could see them through the window, sprawled out across the seats, feet up, necking from the bottle.

'Come on,' the soldier cried again. 'Don't you want to get out of the rain? Girls?'

He grabbed one of the teenagers by the arm and pulled her towards the bus. She whimpered and her friend snatched at her other hand. The umbrella fell to the ground.

With a shout, the final soldier ran up behind the girls and grabbed one of them around the waist, lifting her up and into the bus. He dragged her further back, where his friends were already sitting. She tried to grasp the rails as he hauled her onwards, pleading with him to let go. The other passengers stood frozen.

The first girl was crying as the soldier succeeded in getting her into the bus. He held his gun up to the driver's head, dropping the girl's hand.

'Shut the fucking doors and let's go.'

The bus pulled away; the girl stepped back towards the doors, her eyes meeting mine. She mouthed, *help me*. No one moved. At the back of the bus, the second girl was fighting against three of the soldiers, who had her trapped against the window.

Out of the corner of my eye, there was a flash of movement.

I turned in time to see one of the men who had been smoking pull out a gun. He yanked the scarf up over his mouth, covering most of his face and launched himself into the street in front of the bus, his companions close behind.

The bus screeched to a halt. Still no one at the bus stop moved.

'Open the fucking doors!'

The three men brandished their guns; one of them carried a semi-automatic rifle, snug against his shoulder. He fired at the ground, the bullets sparking and skittering away, some of them ricocheting into the front of the bus. The doors hissed open and the driver emerged, hands in the air. I could hear the cries of the two girls. Without pausing to look back, the driver ran.

Guns leading the way, the men jumped onto the bus. I heard shouting and a shot was fired. Then another. Then more than I could count. It fell silent and we stood like stone, not breathing, only there to witness.

A scream rang out and the two girls burst from the bus, blood on their uniforms, their faces. Hysterical, they fled, clutching hands, their schoolbags abandoned.

There was another shot.

The three men reappeared, scarves still covering their faces. They walked calmly towards the car. I hadn't noticed but it was idling by the kerb, a faint cloud of exhaust hanging in the air. As he opened the door, one of the men turned back to look at us, raising a fist in the air. Then he slid into the car and it peeled away, tyres spinning on the wet street. The bus sat in the middle of the road, doors open, engine still running. The wipers scraped slowly across the windscreen. Nobody moved inside.

It was quiet for a long moment.

Without turning to look at the other passengers, the old woman waiting beside me said, 'Guess we're walking home tonight folks.' Adjusting her hood, she began the slow journey home.

The first thing I did when I got home was turn on the television. The same news show was on every channel. David G. Tubby and Susannah Smart sat under the studio lights, their eyes wide as they read from the teleprompter, prop papers clutched in their hands. I could see the sweat beading on his brow, her make-up beginning to melt beneath the glare.

Today's attacks have been shocking. An anti-government group known only as Lumière has claimed responsibility for a series of random attacks across London. Fifteen members of the Authorisation Bureau have so far been confirmed dead.

But I knew the attacks were not random. Behind them was a careful plan, designed to stretch and confuse the military and engage the attention of the Authorisation Bureau so that we might be able to gain entry to their compound while they were busy elsewhere.

Tubby continued.

In the first recorded attack, a bomb exploded at a military checkpoint. Two gunmen took out a government transport as it escorted a minister to a private meeting with the US ambassador.

Walking home, I had watched the panic growing around me, and something else, like hope, like rebellion. The whispers on the street grew louder as the people found that their voices were not as lost to them as they had thought.

A statement from the First General's office confirms that these attacks will be swiftly dealt with and citizens should go about their business as normal. There is no reason to fear, although citizens are asked to remain in their homes overnight as the military will be out in force.

There was a rumbling noise outside and I ran to the window.

Three heavy military trucks drove along the street, soldiers holding automatic rifles standing in the back. I yanked at the curtains, drawing them shut.

Behind me, the voice on the television changed.

These cowards, who call themselves Lumière, will not be allowed to win. We are not afraid and the government will take back control.

Her voice wobbled. I turned back to the screen and could see that she was upset. She must be a true believer. I wondered if she had family in the regime. She was old enough to remember what it was like before.

As she turned her face from the camera to compose herself, Tubby hurried to fill the silence.

I repeat, citizens are urged to remain indoors and not engage with any activity happening outside their homes. These freedom fighters will not be allowed to overturn the government.

My mouth fell open. The words had barely left Tubby's mouth when he realised his mistake. Freedom wasn't for the individual; it was something the First General had provided for our nation: freedom from the terror outside. The government was all powerful. Anything else was blasphemy.

He shifted in his seat as his wife's head snapped towards him. His eyes darted to one side and there was a sudden shudder as the camera zoomed in, his terror large across his face.

There was enough time to see the security guards march into the studio, before the channel went abruptly off air.

The streets were different. The air was charged as I walked to the university. I saw a woman tearing down the *We're taking back control* posters on the front of her building despite the soldiers on every corner.

My students were no longer afraid to read in public. One girl read *Nineteen Eighty-Four* openly in the quad. She clutched a tattered copy of the book in her hands, not even a photocopy.

I don't know where she could have found it; my heart dropped like a stone. The title screamed from the front cover as she flicked reverently through the pages, engrossed in this forbidden world.

With a surreptitious glance around me, I rushed across the grass and stood in front of her, blocking the book from view. She glanced up as I interrupted her light. It was one of the students from my class; I had encouraged her to read it.

I put my hand on the book and pulled it down, so that she held it face down in her lap. 'It's still not safe for that yet.'

She stared into my eyes for a moment, with a flicker of mutiny. But she nodded and tucked the novel into her bag.

'Soon,' she said, getting to her feet and walking away. I stared after her, frightened and exhilarated by the promise of this thing that I had started.

Thirty-four

Before we could attempt to break into the Authorisation Bureau building and find Simon and Jerome, there were preparations that had to be made. For me, this meant little more than studying an abstract drawing I had done of the tunnel layout. It was too dangerous to copy it exactly, with identifying information, so I had sketched it as a child would: a squiggle of uneven lines, in brightly coloured crayon. It would mean little to the outsider, but I understood it.

Committing the map to memory filled in the time that was otherwise spent waiting. I wasn't privy to the finer details of the rescue plan, only the basic overview. Caleb hadn't told me when it would happen, only that he would contact me when everything was in place. I felt sick all the time.

It was approaching the holidays, so things at university were winding down as the students prepared to return home for a few weeks. No one bothered to celebrate Christmas any more; the meaning had been lost long ago and few people could afford to indulge in the present-buying sprees that used to be so commonplace. But there was still something about that time, another year drawing to a close, with the possibility of change ahead.

The university noticeboards were full of messages from students travelling home for the holidays, searching for a travel partner to share the cost, or people with temporarily empty rooms they wanted to rent out.

That was where I saw the poster on the final day of term. It was the dog that caught my eye. I don't know what happened to it in the end, after it followed me home. We got halfway there and when I turned back it had vanished. Now its likeness was pinned to the board, as it sat beside its owner. He was grinning at the camera. Above the photograph the word MISSING screamed out at me. Face burning, I ripped the poster from the wall, feeling light headed as I read the plea for information. His name was Trevor. He had a wife and a son. I shoved the piece of paper in amongst the books I was carrying and escaped to my office, heart racing.

I was there when Elizabeth brought the message. She knocked on my office door as I was packing up my papers. The 'missing' poster sat on my desk like an accusation. I waved her inside, closing the door as she hovered in the middle of the room, backpack dangling from one shoulder. She unzipped her parka, her cheeks rosy.

Reaching into her coat pocket, she pulled out a scrap of paper and handed it to me.

'From Caleb,' she murmured.

I unfolded it and read the message. It only said:

Three days.
Be ready.

I looked at Elizabeth, my eyebrows raised.

'Monday night,' she said softly. 'That's all you need to know.'

Everything around me seemed to become still. I blinked away an image of the dead man, tried instead to picture

Simon's face; smell the scent of his skin, his hair. Three days; so close and yet, all that time.

I tucked the note into my jeans. I couldn't bring myself to look her in the eye; I might dissolve at any moment.

As she passed me on her way to the door, her fingers brushed against mine. 'It'll be okay.' She squeezed my hand. 'I'll come for you when it's time.'

Outside, it was beginning to snow. I drifted towards the window, pressed my palm against the cold glass. The main door to the building opened below me and Elizabeth jogged down the steps, tugging the hood of her parka around her face. Her feet left impressions in the dusty snow as she hurried away.

I shrugged my arms into my coat and wrestled my bags into a position where I could comfortably carry them. I paused, about to leave the room. Turning back, I screwed up the 'missing' poster and threw it into the wastepaper basket. I shuffled out of the office, switching off the light. There was no need to lock the door; that might imply I had something to hide.

The empty corridor stretched out ahead of me as I made my way to the stairs, spiralling downwards beneath the dull glow of the emergency lights. I stepped out into the quad in a halo of frozen breath, snow settling in my hair.

Elizabeth's footsteps were already barely visible, but I made a game of them, treading carefully in her imprints to distract my mind from what was to come. Three more days.

Thirty-five

The explosion shocked me from a deep sleep. I sat up in bed, clutching the covers around my chest, my eyes wide in the darkness. It took me a moment to orient myself, senses crying out.

Light flickered behind the window blinds. I slid out of bed, the floor like ice under my hot feet. Carefully I tweaked one of the panels so I could peek outside. At the junction at the end of the street, a car had been overwhelmed by flames. They burned high, reaching up into the night. As I watched, three unmarked cars screeched to a halt around it, Authorisation Bureau soldiers tumbling out, picking their way across the debris littering the road. I could hear their shouts ringing along the street.

One of them began waving his arms and I could make out a dull rumbling sound. A tank rolled around the corner, a single soldier atop it surveying the area, weapon in hand. The men circled the car frantically, but they couldn't get close enough. I could almost feel the heat singeing my skin. I leaned closer and my breath clouded the glass. All along the street I could make out curtains twitching as my neighbours watched the drama unfold. Nobody emerged from their buildings.

It took a long time for a fire engine to arrive. By then the flames had consumed everything; only a twisted steel skeleton remained, blackened by ash. Two policemen began to haul charred bodies onto the pavement. Four of them were lined up without ceremony.

Shuddering, I let the blinds fall back into place. A faint whisper of daylight was beginning to graze the skyline. I climbed back into bed, between my now-cold sheets, and knew I wouldn't sleep again today.

There was no reason for me to leave the apartment, but after a few restless hours it was becoming claustrophobic. I had little to do but stare at the clock as the minutes swept slowly by, listening to the aftermath of the explosion in the street.

Every time I closed my eyes for a second I could picture the bodies laid out on the side of the road, burned beyond recognition, hands clawing at agonised flesh. I tried to stop myself from wondering about the source of the bomb, whether Caleb was responsible.

I had to get out. Scrambling into my boots and coat, chest tight, I decided to go and buy milk. I always needed milk.

As I ran down the stairs, boots thundering on the concrete, I wrapped my scarf around my neck, feeling as though I would suffocate. Outside, I turned away from the scene of the explosion. It was beginning to snow again; powdery white flakes floated to the ground, catching in my hair.

I walked for a while, longer than I needed to. I returned with a pint of milk, shivering from the cold, the tips of my fingers turning blue. The clean-up operation was now under way and the residents of my street had begun to slink from their homes, gathering in doorways to whisper with their neighbours.

On the street corner, a woman was wailing. 'My son, my son.' A uniformed woman was trying awkwardly to comfort her, to block her view of the charred metal shell where her boy had died. An eerie silence consumed the street as she crumpled to the ground, snow falling around her.

A group of men from the apartment block two down were smoking outside the fire escape. As I walked by, one of them muttered something to his friend. I caught nothing but the word, 'Lumière'. It was all I could do to stop myself turning towards him in shock. I forced myself to keep walking.

A group of tenants were standing outside my building, more brazen than the rest. They had stepped out into the open and were watching the men at work as they gathered evidence from the blast.

I was about to sneak behind them into the building when a woman who lived on the floor below turned and noticed my approach.

'Awful isn't it?' she inclined her head in the direction of the car bomb.

Before I could reply, someone else said, 'Bloody deserved it though.' A murmur ran through the crowd.

A man spat on the ground. 'Fucking Authorisation Bureau.' He caught sight of me, lurking at the back of the group. 'It was one of their commanders in the car, you know. Couple of his lackeys and the driver got blown up an' all.'

They all watched for my reaction. A chill skittered down my spine. Why were they all looking at me? Did they know I was working with Caleb? Or that Simon had been taken? Did they think I was a sympathiser because of the major? I rarely spoke to anyone in the building.

'I…' Unspoken words seemed to hang in the air. Very quietly, I said, 'Good.'

A fleeting smile worked across the man's lips. As I turned to walk inside, the woman from downstairs reached out and squeezed my shoulder. I could feel the imprint of her hand all the way up the stairs.

The weekend crawled by, each unoccupied minute stretching out into eternity. By Sunday night I was pacing a groove into the floor, nerves a tight, angry knot in my stomach.

It was late when there was a soft knock at my door. I opened it a crack to find Elizabeth, peering over her shoulder.

She pushed past me into the flat. 'Quick, close the door!'

I complied, clicking the lock shut.

Her cheeks were bright with cold and her eyes shone in the dim light.

'What's wrong?'

She made a small, strangled noise. 'I was coming to give you the rest of the details for your part of the plan, but I think some-one was following me.'

I stopped breathing. 'Did you see who it was?'

She shook her head, blonde hair framing her face. 'I'm not sure…'

I stared at her intently. 'Tell me.'

'I think it might have been a member of the Authorisation Bureau.'

I closed my eyes for a second and said a quiet prayer. 'What makes you think that?'

She thought for a second. 'Something about the way they moved. They weren't wearing a uniform but… I could still tell.'

I nodded. 'Okay, where were they? Did they see you come into this building?'

'I don't think so. I knew he was behind me for a while, so I ducked into a couple of shops, as though I needed groceries.

The second time I cut out of the back door and doubled back on myself. It was streets away from here.'

I exhaled slowly. 'Who knew you were coming here?'

'Nobody, just Caleb. He sent me with the message.'

'Right, okay. Well I guess you'd better tell me and then we'll have to get you out of here. We can't be found together, it would ruin everything.'

She agreed. Bending down, she unzipped one of her boots and pulled out a piece of paper. 'Here.' She held it out to me.

I snatched the note and read it quickly, twice. The directions were simple enough. Striding into the kitchen, I switched on the gas hob and held the paper against the flame. It caught light and I flicked it into the sink, watching to make sure it burned. When there was nothing but ash, I ran the tap to flush the remains away.

'We'd better get you out of here.'

I was about to grab my coat when there was another knock at the door. We both froze, staring at each other, eyes wide.

Get in the bathroom, I mouthed, waving my hand frantically at her. She shot across the room as I ushered her inside. As I closed the door, I glimpsed her clambering into the bath tub and sliding the shower curtain across so that she couldn't be seen if anyone looked into the room.

Pressing my face against the front door, I squinted through the peephole. Will was waiting in the corridor, his figure distorted: a giant head and skinny body.

With a sick feeling, I unlocked the door.

'Will!' I pasted a cheerful smile onto my face. 'What are you doing here?'

He gave a tight smile. 'Sister.' I stepped aside to let him into my home.

He strode inside, hands folded behind his back, eyes roaming around the room. He walked to the window and pulled the blinds aside, shoving the toe of his boot under the bed sharply. He peered into corners, frowning.

'Can I help you find something?' I asked.

He glared at me. 'Do you have something to hide?'

I stared back at him blankly. 'What are you talking about, William?'

He hated being addressed by his full name. His bottom lip twisted into a pout. Sometimes I forgot he was still a teenager. 'Don't call me that.' The facade of policeman slipped and he was a boy again, trying to make his daddy proud.

I started to get angry. 'Why are you here? Is it money you want, again? You should go and speak to your dad if you're that desperate.' I marched to the door and held it open. 'Now if that's all, it's late. I'd like to go to bed.'

I willed him to leave. Despite his time in the academy, Will was still a boy, unused to dealing with women. I had hoped that by ordering him around, I'd unnerve him enough to abandon his search.

A tight little scowl on his face, he took the bait and headed to the door. I'd never noticed before, but he was so much taller than me now. He sneered at me. 'Don't worry, I'm going. But you'll be seeing me again soon, *dearest sister*.'

I ignored the urge to slam the door shut and kept my eyes trained on his back as he started down the staircase. I watched to make sure he was gone.

With a relieved sigh, I went back inside and shut the door, leaning against it, knees trembling. A small voice called, 'Clara?'

'It's okay, he's gone. You can come out now.'

There was a shuffling noise and a bang, then Elizabeth appeared, face pale. 'Who was it? Were they looking for me?'

'It was my brother. He's been training to join the Authorisation Bureau. I guess they must have fast-tracked him through the academy or something.' I plopped onto a chair. 'He started to poke around out here as though he was looking for something, but that doesn't necessarily mean it was you. Last time he was here he was pretty desperate for money. I think he's on drugs. For all I know, he was looking for something he could sell.'

She didn't look convinced. 'Bit of a coincidence, him showing up like this, so late at night. He could have followed me here.'

I splayed my hands in frustration. 'I've no idea, Elizabeth. I can't exactly go and ask him.'

She pulled out a chair and sat beside me. 'So… what do we do now?'

'I don't think it's safe for you to stay here. That wasn't part of Caleb's plan anyway, was it? Do you have any friends nearby who you can stay with? It would get you off the streets.'

She thought for a moment. 'Yeah, I know someone a couple of streets away actually.'

'Okay.'

She stood up. 'I'm sorry if I've brought any trouble to you, I was just delivering Caleb's message.'

'It's fine, how could you know?' I stopped. 'You don't think…'

She looked back at me, as a cold feeling crept across my skin. 'What?'

I shook myself. 'You don't think they know about the plan? Why else would they be following you?'

She frowned. 'No… they can't. None of us would tell them and there aren't many people who know.'

I walked her to the door. 'I hope you're right.'

She stepped into the corridor. 'I'll see you soon, Clara. Take care of yourself.'

I squeezed her arm. 'You get home safe, okay.'

She nodded. 'See you.'

Her feet moved more quickly down the stairs than my brother's had. I was about to close my door when a shrill scream rang out. Without thinking I ran into the hallway and downstairs, leaving the front door wide open.

The building's foyer was empty. I didn't stop moving, I ran out into the street, looking quickly in each direction. There was no one there. I stood in the middle of the road, moving in a slow circle looking in every direction; there were no signs of life.

Thirty-six

My instructions were to wait for Caleb on the corner of a street about fifteen minutes' walk from the Authorisation Bureau headquarters. I knew I'd be there too early, wired with nervous energy, drawing suspicious glances, so I circled the streets alone until it was time. Every few steps I checked over my shoulder, paranoid that someone was watching me.

I hadn't been able to sleep after Elizabeth left. I wanted to help her, but I didn't know how. It would only endanger the plan if I tried to contact Caleb before the scheduled time. I spent the whole night on the floor of my flat, curled into a ball, staring at the front door, waiting for the soldiers to pour through it.

But they never came. The day passed by in a haze of anxiety; I imagined every possible negative outcome for the rescue, convinced myself there would be mayhem and death. As the sky grew darker again, I was violently sick. The meagre contents of my stomach stared back at me from the chipped porcelain of the bathroom sink like an accusation.

I washed it away, but I couldn't wash away the sense that something bad was going to happen. Weak and trembling, I dressed as instructed, in dark clothes and sturdy boots, a hat and scarf ready to mask as much of my face as possible.

Then it was time to leave. I took one last long look around the flat, tracing my fingertips across the smooth cotton bedcovers, which were cool from a night without sleep. I closed the door, praying that the next time I crossed the threshold Simon would be with me, his hand in mine.

The streets were quiet. The faint covering of snow had melted, leaving behind only a grey slush. My feet grew damp as the water seeped through the cracked leather. As I waited for Caleb to appear, I studied the patterns the damp left on the material.

I didn't hear him approach or see the place he materialised from. One moment I was alone, the next his hand was resting on my shoulder. I jumped at his touch, my breath caught in a gasp.

'It's just me,' he said softly.

I put a palm to my chest and tried to smile, my face twisting into a grimace instead. Caleb gave me a hug. 'Are you sure you want to do this? If it's too much, we can go on without you. It'll work somehow.'

I looked up at him fiercely. 'No! I have to be a part of it. I have to see Simon again...' Something inside me tore; a rush of emotion hit me so hard I couldn't breathe. I forced it away, forced myself not to cry. 'I have to.'

'Okay.' Caleb took my hand. 'Come on, the others are waiting.'

The nausea returned as I remembered Elizabeth. His hand in mine, I held him back. I took a deep breath, my eyes drifting off to the side, unable to meet his gaze. 'There's something I think you should know... about Elizabeth.'

He listened as I recounted the events of the previous evening.

'I'm so sorry, Caleb. I should have protected her; I shouldn't have sent her back out onto the street like that.'

He shook his head. 'Clara, you didn't do anything wrong. You couldn't have let her stay with you; it would have been too dangerous. And we don't know for sure that something happened to her. One of the others might know.'

I followed him around the corner. He moved quickly, heading for the door of an old electricity substation that was partially obscured by the branches of an overgrown juniper bush. He cracked the door open and slipped inside. Taking a heavy breath, I followed.

It was dark inside; it took my eyes a moment to adjust. The floor was littered with debris and wires hung loose from the ceiling. I could make out a flash of graffiti. A shadow broke away from the wall and came towards us. It was Zeke. As he moved he dislodged a chunk of fallen masonry; a rat escaped, skittering across my foot.

'The others have already started down the tunnel.' Zeke's voice was dark with anticipation. He lifted his arm and held something out towards Caleb; it gave off a metallic glint in the darkness.

'Is that a gun?' I hissed.

Caleb tucked it into the back of his jeans where I couldn't see. 'Don't worry about that, it's only a precaution.'

The sense of doom intensified, gnawing in the pit of my stomach. 'You're not planning to shoot anyone, are you?'

I almost heard Zeke's smirk. 'You don't think we would go in there without weapons, Clara? The guards, they'll be armed.' He paused. 'You don't have to come.'

If I'd been able to see his self-satisfied face, I might have punched it. 'What am I going to do, stay in here by myself while you all go off and get *shot*? No thanks.'

'If you're sure.' He moved away. 'It's this way.'

I followed, with Caleb in step behind me. We approached what seemed to be a solid wall; Zeke clicked on a small torch and pointed it at a narrow gap where one side of the wall protruded further than the other. As we slipped through the gap into the tunnel, my foot caught on something and I stumbled, twisting my ankle and landing heavily on one knee. Caleb's hands reached under my arms and lifted me back to my feet. There was a rush of icy air around my knee where my jeans must have torn.

'Are you alright?' Caleb asked. The torch had bobbed away down the tunnel, where it came to a halt, Zeke waiting for us in silence.

I winced, pulling off my glove and running my fingers down my leg. They came away bloody. I stuffed my gloves into the pocket of my coat.

'I'll be fine.'

'We have to go.' Zeke's voice was insistent. 'It's almost time.'

We hustled down the narrow tunnel towards him, elbows scraping on stone. As we moved further into the darkness I could sense people ahead of us. A voice called out softly and Zeke responded. Several torches flickered on at once, dazzling me. I shielded my eyes.

Those that were part of the plan to invade the Authorisation Bureau headquarters were waiting for us. I could barely make out their faces above their black clothing; with scarves pulled up around their faces, they disappeared into the gloom.

Caleb came up behind me and addressed them. 'Is everyone here? What about Elizabeth?'

There were mumbles of assent at first, but they dropped away as she failed to reply. 'Okay.' Caleb found my hand in the darkness and gripped it.

'If she didn't make it here... we suspect Elizabeth was arrested last night.'

The whispering grew tense.

'Quiet,' Caleb commanded. The tunnel fell silent. 'If she was arrested, the chances are we'll find Elizabeth somewhere in this building. She will need our help; we must look for her along with the others. Okay?'

The others hissed in agreement, still trying to keep their voices low.

'Let's go over the plan one more time,' Caleb said. 'It's important that we all remember our places.'

I murmured along with the crowd, uncertain of the details. 'Our inside man is primed to cause the distraction we will need to get into the building unseen. At precisely 8.53pm, he will short wiring in one of the maintenance rooms on the third floor, causing a small electrical fire. The alarms will sound, attracting the guards. As this is within the evening shift-change window, there will only be a skeleton staff available; the next shift won't have finished clocking in, so when the fire triggers a system lockdown, they'll be shut out of the main building.

'This is when we will enter via the tunnels. We'll split off into three groups, each entering the building on one of the underground floors. Down there, only the main doors are controlled electronically – you need keys to access the cells and we've got copies. Members of each team should have them.'

A ripple of agreement swept through the group. 'Good. Once we're inside the building, each group will need to proceed to their target. We don't know where exactly they're being held in the building, but our insiders have given us as much intelligence as they can. Once we locate the prisoners, we need to get them out as quickly as we can and get back to the tunnels.'

Caleb paused. 'I can't emphasise this point enough: do not wait for anyone outside of your team. Once we get back to the tunnels, we'll be splitting off in different directions to avoid detection. If you get back first, leave. Don't wait for the others. We'll meet at the rendezvous point at midnight, with the prisoners.

'If anyone doesn't make it, we'll know where to find them.'

We stood in silence, the weight of Caleb's words sinking in. Some of us might not be coming back. I shivered, thinking about the gun tucked into the waistband of his trousers.

'Everyone ready?'

The answering voices were quiet yet fierce. It was time.

Zeke led the way; he was the expert on the tunnels. Caleb was somewhere in the middle of the procession as it marched along the narrow corridor. I fell into step behind him, hands reaching out unconsciously to clutch at the brick, to feel something tangible that might guide me.

Caleb must have sensed my discomfort. He reached back and took my hand, towing me along in his wake. I fought to keep myself steady, to avoid treading on him or tumbling to the floor in a quivering heap.

It was a long walk. I never even saw the Authorisation Bureau building before we went inside, like rats tunnelling deep underground.

We entered through a barely remembered door at the end of a dimly lit maintenance tunnel. No one spoke. Caleb signalled his soldiers with brisk movements as they took out their weapons, gripping them tightly in bloodless hands. They separated into three groups and began to jog, one after another down the corridor. The first two groups disappeared into a stairwell and I imagined them climbing higher, to floors where there would be more soldiers. My legs began to shake.

Wordlessly, Caleb squeezed my arm and inclined his head. Our group took off along the corridor, passing the stairway and moving towards a set of double doors. We paused; a brief moment to catch our breath.

Beside the door was a fire alarm, an old-fashioned axe displayed in a glass-covered case. Caleb caught me looking and smiled tightly. Holding up a hand, he tugged off his shirt and hung it over the case, then jabbed his elbow sharply. The sound of glass breaking was muffled. He shook the tiny shards from his shirt and put it back on, before tugging the axe from its case. He handed it to me.

They all watched as I held it out in front of me like a talisman, surprised by how light the metal was. My fingers tightened around the cool handle and I nodded to Caleb. He turned to the door and I sucked in a deep, painful breath.

Caleb raised a foot and kicked the doors, hard. They burst open and eight of us spilled out into the corridor clutching our weapons and looking frantically around.

There were no guards. Caleb called my name and time seemed to speed up. I hurried to his side as we ran along the corridor, pausing at each door to peer through tiny panes of wire-scarred glass. Around us the others were trying door handles, banging on windows, struggling with copied keys or kicking in doors.

There were people inside the rooms, but they were broken. Tears streamed down my face at each new tableau. We weren't there for them, but we tried to help. One man was chained to the wall, his arms above him, head lolling forward onto his chest, swimming in and out of consciousness.

Caleb unlocked the door to his cell but he couldn't release the chains. The key was no use.

'Give me the axe.'

He swung it with a grunt and the blade sparked against the metal restraints, but they didn't give. He tried again and again, but nothing. The prisoner barely noticed we were there.

As Caleb shook his head and marched to the door, I cried, 'Surely we can't leave him here?'

He shrugged. 'What can we do? We have to find Simon, Jerome, Elizabeth… they're the ones we came for. If they catch us here, we won't be able to help anyone.'

With a last look back I followed him out of the door. The corridor felt endless as we pushed forwards, Caleb squinting into each room as I kept moving ahead. Along the corridor one of the others was supporting a man as he staggered out of a cell. He looked back at us and I was shocked to recognise him: the presenter from the news channel, the one who had slipped and called Lumière freedom fighters.

His usually neat, expensively styled hair was bloody and plastered to his head, his eyes almost glued shut with blood and bruises. He was wearing scrub trousers and nothing else. As his rescuer led him away, I gasped. His back was raw, gaping strap marks lashed across his skin, layer upon layer of wounds destroying his flesh. If they'd done this to him, what would they have done to Simon?

Something caught my eye and I stopped; my feet belonged to someone else. The clinical beige of the walls was broken by a long, deep window set into the brick: a viewing gallery of sorts.

I stared through the window, horror building in my chest. The cell was brightly lit, the bare strip lights flickering coldly. A woman was slumped on the floor in the middle of the room, her hands bound behind her back. Her clothes were torn and stained, her feet bare. There was blood smeared on the floor.

She had a bag over her head, but I recognised her. There was a small tattoo on her ankle that I had seen before.

'Caleb.' My voice was a shriek of pain. He looked up. I pointed at the glass, hand shaking. 'It's Elizabeth.'

He hurried to my side and I had to turn away as he looked

through the window, the colour fading from his cheeks. I burned in shame for her, in rage. With a roar, he ripped the axe out of my hands and smashed it against the glass. It shook, but didn't break. He swung again, eyes wild, and a crack appeared. The corridor echoed with the ringing of the axe as it struck the glass over and over. When it finally shattered, glistening shards flew in every direction. Elizabeth screamed as they hit her, the feeble sound muffled by the hood.

I sliced the palm of my hand clambering over the window frame into the cell, but I barely noticed, even as the blood ran along my wrist. Caleb cut her free and pulled the bag from her head. She screwed her eyes shut in the sudden blinding light, shrinking away from us.

'Elizabeth,' I said softly as Caleb stepped back, 'Elizabeth, it's Clara. And Caleb, Caleb is with me. We've come to take you home. I'm so sorry, darling, I'm so sorry.'

She was whimpering, her feet scraping over the shards of glass as she twisted, searching for a way out. I pulled off my coat and went to her, wrapping it around her shoulders. She cried out in pain.

'Elizabeth, can you walk? We need to get you out of here.'

Her eyes began to focus. They found my face and clung to it. 'Clara!'

Her voice was weak. I reached out to pull the coat tight and she began to cry. I looked back at Caleb, gesturing to the ground. 'The glass.'

With a nod, he stepped forward and swept her up into his arms. He winced as her body tensed in pain but he carried her towards the gaping window frame. I quickly climbed back through and helped her into the corridor.

Further along, the rest of the group were helping stumbling prisoners towards our exit. A siren began to wail. They caught sight of us and began to wave urgently. 'Caleb, we've got to go! They know we're here!'

I looked around frantically. 'Simon, did they find him?' There were still half a dozen rooms along the corridor that we hadn't checked. I didn't see him among the people struggling for the door. Panic curled around my heart.

Caleb looked at me, Elizabeth draped across his shoulder, weeping hard. I waved him on, 'Get her out of here. It's a few rooms, I'll check... I have to check...'

I didn't wait for his permission. As I ran, he called out my name. I spun round. 'Get her out of here, Caleb!'

He nodded. 'Hurry!' he called back, his voice already obscured by the screeching of the alarm and his heavy footsteps as they ran, the bleeding girl in his arms.

I knew I didn't have much time. I glanced through each window long enough to ensure Simon wasn't in that room. Tortured eyes beseeched me, but I didn't have time to save them.

He was in the last cell. They hadn't restrained him. He stood in the middle of the room, staring at the door. As he saw my face he gave a shout and ran forward, banging his fists against the glass.

'Simon!' I screamed, pressing my palm against the window. Tears blurred my vision as I tried to take him in. It didn't feel real. In the distance there was a shout and I knew that the guards were coming. My heart dropped; Caleb had the key.

'Step back,' I screamed at him, not even waiting for him to comply before I arced the axe through the air. I was slower than Caleb, my arms weak and shuddering, each blow ricocheting through my bones. But I broke the lock. I got the door open.

He staggered out into my arms in a haze of sweat and blood

and torn clothing, a ragged beard scraping against my face as he kissed me fiercely.

'We have to leave,' I gasped, grabbing his hand and pulling him along. 'They're coming.'

He overtook me, towing me along the corridor. I still couldn't see his face, only the width of his shoulders, tense beneath an ill-fitting shirt, and the hair that had grown long and curled over his collar.

We were almost at the door when I saw her: a young girl, even younger than Elizabeth, staring out through the tiny window of her cell, hand pressed flat against the glass. My hand dropped from Simon's grasp and I stopped, fumbling for the axe.

He turned back to me, almost at the exit. 'Clara, what are you doing?' His voice was shrill with panic.

'I have to help her. Just go, I'll be right behind you.'

He started to come back to me and somewhere a door burst open and regimented feet ran towards us. There were shouts of anger and his eyes filled with fear as he stared towards the noise.

'Go, please,' I screamed, 'I'm coming.'

With a swing of the axe I had the door open and I had the girl with me. Seeing us on our way towards him, Simon hurtled through the double doors and I caught a glimpse of him running hard.

I followed as fast as I could, dragging the girl behind me, her laboured breathing loud in my ear. The footsteps grew louder and I began to pray: *please God, let me make it through this door, let me help this girl.*

We reached the door as they rounded the corner, a dozen men in uniforms, all of them clutching automatic rifles. The girl screamed as I shoved her through the gap ahead of me.

'Run!' With a final glance at me, she disappeared, her feet slapping desperately against the floor.

Before I could follow, there was a shout and one of the guards fired several rounds of bullets. The corridor echoed with the noise. I froze; eyes squeezed shut, feeling the rush of hot metal in the air, waiting for the bullets to tear into me.

But they didn't come. Rough hands grabbed me and forced me to my knees, onto my face on the floor. I gasped as they wrenched a plastic tie tight around my wrists, so tight my circulation stopped. I couldn't feel my fingers.

'Keep your head down,' someone yelled at me. I could see nothing but the polished leather of two dozen boots, gathered furiously around me.

It wasn't until I heard his voice that the reality sank in. I was a prisoner.

'Get her up.'

They lifted me, yanked me to my feet, holding me tightly in position. And it was then that I saw them. Two bodies lay sprawled on the ground, blood slowly seeping from the bullet wounds in their backs.

I let out a scream; it felt like it would rip my chest in two.

The major stood there, his mouth twisted in a nasty little smile. 'Clara, well, fancy seeing you here.'

He walked away from me, towards the bodies, his pace agonisingly slow. Each step was a taunt. He stopped beside them, his carefully polished boots just outside the pool of blood. With his toe, he prodded Simon's leg. A hot burst of anger rushed through me as the major turned him roughly onto his back.

'Oh, Simon...' he shook his head sadly. Tears poured down my face; my knees felt weak. I struggled to breathe, my world falling away. I remembered that last afternoon in the park, the way Simon had smiled at me. I remembered the shock of seeing him bundled into that car, the screech of tyres as it sped away, the pain in my chest as the realisation struck. The pain was there again now, crippling my lungs.

The major walked back along the corridor, eyes on me the entire way. For a long moment he did nothing but stare as the sound of my sobs filled the air. Then he tutted softly.

'What were you thinking, Clara? I always knew you were irresponsible, but I never thought you'd risk someone else's life, especially Simon's.'

I opened my mouth to reply, but I couldn't speak through my tears. Before I could catch my breath, he smiled and drove his fist viciously into my gut. I tried to double over, the air driven from my body, but the guards held me upright. Stars sparked on the periphery of my vision.

'Take her to one of the interrogation rooms,' the major commanded.

'Yes sir,' they answered and I was dragged away, spluttering and fighting for breath, the toes of my boots squeaking on the shiny linoleum.

Thirty-seven

Somewhere above me a light flared angrily. It burned its way into my consciousness, demanding my attention. I kept my eyes closed as I surfaced from a sweaty, drug-induced sleep, but still the light seared pulsating red rings into my retinas. I tried to bring my arm to my eyes for protection, but I couldn't move. My limbs were heavy, still suffused with barbiturates. I tried to shift positions but I couldn't. I was tied to the bed. Panic overwhelmed me.

My eyes flew open and everything went white. I twisted my head to one side, trying to find a place away from the light, but I couldn't escape. As I struggled to regain my sight, a tinny clicking sound rang around the room.

'Ah, you're awake. I'm so pleased.'

A chill shuddered across my skin as my stepfather's disem-bodied voice washed over me. Squinting against the glare that consumed the room, I tried to figure out where I was. I lay on a narrow bed in the centre of a cell, a row of strip lights directly above me. My arms and legs were cuffed and fastened to the bed; another strap circled my waist. I flexed my fingers, testing the leather. It didn't give.

Cold air rippled along my legs. I managed to lift my head

enough to see that I was no longer wearing my own clothes. Instead, someone had dressed me in a plain hospital gown; I could feel the ties at the back digging into my flesh, the rough scrape of a woollen blanket against the exposed skin where the material didn't meet. I wasn't wearing any underwear.

Panic hit me once more as I pictured what had happened. Images assailed me; the smell of bullets burning filled my nostrils. Was it only yesterday?

I wondered. I had no way of knowing how long I'd been lying here. I couldn't rely on anyone to tell me the truth.

Tears slid from the corner of my eye as I thought about Simon. I worried about Caleb and the others and if they'd managed to get away. I could only hope they would come back for me. But this time, the guards would be expecting them. They would know that the tunnels had been used to access the building. My tears intensified.

The major's voice echoed once more through the speakers. 'Don't cry my dear; we've got so many fun things planned for you today. You wouldn't want to miss them, would you?'

I strained against the restraints, my eyes darting around the room. There was a long, low window cut into the wall, much like the one that had been in the cell where we found Elizabeth. I tried to catch sight of the major on the other side of the glass, but there was nothing but my own reflection. I couldn't bear to look at myself.

I lay down in defeat, imagining the twist of his mouth as he smirked, watching me from behind the mirror. I wondered if he would be alone, or if there would be others there with him, planning the best way to torture me.

I forced the terror somewhere deep down inside myself; it was the only way to keep from crying out. I tried to set my mind free, wandering outside somewhere, away from thoughts of what the next few hours might hold for me. I pictured

Simon's face, tried to remember the feel of his arms around me. But images of his dead body kept intruding and I felt sure I'd soon be joining him.

It felt like forever until the major came for me. I lay there alone in that white room, feeling eyes crawl across me, eyes that were hidden behind reflective glass. Exhaustion flooded my veins, an after-effect of the drugs that were still hazy in my bloodstream, but the glare of the overhead light wouldn't allow me to sleep.

Despite all the waiting, I wasn't ready when the key clanged in the lock and the heavy door swung open. To my surprise, Will was the first one to enter the room, his eyes fixed on the floor. The major appeared close behind, almost casual without his uniform jacket, shirt sleeves rolled up to his elbows. The muscles in his forearms flexed as he closed the door behind them. I caught a glimpse of a guard standing outside the room, automatic rifle clutched in both hands.

Without speaking, the major crossed the room, somewhere behind me. I couldn't twist my head back far enough to see what he was doing and the angle in the mirror wasn't right. Will loitered in the corner of the room, trying his best not to look at me.

There was a scraping sound and the major reappeared in my line of vision, dragging a metal chair behind him. He positioned it carefully: close enough to the bed so that he could reach out and touch me, but far enough away that I had to turn my head awkwardly to see him.

With a heavy sigh, he settled himself into the chair, hands resting on his thighs, feet stretched out towards me. I stared straight ahead. I would not be the first to speak.

He smiled at me. 'I always knew you were rebellious, Clara.

When we first met, you looked at me like you hated me. I suppose you still do.'

I couldn't help it; my face must have betrayed my surprise. It seemed to please him. He smiled in that knowing way that always infuriated me so intensely.

'You thought you were so clever, but everything you ever thought… it was written across your face. Why do you think I sent you away to school? I couldn't stand to look at all that resentment for another moment. It was bad enough by then, having to look at your mother every day.'

In the corner, my brother's face twitched, but he didn't say anything. I scowled at the major, jamming my lips together. His amusement only grew. 'You're so like her, you know.'

I tried to hold onto my anger, to stop it from escaping. I bit my lip until the taste of iron filled my mouth. All the while he smirked at me, until I couldn't keep quiet any longer. 'I'm nothing like her!'

His eyes sparkled. 'Oh you don't see it, but it's obvious to everyone else. You have that same stubborn, destructive streak. The only difference is, she's never managed to find a constructive outlet for her pain, so she drowns it in drink. She's made herself a victim by wallowing in her own misery. Of course, she's responsible enough for it. She told me all about the conversation you had about how she annulled her marriage to your father.'

He stood up and moved slowly towards the wall. I followed his movements out of the corner of my eye.

'I expected you to blame me, but it seems you've more sense, after all. You can see the part she played in it. For all the things I did to your father, and I don't deny them, she was responsible for the annulment.'

I listened as he spoke, my jaw clenched tightly shut. A vein pulsed beside my eye, causing it to twitch. I blinked hard, trying to make it stop. When I opened my eyes, he was watching me.

'She always loved him, you know. Even after we were married. I often think that's what drove her to drink, despite everything else. Her guilt. She abandoned your father, even though she loved him so intensely. She certainly never loved me that way.' He smiled bitterly. 'Oh she made a good show of it. It's ironic really, considering she never made it as an actress. Our relationship was her grand performance. And she did it all for you.'

I couldn't help it; my eyes flickered to his face. 'Don't look so surprised, Clara. She must have told you. I was the only way to keep you safe.' He gave a burst of laughter. 'If only she could see us here, now. What would she say? Who do you think she would blame first?'

I forced myself to stay silent, even as his words raced through my mind. Behind him, Will was fighting with his own emotions as he listened intently to everything his father said. I'd never considered what my dad must be to him: some ghostly figure skirting the edges of our lives, like a fairy-tale warning of what might happen if you misbehaved. I wondered if he'd ever thought of our mother that way – as someone else's wife, with this whole alternate life that existed long before he ever did. Perhaps he felt as unwanted as his father did.

It was silent for a long time.

'I suppose we'll never know,' the major said softly. He turned to face the glass and made a sharp movement with his right hand, dragging a finger across his throat. Then he left the room. Will followed, throwing me a quick glance over his shoulder.

They turned out the lights and left me there in darkness.

I didn't see them again for some time. Each time the door opened, I expected to see the major and felt almost disappointed when some anonymous soldier entered the room instead.

But when he did reappear, I knew immediately that something was wrong. His face was grey, a fine sheen of sweat on his skin. There was a dark stain on his shirt that frightened me.

He came storming into the room, breathing heavily. I felt the intensity of his stare as it settled on me. If I'd felt vulnerable before, it was nothing beside this.

'I hope you're happy.' His words cut across the room and I was too afraid to reply. But I couldn't look away. Something awful woke deep in my stomach. As I waited for him to continue, my sense of time – already stretched and distorted – threatened to snap completely.

He was in a frenzy and I was afraid of him, of what he was about to say. I swallowed hard.

'After you were captured, an arrest team was sent out to speak to your mother, without my knowledge. The association with you and your father counted against her, even more than her relationship with me. The regime never forgets.'

He began to pace and I noticed a tremor in his hands. The fear in my gut intensified. He wasn't in control here.

'They were actually quite delicate with her. She was asked to accompany them to headquarters; as it was early in the day, they gave her a few moments to go upstairs and dress. Instead, she went into the safe and took my gun. While they waited downstairs, she shot herself in the head.'

A faint gurgle of pain curdled on my lips. My fists tightened and the bite of broken nails cut into my palms. But he wasn't finished.

'Of course, your mother has never fired a gun in her life.

Frankly, I'm surprised she managed to take the safety catch off. Unfortunately, it seems she wavered at the last moment and her hand slipped. The bullet destroyed her face, but she isn't dead. The arrest team were able to transport her to hospital. She's on a ventilator. She'll die, but it may be a slow process.'

He sucked in a breath. 'I've been to the house. It looks like a fucking abattoir.'

The coldness of his words was like a slap to the face. I screwed my eyes shut, trying to force away the images that threatened to overwhelm me. I had no one left.

Thirty-eight

The next day, they took me into another room, a bag over my head as I was dragged from my bed and hauled out into the corridor. My legs were weak and I couldn't make them work properly, my feet scrambling uselessly to keep up.

I was jostled through a narrow doorway, a guard gripping each arm tightly, my hands cuffed in front of me. A third soldier ripped the bag from my head and I blinked, the light blinding. I was in a room with white tiled walls and a bare concrete floor. This room had no observation panels. There were no cameras. No one would see what happened here.

A thick metal hook hung from the ceiling. It was the only thing in the room. They pulled me towards it and another guard came in carrying a heavy chain. He slung it over the hook, pulling it down and attaching it to my handcuffs. His arms straining, he heaved on the chain, dragging my hands skyward. The breath left my body abruptly as I was pulled upwards until my toes were scraping the floor, unable to find purchase. My shoulders were wrenched unnaturally as the chain forced the joints back too far. There was an ominous popping sound and a wave of pain rushed through me.

And they left. I hung there, like a piece of meat in a slaughterhouse, unable to stop my feet from rasping across the concrete, over and over, panic suffocating me. I couldn't breathe.

They left me there. They left me there for so long that I became delirious. My head lolled against my arms, my body spinning softly, first one way and then the other. As the room spun around me the shadows lengthened and grew unnatural.

The air in the white room was stifling. My underarms were soaked in sweat; I could smell it, pungent and sour. Sweat leached from my forehead; my lips grew dry and cracked. My tongue felt swollen and furry in my mouth. I tried to plead for water but my words were too slurred to make sense. I tried to remember the last time I ate something, but the moment eluded me.

Eventually I began to cry, a low desperate moan, my mouth hanging open, chest shuddering. My thighs grew warm as I pissed myself.

The lights cut out. For a brief moment I wondered if I had gone blind. I wondered if I was already dead.

I came to in a spray of ice-cold water. It lashed against my face, like needles against my skin. It soaked the thin gown and left me trembling, the force making my body spin, fresh agony jolting every joint, every muscle. But still I gulped at the water desperately, trying to angle my head to catch it in my mouth. I couldn't see who wielded the hose, the pressure forcing my burning eyes to close.

When they shut the water off, I was bereft. Thirst clawed at my throat, making me gasp. The gown was plastered to my skin, cold and heavy. I began to shiver violently, my teeth clattering together so hard I thought they would break.

I slipped into unconsciousness.

I woke to a needle in my arm. I groaned and tried to make out the face of the man plunging this syringe into my flesh, but his features swam before me, dissembling. He seemed alien, his eyes huge and black in the smooth grey of his face.

My vision cleared and it was a doctor with a mask over his face, identity void. He looked me in the eye and fear rattled along my spine; he was studying me. I imagined him pulling a scalpel from his pristine lab coat and drawing it across my chest in a vicious Y, peeling back the layers of meat until there was only bone and viscera.

My heart began to race, the blood thundering in my ears. A strange crackling sound filled the room; it was my breathing. It didn't even sound human.

His eyes shifted and slid, his face melting. I went into the light.

I was naked strapped to a table, the metal cold beneath my trembling limbs. My eyes were wrenched open; I couldn't blink. I stared into the strip lights, purple stains writhing across my retinas. Hysteria brought the memory of reading *A Clockwork Orange* late at night, trying to force my eyes to stay open as I flicked through the pages beneath the covers, a torch in hand. A crazed laugh exploded from my lips.

Shapes moved above me and I felt the bite of steel, cutting deeper.

I screamed, falling into blackness.

Thirty-nine

The light hurt. I opened my eyes reluctantly, from a dream I couldn't remember. My whole life was a dream. This room was the nightmare.

I was slumped in a chair, my hands and feet shackled to a metal ring buried in the floor. Someone had dressed me in the hospital gown; I could feel the scrape of the chair against my back.

Will was sitting in a chair beside me. His face shone with tears. When he saw that I was awake, he reached out and took my hand.

'Mama…' the word was ripped from me.

His voice broke. 'She's dead.'

The bottom fell out of my heart.

'When?'

He glanced away. 'A few days ago.'

I began to cry. 'Did you see her? Was she… do you think she was in pain?'

A shadow passed over his face. 'She never woke up, after…'

It was too horrible to think about, but we did anyway, sitting together in silence, our hands gripped tight. We'd never been close, but he was my brother. Whatever had happened, I knew he loved our mother as much as I did.

Before he left, he hugged me. He hugged me and said good-bye. I think that scared me the most.

I fell in and out of sleep, close to giving up. When I next woke, the major was watching me.

I gave a start, jerking back in the chair, chains rattling. Seeing me awake, the corners of his mouth twitched.

'Ah, you're back with us, in the land of the living.' He smirked, but his eyes were cold.

'Why didn't you tell me she was dead? She's my mother.'

He snorted. 'You forfeited the right to any information about *my wife*.'

I didn't even have the energy to scowl at him. I let my head fall forward, exhausted. I couldn't feel my fingers; the handcuffs were so tight that the blood had long since stopped circulating.

The major's dress shoes clicked on the concrete as he began to pace around me.

'I'm afraid it's time I asked you some questions. You've had enough time now to get used to the way we do things here.'

I pulled my head up slowly and stared at him. He was rolling up his shirt sleeves carefully. '*The way you do things here*. You say it as though it's something normal, that you can be proud of.' My voice was weak, but it was full of anger. Each word brought its own stab of pain. 'You torture people. There's nothing but shame in that.'

He began to loosen his tie, pulling gently at the knot. He tugged it up over his head and tossed it to one side of the room.

'Shame. That's an interesting word. Is it shameful to serve your country? To root out anarchy and seek to keep the people safe? To stamp out those who would do nothing but harm to

317

others? Is it not shameful to build bombs and shoot men who are simply going about their jobs, protecting people?'

'Is that what you think I did? Killed someone?' I tried to shake my head but pain flooded through my body and I inhaled sharply.

The major continued to observe me.

'I didn't kill anyone.'

He shrugged. 'You didn't pull the trigger, perhaps, or wire a detonator. But if you associate with those that do, you're as guilty of the crime as they are. Ask your mother, ask Simon, or your student Jerome.'

'Is that what you tell yourself, to feel better? When you've been in here all day torturing someone.' I began to shake with emotion. 'When you beat someone, hang them, cut them, make them bleed. Rape them. Is that justified?'

He sighed. 'I'm not here to discuss morality with you. The simple fact is, you're a criminal, just like your father and your lover before you.' He began to pace again. 'To think that I allowed you to live under my roof for all those years, in my home, with my son. I made sure you were fed, clothed, that you had a good education. I kept your damned mother from drowning herself in a bottle of brandy. And this is how you repay me. You throw it back in my face with this... *rebellion*. You must know I can't let you go unpunished.'

Rage swelled in my chest. 'All you've ever done is destroy my life, from the first time you walked into our home and dragged my father away. You destroyed him; you destroyed my mother so badly that the only way she could stand to be married to you was to drink herself half to death. And now you want to destroy me. When will it end?'

His eyes were black. 'It doesn't end, none of it. Not for you. You won't leave this room. The only question is how badly you will force me to hurt you.'

318

I stared at him. I could feel the bruises blooming on my face, the raw flesh on my wrists where the restraints had cut in. My chest hurt with each breath; I had at least one broken rib. And that hadn't been the only bone to break.

'What does hurting me achieve? Do you want to punish me for my mother, because no matter what you did or said or gave her, she never really loved you? Not like she loved my father. However much she pretended to want you – perhaps she even convinced herself for a while – it was all to stay safe, to have a home. You spent years causing him pain, trying to take him apart. But you could never obliterate him; he was always there, in our lives. He's never been gone, not really. And whatever you do, you'll never *ever* be half the man he was.'

I wasn't ready for the pain that came when he drove his fist into my stomach. I doubled over, the air forced out of my lungs. My ribs burned and I couldn't think of anything except the sheer bloody agony.

When I came back to myself he was examining me, his face a twisted mask. I knew that I was just a piece of meat now, to be butchered. Whatever questions he might ask, he didn't expect answers. The only goal was to take me apart, finally, piece by piece.

'The others – the ones who brought you here – we need to know where we can find them. What their plans are.'

All I could do was stare at him, my face blank, my body prepared for pain. I gave no answer.

He hit me again and I wanted to scream, but I wouldn't give him the satisfaction. He saw my resolution and jabbed me twice in the gut, with the practised moves of a champion fighter.

I couldn't have answered him, even if I wanted to. I coughed and spluttered, gasping for air. He waited for me to regain my composure before he asked again.

'Where do they operate?'

I looked him in the eye. 'I don't know what you're talking about.'

This time he hit me in the face. My head jerked backwards, the world around me spinning. I spat blood onto the floor, marking the polished leather of his shoes. He stared at it, expressionless.

I saw it then, the thing that had driven my mother to lose herself in alcohol. It wasn't the guilt; she felt that every day, but she had learned to live with it. No, it was him. He must have hidden it well at first, and she allowed herself to find hope, to take on the role of wife. To bear his child. But one day she saw it. That something inside him was broken; he relished the misery of others, delighted in their pain. It made him stronger. He used it to measure his manhood. It made him rich; made him important. By spending her life in a haze of liquor, my mother took herself out of the game. It was no fun to have a victim who couldn't appreciate their own anguish. She allowed him to send me away, to a place where I would find a modicum of safety. But she couldn't save both her children. Will had always been his father's son.

'Do you make him do this too? Does he enjoy beating women?'

My stepfather's head tilted to one side quizzically.

'Will,' I said. 'My brother.'

His smile frightened me. 'I've never needed to make Will do anything. He has certain... talents. He is above the pain of others.' His eyes shone. 'Take your friend. That pretty blonde girl, the one we caught coming out of your apartment so late at night.' He wagged his finger at me. 'You were up to no good with that one.

'Well, we got the truth out of her. It didn't take long at all. Will was instrumental in that interrogation.'

I swallowed back the urge to vomit.

'You encouraged your *teenage son* to do that to a young girl. *What is wrong with you?*' My voice was an open wound.

His smile widened. 'That bothers you does it? Making a woman bleed…' He took a step closer to me, touched the tip of his finger to my cheek and drew it slowly downwards. 'Perhaps I was wrong about you. Perhaps we can find another way to make you break.'

The finger slid under my jaw and along the curve of my neck. Underneath the collar of the soiled hospital gown. My entire body went cold.

'I've always thought that you looked a lot like your mother.' The hand came up and caressed my hair. 'You're not as petite as her, or as delicate. You look like you could withstand much more than she ever could.'

I refused to look at him. He would not know that I was afraid.

He leaned down and put his lips close to my ear, whispered, 'I don't need to see it on your face. *I can smell it on you.*'

Before I could react, he stuck his tongue in my ear. I jerked away in disgust, but there was nowhere to go. My whole body strained to put as much space as possible between us. My arms felt as though they would break.

He stood up straight and began to laugh. 'You can't get away from me, you know. There's no way out of this room. You could scream and scream all day, and no one would come.' He laughed louder. 'Well, they might. But I don't think it would work out well for you.'

A single tear broke free and rolled down my cheek. I forced myself to look him dead in the eye, to lift my chin.

'You don't scare me.'

He moved closer, one hand on each arm of the chair, his face close to mine. His breath was hot and musty on my skin. 'I should.'

He jerked forward and his forehead connected full with my face. I'd never felt pain like it, exploding in my skull so intensely that I was blinded. Every sense was focused on the hurt; it was the only thing.

I don't know how long I was insensible, but something had changed. The chains were gone. My hands were no longer cuffed. I looked at my arms, barely able to recognise my own body, torn and scarred. Blood poured from my nose; I struggled to breathe.

'Of course, you're not so pretty now.' He pulled a sad face. 'Now, *that's* a shame.'

He resumed his pacing as I struggled to my feet, my legs feeble beneath my diminished weight. I took one step towards the door, and then another. I moved slowly backwards. I wouldn't turn my back on him.

'It's more fun this way. When you have a chance to fight.'

I gave a sob, the emotion echoing through my body from somewhere deep in the core of my being, somewhere primal and long forgotten.

'Just try and run, little girl. You're back in my house now.'

The fear consumed me and I did as he said. He didn't even have to chase me, I moved so slowly. The door seemed so far away; with each step I took he came closer. And then his hands were on me, pulling me down. I screamed and clawed at his face, gouging his eyes, but there was no strength in my arms. He grabbed my wrists and pinned them easily above my head with one hand, yanking at the hem of the miserable scrub gown with the other.

I screamed louder and struggled beneath his weight. I could feel the chill of the concrete on my skin, exposed and hurting. But I didn't care; I had to get away. I struck his face, harder somehow, and he growled at me, driving his fist into my body, my face. Blood flamed on my flesh, knuckle-shaped bruises darkened.

There was a crash as the door opened suddenly. Will stood in the doorway, staring at us as we grappled on the floor, his lip twisted in disgust.

'What are you doing?' he cried.

The major glared at him, his normally coiffed hair in disarray as he fought to keep my hands pinned. '*Get... out.*'

'You can't – that's my *sister*.' Horror filled his voice. He took a step forward, but before he could intervene, there was a burst of noise somewhere outside the room. There were shouts and storming feet; a burst of gunfire.

Will's attention shifted. He clutched at the gun on his hip, pulling it free from the holster. Shifting to a slight crouch, he edged towards the door, the gun clutched in both hands. He disappeared into the corridor.

My stepfather's grip on me loosened, the hunger in his eyes dulled as he glanced towards the door, panting.

In the distance there was a cry of, 'Guards! Guards! Stop!' and more shooting. I barely noticed when the major's weight disappeared and I was no longer pinned to the floor. The air was cool on the top of my thighs. Clutching at the thin fabric, I wrenched the gown back into place, my legs shaking.

He pulled his gun from a holster on his ankle; I hadn't even noticed it was there. Cautiously, he peered out into the corridor. Uniform feet ran past; he left the room and relief surged through me, but was quickly overtaken by panic. I had to get out.

I didn't know what was happening, but it had to be big. Hope coursed through me; what if it was Lumière, come to rescue me? Crying, I dragged myself to my knees and began to crawl towards the door, my shattered body fighting to escape.

I reached the door frame and clutched it, dragging myself to my feet, ignoring the shots that rang out along the hall. But before I could get through the door, the major reappeared. I cried out in despair, but he didn't look at me. I staggered away, every instinct telling me to run, as he backed into the cell.

A gun appeared; it was pointed at him. Another man came into view; a man with long hair fastened back in an elastic band, his thin body tense, the expression on his face hard. In his other hand was the major's gun.

I studied him, holding my breath. The moment felt unreal. It was my father.

A low wail escaped me. 'Daddy!'

He looked at me, blankly at first, then with an air of recognition spreading over his face. 'Clara? Is that you?'

I began to cry.

With my father's attention momentarily fixed on me, the major took his chance and surged forward. He tackled my father, who was blocking the doorway. Despite his slender frame, he didn't give way. They collapsed to the ground in a blur of arms and legs, grunting with rage as they each tried to take control. The major's gun clattered to the floor and skidded off into the corner of the room. Neither man seemed to notice, they were so intent on their struggle.

In a daze, I stumbled across the cell. The gun was heavy in my hand. I had never fired one before. I stared at it, turned it over in my hand. It wasn't connected to me; it was outside my control. Without thinking I walked forward and pressed the gun into the back of the major's head.

'Stop.'

They both froze. The major's body was rigid. My father slid out from underneath him and got up. There were tears in his eyes.

'Clara, my Clara, are you okay?'

I didn't take my eyes off my stepfather. 'I'll be okay, Daddy.'

The major was tensed, his palms pressed against the rough concrete floor, ready to spring to his feet. My father followed my gaze. One foot took the major's arms out from beneath him, his face scraping painfully as he hit the floor. He looked at me over his shoulder, eyes rolling upwards.

'Get up.'

He did as I said. This time he was the one to meet my gaze.

'I wasn't...'

I didn't even think; I pulled the trigger. My hand recoiled painfully as the major's forehead exploded, blood and shards of bone splattering the wall. His body fell to the floor with a heavy thud, legs twitching. I didn't feel anything.

I looked down at the gun clutched in my hand, as though it belonged to someone else. When I let go, it clattered noisily to the concrete. A spray of blood stained the front of my surgical gown. The major's, mine, it all blended together in a mess of pain.

My father was watching me silently. We stood there, unspeaking in the midst of chaos. I was calm.

It took me a moment to realise that my brother had come back into the room, the gun still clutched in his hand. He saw his father's body sprawled on the floor and he cried out. He looked from me to my father, to the gun in his grasp.

'No – no, you didn't.'

'Will...' I began, holding out my hands towards him.

But he wasn't looking at me. He was fixed on my father, every muscle coiled as though he was about to pounce. He stared at his face.

'I know who you are. You're Clara's father. You're the one...'

My dad lifted a hand in an effort to appear conciliatory. 'Now, son...'

It was the wrong thing to say. I blinked and Will had raised his gun, had pointed it at my father. There was a sharp pain in my chest as he yelled, 'I'm not *your son*. I'm his... *his*...'

I couldn't breathe. My brother's hands shook as he tightened his grip on the gun. 'He should never have let you leave here.'

His finger tightened against the trigger, but he wasn't quick enough. Without breaking eye contact, my father brought his gun up and fired. I screamed as the bullet caught Will in the shoulder, sending him spinning off balance. His own shot went wide, the bullet embedding itself in the wall.

As he landed hard on the floor, he began screaming in pain. My father strode forward and kicked the gun out of his hand, where it skittered out of reach. Will's fingers clutched weakly at his shoulder as the blood poured from the wound. He began to cry.

'You shot me, you shot me.'

For all the uniform, all the anger, all the things I knew he had done, in that moment he was a boy again.

I looked at my father stupidly. 'You didn't kill him.'

He looked down at my brother, something like pity in his eyes. 'He's a boy. He'll have to answer, but... no.'

There were so many thoughts crowding into my head that I struggled to focus.

Then he crossed the room in two strides and took me in his arms. I allowed myself to collapse against him, but he did not stagger beneath my weight.

I cried into his chest as he stroked my hair. It was so familiar, even after all this time. He still smelled the same. It took me a while to realise that it had fallen quiet. The gunshots, the shouting, it had all stopped. The only sound was Will's whimpering.

I pulled away to look at my father. For a moment, I was eleven again. He touched my face softly. 'It's time to go home.'

We left Will there, locked in a cell with the body of the major. My father gave me his coat; it hung loose around my shoulders, but I found the scent comforting. He led me slowly along the corridor, supporting me as I struggled to make my legs work normally. The adrenalin had left my body and I could feel every inch of my skin, every cut, every bruise. I concentrated hard on my feet and making them move forwards.

We found the others in the guards' room, where the walls were lined with monitors. I could see every room, every cell. I could see the people locked inside. I found my brother, sobbing as he clutched his father's body. I had to turn away.

They were all looking at me: Caleb, Zeke and the others. Even Elizabeth was there. Her face betrayed her time in this place, but she held her chin defiantly. When I caught her eye she smiled, rushing across the room to touch my face.

'Thank you, Clara. Thank you for coming for me.' She pressed her forehead against mine and I couldn't hold back any longer; I began to weep. She took my hand and I squeezed her fingers tightly.

I looked round the room at them all. 'You came back. *You came back.*'

Caleb smiled sadly. 'We couldn't leave you here. If it wasn't for us…'

'No.' I was surprised by how firm my voice sounded. 'You're not to blame, Caleb.'

I tried to say more, but I began to feel weak. My eyesight started to blur and the blood rushed from my limbs. The babble of voices around me intensified and someone caught me before I could fall. They lowered me into a chair.

'Is she alright?'

'What should we do?'

'She needs a doctor.'

Simon was kneeling on the floor in front of me, peering earnestly into my face.

'Simon?'

He held a finger to my lips. 'Don't talk, sweetheart, don't talk. You need to rest.' His voice shook. Other voices murmured around us.

When I came back to myself, my father was looking up at me, his eyes full of concern and fear. And it all came rushing back. I pictured Simon's body cold on the floor, mouth slack and bloody. The last spark of life inside me flickered and for a brief moment I thought it would go out.

But my father took my hand. His grip was firm, the skin of his palms rough from years of toil. He squeezed my fingers tightly, anchoring me to him.

I leaned forward and flung my arms around him. 'I thought I'd never see you again.'

He kissed my hair and it all fell away; I was eleven years old again.

They took me home through darkened streets, through a night thronged with people, crowds everywhere I looked. Caleb drove slowly, as my father and I sat together in the back seat. He would glance at us in the mirror from time to time. I leaned against my dad, not speaking, but thinking about everything we'd lost and what might happen next.

As we waited at a crossroads, people milling in every direction, Caleb flicked on the radio. They were singing. There was laughter in the streets. My heart was raw.

The end

There were a lot of funerals. Over time the gravesides blurred into one. My father came to stay with me and, without him, I'd have drifted away.

He helped me plan a goodbye for my mother and for Simon. The morning of his funeral was bright and cold, the light so intense we could see the dust motes moving slowly in the air. I wore a new dress, one that masked the jutting bones and still-smarting wounds marking my body. I felt older, weaker, not full of the hope that seemed to charge the people around me.

There was a different news show on the television now, but the presenter anchored it to the past. David Tubby had dropped the G, but he hadn't yet lost his bruises or the haunted look in his eye. He was alone now; his former wife and co-presenter had become the news, arrested along with the other supporters of the First General's regime.

The interim government has announced a General Election, to be held on Thursday 2 May. Members of the public will receive registration forms over the next few weeks. You are all encouraged to fill them out and confirm your vote. We need your voice.

State-supported funerals for those killed by the former regime continue. The Acting Home Secretary, Caleb Morris, has pledged funds

329

for a memorial in Hyde Park that will pay tribute to all the disappeared.

In other news, a diplomatic mission has been sent to Russia, where it is suspected the First General is in hiding with two of his sons.

My father put his hand on my shoulder.

'It's time to go, Clara. The car is outside. Caleb will be waiting.'

I closed my eyes and drew in a deep breath. Simon was everywhere. I could still feel him in the apartment, on the streets we used to walk every day. I still expected to see him each time I turned a corner. His shoes waited by the door, but I couldn't bring myself to put them away.

The television fell silent and my father took my hand. I swam back out of my memories, into the light. Every line on my father's face reminded me of the time we'd lost, of all the love that was gone.

'It's time, Clara.' He squeezed my hand.

I tucked it through his arm and let him lead me out of the apartment, onto the street outside, where a sleek black car was waiting. Waiting, with a crowd of people all dressed in black. As we walked towards the car, they began to whisper. I couldn't make out their words at first. It was his name: they whispered Simon's name, and the names of a thousand others all lost to us.

We teach our children that history is always written by the victors. But now, when we stand at the front of a lecture hall, all those expectant faces turned towards us, we only tell the truth, as we have lived it.

We don't shy away from the pain, the darkness, the shame of it. We remember the world before this happened. It wasn't perfect, but if we're ever to reconstruct it, we need them to understand the reasons why. We need them to remember the ones we lost; whichever side they were on.

I don't need to choose the texts I share with my students. They chose me. They've been there, throughout my story, waiting for the moment that they can reach out to another generation. We find meaning in the words.

I walk into the classroom, my students already gathered there, chatting amongst themselves. They see me arrive and begin to settle down as I arrange my things on the desk at the front. I come around it and perch on the edge, preferring to remove that barrier between us.

In my hands I hold a book.

'Okay everyone, today we're going to be reading *Nineteen Eighty-Four* by George Orwell. I hope you all managed to get hold of a copy from the bookshop.'

I could have laughed at the novelty as they pulled them from their bags, running their hands over the covers, over the fresh ink. We weren't in black and white any more.

'Right, who wants to begin?'

Acknowledgements

Crowdfunding a book is all about taking your readers on a journey with you through the publication process, and it has certainly been an adventure. Heartfelt thanks go to each person who pledged for this book and helped to make my dream of becoming a published author a reality. I can never thank you enough, but I hope you understand how much I appreciate your contribution.

And while I'm talking about crowdfunding, one of the main reasons I got through the process was the support of the Unbound Social Club. Thanks to you all; reading your books has been a delight!

But before there was Unbound, I spent many years working on this book. I'm fortunate to know other talented writers and offer thanks to those who gave feedback on the early drafts of this book: Frankie Thompson and particularly Martin Feekins, for being a friend and for offering your time and insights to help me improve this book.

My friend Louise, I don't think you realise it, but in allowing me to spend the last few years tagging along with you to gigs and events, you've filled a hole in my life that has brought so much creativity and joy to it. Thank you!

And for Yaffa, thanks for being an early supporter of this book and for graciously arranging my first author event. You're much missed.

Thanks also go to James and Laura from Writers' Block NE. I loved being a part of the programme while writing my next book. And without WBNE, I wouldn't have ended up joining my current writing group, who have been a great source of writing chat, support and inspiration. Thank you Lisette, Mary, Marita, Katharine and Lindsay. I'm looking forward to talking about writing with you all for a long time to come.

A huge thank you goes to Kwaku Osei-Afrifa for commissioning this novel. I don't usually thank people for making me cry at work, but you made my day (and possibly a large chunk of my life) by giving me an opportunity to publish this book. You're a star!

Thanks also go to the rest of the team at Unbound, particularly Sara Magness and Xander Cansell for their support in the run up to publication. And thanks to Craig and Andrew for being wonderful editors – this book is in much better shape than it was due to your guidance and advice.

Two literary awards also played a big part in helping me with this book. Thanks to the Bath Novel Award team and also New Writing North for choosing this novel to win a Northern Writers' Award, which allowed me to take part in The Literary Consultancy's Free Reads scheme.

Thanks also to my friends, family and colleagues for their support over the years and particularly to those who pledged for this book. I couldn't have done it without you.

And for Ste, because this book simply would not exist without you. Thank you for being such a supportive husband, for listening to me rambling about this book, about crowdfunding and about my hopes and fears. And thanks for understanding that sometimes I disappear, when my head is lost in whatever story I'm working on, and for giving me the time I needed to complete this book.

ADDITIONAL CREDITS

The author would like to acknowledge the financial support of a New Writing North, Northern Writers' Award, supported by The Literary Consultancy, Northumbria University and Arts Council England.

Unbound is the world's first crowdfunding publisher, established in 2011.

We believe that wonderful things can happen when you clear a path for people who share a passion. That's why we've built a platform that brings together readers and authors to crowdfund books they believe in – and give fresh ideas that don't fit the traditional mould the chance they deserve.

This book is in your hands because readers made it possible. Everyone who pledged their support is listed at the front of the book and below. Join them by visiting unbound.com and supporting a book today.

Dan Allick
Helen Anderson
Karen Attwood
Lisette Auton
Sharon Barker
Bath Novel Award
Paul Breen
Stephanie Bretherton
Claire Buchan
Lesley Burdett
Miles Campbell
Lindsay Cannon
Henry Carden
Mark Ciccone
Ann Cofell
Peter Cumiskey
Melissa Davies
Laura Degnan
Rachel Doherty

Pauline Durie
Robert Eardley
Kathryn Eastman
James Ellis
Hannah Grey
Alex Griffiths
Craig Griffiths
Claire Handscombe
David Hanratty
Sam Haysom
Jennifer Heil
Grace Helmer
Amanda Hodgson
Kaye Hudson
Karen Hutchinson
Amanda Johnson
Helen Johnson
Holly Johnson
Amanda Kenmir

Ruth King
Chloe Lawrence
Ewan Lawrie
Allan Lord
James Lord
Will Mackie
Gwen McGinty
Glen McNamee
Lyndsey Middleton
Simon Miller
Trevor Millum
Kathleen Moore
Christina Morrison
Alex Murdie
Samantha Murdie
Carlo Navato
Robert Nichols
Ros O'Sullivan
Annemarie O'Donnell
Elizabeth Ottosson
Yaffa Phillips

Aileen Quealy
Paul Robinson
Colin Robson
Lynsey Searle
Joanell Serra
Ste Sharp
Lucy Sinclair
Jennie Smith
Tony Stowe
Julie Sykes
Angela Thomas
Sue Thomas
Emma Todd
Dan Turner
Alexandra Turney
Paul Vickers
Alison Watson-Shields
Hannah Whelan
Jule Wilson
Joshua Winning